A COLD KILLING

DEFOREST DAY

Carroll & Graf Publishers, Inc.
New York

First Carroll & Graf edition 1990

Carroll & Graf Publishers, Inc
260 Fifth Avenue
New York, NY 10001

Library of Congress Cataloging-in-Publication Data

Day, DeForest.
  A cold killing / DeForest Day.—1st Carroll & Graf ed.
    p.   cm.
  ISBN 0-88184-577-9 : $17.95
  I. Title
PS3554.A95906   1990
813'.54-dc20   90-33997
                                                    CIP

Manufactured in the United States of America

A COLD
KILLING

for b. w.,
who said I could.

CHAPTER 1

The telephone rang. More precisely, it chirped; the pseudotech insect noise bothered Defoe each time he heard it, but the cordless feature of the instrument overrode its obnoxious voice. Still, he missed the honest ring of an electromagnetic clapper against a bell; it let you know, by God, that it was the *telephone* intruding and not the front-door chimes, the alarm clock radio, some disc jockey once again testing the Emergency Broadcast System, or heaven forbid, the microwave announcing that your TV dinner was thawed. Since Defoe owned none of the above he was not in the least confused when the instrument tugged at his auditory sleeve.

"Defoe here." He picked up the receiver from its base by the central stairway in the living area of the converted Pennsylvania bank barn. When he went down to the lower level he took the handset with him; when he went up to bed it was a matter of habit to carry his connection with the outside world upstairs and plunk it on the floor. It was one of the aspects of his business that he needed to be in almost constant contact with civilization.

"Chase! It's your uncle Bill. How's the boy?"

Defoe smiled and carried the phone back to the kitchen area. Bill Pickering, seventy-three years old and still at the helm of a major insurance company, continued to call Chase Defoe "boy" more than forty years after the Episcopal Bishop of Connecticut had doused the squalling infant with ice water and entrusted his soul to the care of William and Martha Pickering, residents of the town of Hartford and ex-roommate—the former and ex-flame—the latter of Chase's father, George Phillip Clinton Defoe.

"Hello, Bill. I was thinking about you a couple of weeks ago; I had lunch in New York with a classmate, Chappy Fenton; I gather you know him."

"Yes, Goldman Sachs; bright lad, Chase. Should go places."

Defoe chuckled softly. "Bill, Chappy and I will be in New Haven for our thirtieth reunion next year. If these 'boys' and 'lads' are going anywhere, we should have started long ago!"

Bill coughed and quickly said, "I'm sorry, Chase, I didn't mean to imply—"

"No, of course you didn't, Uncle Bill, I know that. You forget, it's my *father* who thinks I haven't made my mark in the world, not me! Remember, he's the one annoyed that I'm not undersecretary of something or other at State. I tried his footsteps, Bill, and found them rather muddy and pointing in directions I'd rather not explore. But you didn't call to discuss careers that might have been. How are things in Hartford?"

"Your godmother and I are well, as well as can be expected for two doddering old fools. She's as involved as ever in Good Works, and I'm still trying to figure out why the devil I ever took up golf! Jack and Nancy and the children flew in for the Labor Day weekend. But the reason I called, son, is that I'd like to ask a favor of you, if it's not too inconvenient. It's the sort of thing you'd enjoy, I think, what with your interest in security."

Defoe opened the refrigerator and took inventory of the perishables. "Interest in security." He shook his head and smiled. *He's like my father*, he realized. Even after nearly twenty years in Naval Intelligence they both still thought that he was indulging himself with some sort of hobby.

"You've piqued my interest, Bill, tell me more." He began to remove items from the refrigerator that would not survive a fortnight's inattention: a clutch of eggs, a piece of Brie that was already approaching senescence, two bottles of beer. And in white freezer paper, a pair of pork chops, nearly thawed, that he had brought upstairs from the chest freezer the previous day. He hoped they were not freezer-burned beyond consumption. Freshness was a fetish for Defoe.

"It's an insurance claim; we provide the primary coverage on a trucking company and they've had three loads stolen in the last four weeks. One of the consignees is screaming for a fast settlement; apparently they lost a container of French designer clothing. Valued at a million or so, and, the way I understand it, the usual procedure is for these importers to pay for it up front with a letter of credit, even before the garments are shipped from Europe.

"It's all straightforward enough, Chase, routine. The problem is, our man down there, an independent adjuster, had a heart attack yesterday. He's in a hospital in Allentown. They tell me it's not critical, but he certainly won't be doing any more work on this for a while. You're not too far from there, are you?''

"About half an hour, forty-five minutes.''

"Yes, I thought it was your neighborhood. What I'm asking, son, since we're being pressured to resolve this quickly, is for you to talk to this investigator and tie up any loose ends on the claim. I gather he's satisfied that it's legitimate, but with the amount involved we'd feel better if it was wrapped up before we make a payout; getting money back after the fact is rarely successful. It shouldn't take more than a couple of hours of your time. Just see him in the hospital and then put his paperwork into some sort of order for our claims department.''

A cheese omelet made with the Brie and cook the pork chops in beer. Perfect. "No problem, Bill, I'd be happy to do it. Only it really will have to be a couple of hours work; I'm leaving for South America tomorrow. I'll be gone for two weeks.''

"South America!''

"Yep. The whole continent; I'm going to sweep all the embassies of one of our less stable allies down there. A training mission, really. I sold them the equipment, and I have to to teach their people how to use it. Eleven countries in fifteen days. Who's your man and what hospital is he in?''

"Askew, Harold Askew. He's in . . . I have it here someplace— Sacred Heart. He has all the data, Chase, and he's a good man, been associated with us for nearly twenty years. I don't anticipate any problems. Ordinarily this could wait until he was back on his feet, of course. But, as I said, the consignee is screaming at the trucking company and they, in turn, are pressuring us. IGT is a longtime account and we want to keep them happy.''

Defoe jotted "Askew" and "Sacred Heart" on a scrap of paper. "I'll go see your adjuster tomorrow. Give my love to Martha.'' The chops were braising in the beer and Defoe broke the eggs into a bowl.

CHAPTER **2**

Twenty-five miles northeast of Defoe's barn a man in a green polyester shirt and matching trousers stood against a locust fencepost beside another barn, his hands behind his back.

A hundred feet closer to the old stone farmhouse the man in the plaid shirt stood in the rutted, hard-packed dirt driveway that separated the two buildings. He looked over his shoulder at the figure by the barn, then turned back to face the man in the motorcycle helmet.

It was a Bell TX, black, its smoked visor obscuring the features of the face inside. Black leather—jacket, pants, boots, gloves—covered the man completely, so that he seemed a huge arachnid beside the black motorcycle, hot metal ticking quietly as it cooled in the crisp October air. "I am terribly displeased, Skean," he said in a muffled voice, "by this involvement of personnel."

"You can take off the helmet," the man in the plaid shirt replied. "There's nobody here but me."

The bike was one of the kamikaze crotch rockets; a hundred horsepower and a top end around a hundred and sixty; it had made the trip from Central Park West to the isolated farm below Allentown in ninety minutes.

Skean knew the man was going to be pissed, but the call had to be made; he went into the farmhouse, fishing through his wallet for the slip of paper with the New York number on it. The switchboard transferred him to the man's office and a secretary put him on hold. Skean looked out the window at the big Ford with the sleeper box and forty feet of cargo trailer behind it as he listened to canned music over the telephone.

Joe Skean had been sitting at the scarred wooden table with the enameled steel top that served as desk, dining table, and nerve center of the operation still known as Hunter's Game Farm when Hunchie had pulled into the farmyard with the Loadstar.

Two quick hoots on the airhorn raised a score of pigeons from the sagging slate roof of the barn and made the pigs dance in frenzied circles behind the high board fence that screened them from view. Wild boars that behaved like domestic hogs were of little use to sportsmen. Skean's head came up from the stacks of twenties and fifties on the table in front of him. He ran a cash business.

Hunchie climbed down from the cab and headed for the run-down farmhouse. His name was based on his physique; five ten and two hundred and fifty pounds, most of it in front—pendulous breasts over a drum-tight beer belly—his shoulders had gradually moved forward until his head and neck met his chest in one amorphous mass, so that he measured barely five feet eight as he rolled across the barnyard, his short legs moving like a beached sailor after six months at sea. In his late forties, he was bald in front and on top, and wore his hair long at the sides and back, where it hung in greasy ringlets. He had spent nearly twenty-five years behind the wheel, making transcontinental runs for Mayflower and then United Van Lines, until his alcoholism finally forced the company to fire him. He now drove for a tractor and farm implement dealer, hauling new and used equipment to and from local farms. He lived in a single room on the third floor of the Garville Hotel, a dilapidated stone structure with a two-century genealogy that stood beside a senescent route linking Philadelphia and Reading. The first floor housed a bar with a kitchen of questionable competence; the owner's apartment and a handful of rooms rented by the week occupied the upper floors.

Skean met him at the door. "What the *fuck* are you doing here?" His dark eyes shone like his straight black hair, carefully combed into a series of waves that were held in place with a coating of Vitalis.

"We got problems, Joe." Sweat beads stood out on his forehead. "Man, I need a cold one."

"We got *problems.* Goddamn right we got problems, anyone sees that fuckin' IGT truck within ten miles of this place."

Hunchie went into the kitchen and opened the refrigerator. Black fingerprints surrounded the handle; the inside was no cleaner. Except for a carton of milk, thirteen cans of Miller, and a sour smell, it was empty. He opened and drained a beer in one long, fluid motion, then took two more cans back outside. "We got more than the truck here, Joe. We got a driver."

Skean turned and looked at the big green-and-white rig sitting in his barnyard and felt a sinking sensation in his gut. It had sounded so easy when the motorcycle man had first laid it out for him. Low risk;

that's what he had emphasized. Nobody needs to get hurt and Skean stayed one step away through the whole thing.

He and Mobay had gone partners in the game farm, after Graterford. Mobay had told him about the owner, inside. Crazy old guy, Mobay said, and Mobay ought to know, he worked for him. Part-time; fixing fences, driving a little, and butchering. Mobay did a lot of butchering. That's what he went into Graterford for. The charge was possession of stolen property with intent to sell; what it was was Mobay had a truckload of freshly slaughtered registered dairy goats that the crazy old guy had arranged for his young associate to deliver to a restaurant in Philly that specialized in venison. Goat was the old guy's forte; mystery meat he called it. You wanted spring lamb? He had some nice hind quarters. When horsemeat had been the rage back in the seventies, goat had filled in nicely. Venison steaks? Pour a cup of blood over goat cutlets and you had venison at twelve dollars a pound.

The problem, for Mobay, had been the source of the goats. Registered goats, show goats, he had learned from the State's attorney in open court, are tattooed inside their ears. And the number is on file with the American Dairy Goat Association. The bitch that owned the goats had enough money and her husband had enough clout that every state cop in the Commonwealth had a printout of those numbers in their patrol car.

The crazy old guy was half dead from lung cancer and the assistant DA went with Mobay, a twenty-three-year-old wild man; six feet seven, two hundred and seventy pounds and dumb enough to take the fall.

Joe Skean was five years older and a hundred pounds lighter and doing five to ten for manslaughter. He was the concubine of a black lifer from North Philadelphia; a chance remark in the dining hall about the stew tasting like deer meat had led to a muted conversation across the table between Skean and Mobay.

"Deer meat?" Mobay looked out under lowered brows at the darkly handsome inmate across from him. "What do you know about deer meat, city boy?" The last word came out more like "thittyboy"; the four upper teeth between his canines were missing.

Skean had a gold stud in his ear and a slave bracelet on his wrist. "Shit, big boy," he answered. "I ate more deer than you ever will."

"Where do city boys get deer? *Shit*, yourself." He laughed quietly. "Road kills, most likely."

"*City* boy? The fuck you say. I was raised outside of Shamokin; deer and rabbit and the chickens me and my brother stole was the only meat we ate. I bet I jacked more deer before I got my junior license than *you* ever *saw!*''

"Shamokin, huh? I lived up Tamaqua when I was little. I still got people up there. Coal crackers. My daddy was in the mines, before he went off. Ma moved usth back down here when I was eleven, moved back with her people. Dutchy, she is. I'm half.''

"What you in for? I seen you around the yard.''

Mobay sopped gravy with a slice of white bread, folded it in half, and put it in his mouth. "I had a truckload of deer meat, b'lieve it? Only it wasn't deer, it was goats. You know they tattoo them fuckers?''

"*Goat* meat. You have a lawyer?''

"Yeah, they give me one, from out of Reading.''

Skean looked across the table in disbelief. "Jesus Christ. What are you doin'?''

Mobay lowered his gaze to his plate, played with his spoon. "Three to five,'' he muttered.

"Three to fi—*Jesus.* You been in before, right?'' Skean reached in his shirt and pulled out a crumpled pack of cigarettes. He lit one, then offered the pack across the stainless-steel table.

Mobay shook him off. "Naw. I use to chew, but in here . . .'' He looked up. "No. This is my first offense.''

"First time up to bat and he draws trips. Man, the judge musta had a hard-on for you!''

Mobay shook his head. "Naw,'' he said slowly, "it was them goats. They were registered. Show stock and all. And that bitch that owned them . . .'' He shook his head. "I think she was, too.'' He stood up and extricated his massive thighs from the bench that was a part of the table, leaned across, and loomed over Skean. "What you want to mess around with those shines for anyway?''

Skean glanced to his left and stood, picking up his tray. "Meet me in the yard.''

Joe Skean left school at fifteen and home a few weeks later. Ninth grade, second time around—discipline and attendance, not scholarship, had been his nemesis. The final, long-forgotten infraction had resulted in banishment to the library with the task of copying a full page from the dictionary into his spiral notebook. The page of choice had been his and he flipped open the big Webster's and leaned forward, idly turning leaves until the notion of looking for his name gave his fingers direction.

Suddenly, at the top of a column, there it was: "skean. n. a knife or dagger formerly used in Ireland and the Scottish Highlands.'' Joe knew his father's people came from over there, in England some-place; he remembered his mother talking about it when he was little. The next entry read ''skean dhu: a small knife worn in the top of the stocking in the full dress of Highland males.'' He chewed his thumb and puzzled over the entry until he had it deciphered. An image came to his mind, an old movie, World War II soldiers, those Scottish guys with the skirts and knee socks, that's what it meant. And the crazy sound of bagpipes and rifle fire and running over Nazi lines with fixed bayonets and . . . Jesus! The hair still went up on the back of his neck when he thought about the sound of bagpipes. *Skean*. A freakin' bootknife is what it was. He smiled and slid his hand into his pocket, wrapped his fingers around the Buck lockback, and surrepti-tiously transferred it to his high-topped work shoe.

Joe Skean stood, closed the dictionary, and never looked back. He left home and moved in with an older guy who lived in a trailer connected to a junkyard. He learned a lot of different things over the next few years.

The lockback was long forgotten when Skean went up on the manslaughter charge. The knife that put him inside was a double-edged carbon steel commando model that rested in a leather-and-elastic harness between his shoulder blades. A mail order treat from a soldier of fortune magazine, it had been introduced in court and played a major role in the Commonwealth of Pennsylvania's denying a plea of self-defense.

The slender, feral Skean had quickly been appropriated by the black lifer who dominated the tier. The white convict briefly calcu-lated the odds and chose selective rather than communal subjugation. Requital would wait. In the meantime, the sensual was satiated.

''So you stuck the fucker?'' Mobay shook his head in disbelief.

''Hell, he called me out, I *had* to.'' Skean shoved his hands into his pockets and looked up at the high wall that blocked the view of the fertile fields outside the prison. More than a thousand acres of rich Montgomery County farmland surrounded the penitentiary, fields that had once been productive feeding the Commonwealth's correc-tional system, but now lay idle under a new penal philosophy.

Mobay, like most truly big men, had seldom been challenged, and was tolerant of the few aberrant ones, usually drunk, who felt the call to take a shot at the great oak. An effortless swipe with a big paw generally subdued the raucous assailant. That Skean would feel the need to stab, to kill such a person, was hard for him to understand.

A few weeks later, Mobay casually approached his new friend. ''If you want," he said, "I could see that the shine left you alone. I mean, if you wanted me to," he added quickly.

Skean computed time, hard time, good time, and time off for good behavior; release dates for himself and Mobay and the chances for parole board approval for early release. If Mobay was out before him, he was dead. "Do what you can," he said.

The black lifer slipped and fractured his skull after mistaking Mobay's slow and pleasant demeanor for some lesser attribute. Skean traded an assistant warden a choice tidbit of information for a change in cellmates. Six months later the two friends were released within a week of each other.

Hunter, the crazy old man, hung on at the game farm, subsisting on Social Security checks, his chicken-wire pens of quail, pheasant, and wild turkeys, and the grace of a paid-up mortgage. He died, coughing blood, a month after Mobay and Skean moved into a vacant bedroom.

He was without heirs and they buried him behind the barn in the easy topsoil and Skean practiced his wavering signature until they were assured that the meager monthly check would continue to fund their blossoming business. Hunter's Game Farm would prosper once more.

They strung high tensile fence and cleared brush and established a herd of deer. The old man's client list was a hodgepodge of restaurants, exotic bird fanciers, and private shooting clubs in need of a steady supply of stock for their hunt-for-pay customers. The man with the motorcycle had a seven-hundred-acre shooting preserve in the Adirondacks and bought five hundred ringnecks each spring for release. He and his friends shot them in the fall over pointers and Jack Daniel's. The New York climate is too harsh for pheasants to winter over.

"I'm sorry, Mr. Skean; he's in a meeting. Leave your number and he'll get back to you."

"Goddamnit, lady, tell him it's an *emergency*. Get him on the phone, I gotta talk to him." She put him on hold without comment. A few seconds later there was a click.

"Skean? What the devil's so important that it can't—"

"I'll tell you what's so important. We got a driver here. Hunchie pulled in five minutes ago with the rig and he says they've got the driver, too. What the hell am I supposed to do now?"

"What? Ah, *Je*-sus. Hold on a second." Skean could hear him talking to someone. The office was big, thirty floors above Seventh Avenue, and decorated in Ralph Lauren Macho; acres of leather and other less civilized bits of dead animals—hides, tusks, horns—scattered about in artful disarray. The man leaned back in his desk chair and picked up a scrimshaw and brass letter opener and balanced the point on his leather desk blotter. "How did it happen?"

"I don't know; I told you, Hunchie just now pulled in. All he said was they had the driver. Hold on and I'll go ask him."

"Never mind, that part's not really pertinent. You got him, that's where we are." He paused for half a heartbeat. "This Hunchie and, I assume he had an assistant, how . . . ah—reliable are they? What I'm asking, Skean, is can we depend on them if the situation should deteriorate."

If the situation should . . . Skean chewed his lip. What the fuck; did he think the freakin' *phone* was tapped? The guy always talked like those Washington dopes on the news; Senators and Secretarys of stuff. What he meant was, would Big Red and Hunchie cop a plea. And the answer was hell yes; neither of them had probably faced more than a DWI. Throw them in a lineup for this goddamn driver with a bug in their ear about five big ones for grand theft and they'd sell their mother to get out from under. "I'm afraid they could . . . ah—crap out on us, if you see what I'm saying." What he didn't say was that Hunchie and Gloeckner could pass the ball to Skean, but had no knowledge of the other man's identity. But he didn't have to know that, right now. And he also didn't know Skean's degree of commitment to the Code of Silence, that underworld bullshit that was more honored in the breach than the observance. Well, let him dance with tight underwear for a while; see which way this thing goes.

"I was afraid of a problem of this sort developing. Quite frankly, Joseph, I had reservations about this from the start, reservations about your . . . ah—abilities to coordinate a project like this. If you remember, you assured me that you knew some talent who could . . . who had the experience to handle this type of thing. It appears now that you were mistaken, or at least overestimated the capabilities of these people." He paused, drummed the letter opener on the edge of the desk. "You'll have to take care of it."

"Ho, wait up a minute! You told me right from the start there wasn't going to be nothin' heavy going on with this deal. Just a little push and shove and some driving. And I stay one step back from it."

"Yes, but then it's *your* boys that picked up this driver, am I right? I mean, I made it perfectly clear initially about how they were to go about it. And now you're telling me they've got personnel involved. This is not good, Skean. It's not good at all." He dug the point of the letter opener into the edge of the blotter, leaving little indentations in the lather. "I've got a major financial investment in this project, Joseph. This trucking thing is all a part of the whole situation up here. And it's not a situation I can just walk away from."

"I can appreciate that; the only thing is, I, I got an investment in this, this thing, too. You see what I'm saying here? What I mean is, I got my ass invested here, is what I've got. I was inside once, I told you that. And I see it heading where I just might be looking at the possibility of going back down there, I violate my parole."

"Skean, calm down; nobody's going anywhere. Put that driver somewhere safe and get that truck headed in the direction it's supposed to be going. I'll be there in a couple of hours and we'll take care of this." He hung up without waiting for Skean's response, leaned back in the chair and put his feet up on the desk. "Let's see . . ." he said softly, his eyes fixed on a sinuously twisted pair of kudu horns across the room, "the ACP. Yes; a classic for what could be, after all, a classic situation. And a barrel swap will obviate any potential involvement. Perfect!" He smiled and punched a button on his telephone. "Sweetheart, cancel the spring forecast meeting; I'm leaving for the day. Emergency in the field. Set it up for tomorrow morning."

Skean dropped the receiver on its cradle and rubbed the back of his neck. He blew out a long, slow breath, closed his eyes and concentrated on the orange afterimage of the bright doorway in the unlit kitchen. It was a trick he had learned as a kid; lie in the sun, staring up into the sky. Then close your eyes, tight, and watch the light show. Freebie acid trip. For Skean it helped when the outside got too fast. He went out to the truck, its engine idled, smoke burbling from the twin stacks. "You mind telling me what the hell happened?"

Hunchie dropped his cigarette in the dirt and stepped on it. He looked up at the open window on the passenger's side of the tractor. "Red! It's settle-up time."

From inside the cab, in the back, in the sleeper box, Skean heard a muffled voice. "Be cool, motherfuck; I'll pop you again." Red clambered down and slammed the door, hitched his jeans up on his hips and took a sip of the beer Hunchie had brought him.

"Hey, Joe." Red Gloeckner looked like a piece of raw meat; carrot-colored hair over a perpetually sunburned face. Even his freckles had an auburn tint that blended with the deeper red of the scattered blotches that would occasionally blossom into a full-fledged pimple. He worked as a mason's helper, when the weather suited, and could carry a pair of thirty-five-pound cement blocks in each hand. Up a ladder. But mostly he liked to hunt and drink and fuck.

He was twenty-five, looked younger; pudgy cheeks above full lips that he constantly wet and pursed as though he was about to whistle.

He had high cheekbones and the flat face of the Sioux; he was a conglomeration of parts and genes, Germanic and English and Irish and a rumored touch of Amerind. A real hybrid American; a less charitable soul might have called him a bastard. His pugnacious attitude did little to deny that characterization.

"All right; between the two of you, you think you can come up with some kind of a story for me?" Skean looked first at Hunchie, then at his young helper who towered over both of them.

"Hey, Joe, it wasn't our fault! How was we to know there was two of them? I mean, there wasn't never before."

"Hunchie, what the hell's he talking about; two of them?"

Hunchie finished his beer and crushed the can between his palms, then set it gently on the running board before answering. " 'S true, Joe. It went just like the other times. We picked him up at the terminal and followed him, just like you said; wait until he makes a stop on his own. He pulled in at Midway, same as that first one. About four hours out of the terminal." Hunchie shrugged and continued. "Red took him in the can."

Gloeckner took over, interrupting Hunchie's narration with an earnest voice. "It's like he said, Joe. We pulled into Midway right on him, watched him park the rig, and I followed him inside, just like you told us. Honest, it went down like before. He went into the pisser and I was right in there with him. It went beautiful; nobody's in there, 'cept us. He's fishing his root out and I popped him in the kidneys a shot." Gloeckner laughed a dry chortle. When he smiled, his lips rode up above his teeth, exposing his pink gums. "Like to fold up on the floor, only I hustled him into a stall, bounced his head off the hopper once to keep him down, and beat it back to the truck." He looked down at Hunchie and grinned. "You tell him the rest."

Hunchie lit another cigarette before speaking. "While our young man here was in the crapper with the driver, I was opening the cab up. Nothing to a Loadstar. Fords! I climbed up, leaned across and unlocked the other door. He'd left her going; I didn't have to worry about that. Anyway, Red had got the keys, in case. So I took her across the overpass, and got back on 22, heading back east. About, I guess, a minute later, it seems like, this guy comes up out of the sleeper box. Scared the shit out of me. 'Hosey', he says. 'Where's my coffee?' Jesus Christ!" Hunchie laughed and looked at Gloeckner. "Ol' Red about jumped out the truck! Well, this guy looks at me and looks at Red and says, 'Hey, who're you guys, you're not Hosey!' Well, no shit, and the guy tries to climb up front and I'm all over the Interstate with this dumb fuck hangin' on me and Red whacks him a couple and there you are. He's got the uniform on, I guess he's a company man. Relief driver or maybe they figured two guys on these Interstate runs on account of the other times. Anyhow here he is. He seen us good, Joe.''

"Yeah, I figured that part already. Listen, it's fixed, I talked with the guy, we'll get it straightened out. Red, put him over by the barn there.Tie him up or something. Ice him down. Then I'll take care of that part of it. Now what you got to do, is finish the job, like I told you. Hunchie, get this load the hell out of here and head like we said for New York. They're waiting for you up there, you know that. Right?'' He reached out and grasped Hunchie's bicep. ''Nothing different, just like the last one. Don't worry about this end of it, just get the load up there. Now I realize what you're probably thinking, your probably thinking that other damn driver's out of the crapper and screaming to the cops about his load, right? Sure he is. But, only the way I see it, it's about dark by the time you get back onto the Interstate, anyway, we're gonna peel the IGT decals of this rig right off now. You remember how I told you we could do that? Red, you get that son of a bitch out of the truck and do like I said. And Hunchie, turn this thing around. I'm gonna go look for that can of acetone I got. Like I told you, it'll soften up these truck decals and they'll peel right off and you'll be just another eighteen-wheeler heading into New York. Besides, the cops'll never figure on the truck heading right the hell back where it came from.'' He waited until Gloeckner was out of earshot. ''I'll see the man about puttin' a little more sugar on it, on account of all this.'' He turned away as Gloeckner climbed back up into the truck and dragged the semiconscious man out.

"Fuckin' amateurs!'' Skean muttered, and headed for the house. Somewhere, either in the kitchen or in one of the other first-floor rooms, among the accumulated trash of the past decade, was a gallon of acetone.

The man peeled off the black helmet, ran his hand through his hair, and released the latch that allowed him access to the tool compartment beneath the seat of the motorcycle. Skean watched him remove the sheepskin-lined pistol case in silence. The man zipped it open on the motorcycle's gas tank, revealing a Colt Government Model .45, two magazines, and an extra barrel. ''The 1911 ACP,'' he said, picking it up. ''I qualified with this particular weapon; ROTC. Did you know I was Airborne? Down there in redneck land. Ever been in North Carolina?'' He did not expect an answer from Skean and continued his monolog as he prepared the pistol. ''I made my bones with this; Southeast Asia, where I learned to appreciate handgun hunting. I was OIC of the motor pool, not much action there, so a few of us second lieutenants ventured into the jungle at night for sport. I enjoyed the challenge of the Cong. You are a hunter, Joseph, you would have loved it. But then you were in prison, weren't you.'' He selected one of the magazines and tipped it toward Skean. ''Two hundred and twenty grain Winchester Silvertips. See that hollow point? They just plain explode when they hit; turn themselves inside out.'' He held up his fist and made it burst open into widespread fingers. ''The tissue damage is awesome. Great self-defense round; even in .22 Magnum. But for a serious situation I like the ACP; an absolute classic, and properly tuned it's flawless.'' He shoved the magazine into the handle of the pistol and worked the slide, chambering a round. He thumbed the safety and offered the weapon to Skean, butt first. ''Like to do the honors?'' He smiled and brought the automatic back to his side. ''I thought not.''

CHAPTER 3

A hundred and twenty miles to the west an agent of the Pennsylvania Game Commission sat on a barstool and formed the apex of a triangle that connected him with Hunter's Game Farm and Defoe's barn. His hair stuck out like bits of straw from under a worn and dusty tractor cap as he wiped his hand across the stubble on his chin, then tilted the green Rolling Rock bottle toward the ceiling. "Ah don't kere *what* them animals had done to them, long as they kin walk good enough to get through the auction ring, friend." He finished the beer and set the bottle on the table. "Don't matter to *me* what them perfessors of yours been doin'."

The other man wore a set of blue coveralls with "Penn State" embroidered on one breast and "Jim" on the other. He looked around the dim bar, nearly empty in the early afternoon, and said, "Keep your voice down, for Christ's sake. I'm supposed to destroy *all* the experimental animals, after the project is run. Even the controls. I could lose my job if they found out I was selling them."

"Yeah, yeah, I hear ya," the agent said. He pulled a folded wad of bills from his pants pocket and peeled off a twenty, waved it toward the bartender for another pair of beers. "We gonna do some business or not?"

The man in the coveralls looked at the roll of bills. "Yeah. Tomorrow night. Eleven o'clock, C Building. You bring the fifteen hundred and your truck and I'll take care of the rest."

The agent picked up a fresh beer and touched his bottle to Jim's. "You got yourself a deal, friend," he said.

15

CHAPTER **4**

Defoe's telephone chirped again as he adjusted the burner.

"Defoe here."

"Attorney Oberholtzer for Chase Defoe, please." A female voice.

"Defoe here." He peered through the glass doors, spotted the second bottle of beer, and opened the refrigerator.

"Mr. Defoe?"

"Defoe here." He gave the omelet pan one final flourish and pulled it off the burner, then opened the bottle of beer.

"Please hold for Attorney Oberholtzer."

Defoe slid the omelet onto a plate, forked the pork chops beside them, and took a pilsner glass from the cabinet over the sink.

"Chase?"

"Defoe here." He carried the beer and the glass in one hand, neck of one, stem of the other between his fingers, and the plate of food in the other, and tilting his head to one side, kept the telephone receiver in place. At the counter opposite the stove he hooked a stool under his rear and sat, unloading his hands, then took the telephone with his left and poured beer with his right. It welled up in the glass, producing a full head.

"Chase! Tough man to get hold of. Been trying to get through to you since noon."

"Hello, Peter; excuse me, Attorney Oberholtzer. Getting to be quite the important advocate; a secretary places your calls now."

"Come on, friend; I've been in court all day and I have a township meeting tonight. We're trying to tie up some loose ends here before the weekend. I'll be out of here for a week, ten days, and there's a lot of last-minute things to resolve."

"I forgot, it's that time of year again."

"Yeah, I'm off to Alaska this time, shoot hell out of the moose population. That's not why I called, but while we're on it; that double rifle of your grandfather's? The one you won't sell me, the .458 Weatherby. Any chance I can borrow it for this trip?"

Defoe cut a piece of omelet with his fork. The melted Brie oozed out. "Peter? I hate to have to be the one to tell you this, but there haven't been any mastodon in Alaska for about ten thousand years."

Laughter came from the receiver. "No, but there's still a chance for a Kodiak permit. Yeah, I know, I have the H&R that's probably more appropriate, but see, this guy, this client, this *asshole* that I'm flying up there with, he's one of your old school-tie compatriots, and he's always got some kind of shit to pull whenever we get together to shoot a few birds. His father's Purdy a couple of weeks ago. Daddy had just given it to him, the old boy doesn't hunt much anymore. That kind of stuff. So I thought, just to see the look on his face would be worth it, I pull that seventy-year-old fitted pigskin case out of the baggage compartment of the Cessna and casually mention that yes, it was Granddad's; I don't get to use it much anymore, now that Africa is about closed down to the, ah, *traditional* sportsman, so I thought, one last time . . . Etcetera etcetera."

Defoe laughed. "I'd like to be there. How do you plan to explain the inlaid initials on the stock?"

"My mother's side of the family."

"Thinks quickly on his feet. I seem to recall that's what initially impressed me about you. Now that we have this parenthetical digression satisfied, tell me the real reason that you called."

"Why I called. I'd like a few hours of your time. This courthouse project. I remembered you said you'd be out of town and I wanted to touch base before you left."

"Tomorrow. South America for two weeks. I'll be hunting bugs. More exciting than moose, if you want my opinion. Why don't you stay home; for half of what this trip is going to cost you, my neighbor will let you shoot one of his Holsteins. I imagine the excitement level, not to mention the skills required, are about the same. What courthouse project?" Hot Brie, melted with eggs, was revolting. He shoved the omelet aside; cats would think it divine. He cut a piece of pork chop and forked it into his mouth.

"The new annex. I'm representing one of the architectural firms that will be bidding the job. Presentations to the commission are this week. Don't you read the papers?"

Defoe sipped his beer. "As infrequently as is decently possible. Tell me about it."

"Hundred-million-plus project, half in Federal dollars. There's a lot of competition for it, but these people out of Baltimore have a good shot at the job.''

''And you're greasing the way.''

''As an attorney with an intimate knowledge of the workings of local government, they felt that I could be of some assistance in helping them to secure the contract.''

''You're reading that from a press release, right? How do I figure into this?''

''Listen, off the record, Chase, I think it's about wrapped up; I've been talking this thing for some time now with the people who decide. But this final presentation, a scale model of their design and the complete set of blueprints, well, I'd feel better knowing that you'd looked over their security system. From what they tell me it's pretty sophisticated; closed-circuit cameras, metal detectors built into all the entrances. Even electronic explosive sniffers. Hell of a thing, Chase, when our courthouses are turned into fortresses, right? Anyway, I don't know diddley about this stuff, and neither does anyone on the commission. So if my people's plans had been scrutinized by the finest systems designer in the world . . . well, we'd have a leg up.''

''Flattery will get you everywhere. You want me to look over their proposal, see if I can find any weak spots, is that it?''

''Something like that. Shouldn't take, as I said, more than couple of hours; can you look these plans over before you leave?''

''What's your hurry, Counsellor; you got somebody else on hold?''

''I got three lights blinking at me and a girl standing here with an armload of papers.''

''And a date with a moose. Sure, fine; how do you want to set it up? My flight leaves tomorrow afternoon.''

''If it's okay with you, I'll drop off the plans tonight, and pick up that gun. Then you can look 'em over, and I'll come back out for them in the morning.''

''No problem. I should be here, but if I'm not, you know how to get in.''

Defoe opened the back door and put the dinner remains down for the cats. ''Hey!'' he called, scanning the alfalfa field beyond the gravel parking area. ''Last home-cooked meal for a while, you two. It's live off the land for a couple of weeks after tonight, better come and get it.'' He went inside to wash the dishes.

CHAPTER 5

The man in green looked up and saw the man in black slowly walking in his direction. One eye was nearly swollen shut; the side of his face was raw and turning purple from its impact with the side of the truck. He had to turn his head to bring the image into focus. His hands were tied behind his back; lengths of baler twine were looped around the fencepost. His arms jerked upward instinctively and he tried to twist his body away as he saw the man stop and face him, fifty feet away.

He held the pistol with both hands, the left cupping the fingers of the right, elbows slightly bent and locked. His head leaned to the right, his dominant eye aligned with the black oxidized combat sights.

The sharp report of the pistol echoed off the stone farmhouse and repeated three more times; each diminished in intensity as it rolled over the wooded valley. He brought the muzzle back down on the target and fired a double tap; the second bullet impacted an inch above the first. The third hit four inches higher, entering the driver's neck. Death was as instantaneous as it can be; in a fifth of a second a fastball travels thirty feet, time enough for a major-league batter to watch the seams roll, decide where it will break over the plate, and look it into the catcher's glove. A fifth of a second can stretch to infinity for a dying man.

Skean watched the man pick up the three ejected brass cartridges from the dusty barnyard. The driver hung forward, his bound hands holding him against the post.

A steep bluff angled behind the barn and curved toward the house. It dropped fifteen feet to a tangle of second growth and a riot of thorns that grew through and around a rusty accretion of abandoned automobiles and defunct farm equipment. He threw the three casings out over the tangle of vegetation, then walked back to the motorcycle where he methodically began to strip the weapon. He watched Skean's eyes as he depressed the recoil spring plug and rotated the bushing past it, then released the plug and the spring, aligned the slide stop and the dismounting notch by feel, pushed out the stop, moved the slide forward and off the frame, and dropped the still-warm barrel into his leather-covered palm. Only when the seven separate pieces of the automatic lay on the oiled sheepskin did he look down. "The ejector," he said quietly, "can make certain . . . ah—unique marks on the shell. Something to remember if you use an automatic, Joe. The barrel, of course," he continued, holding up the warm piece of steel, "we all know from the detective novels, has lands and grooves that impart their individual imprint to the bullet. Without the shell casings, or," he continued, throwing the barrel in a high, looping arc out over the bluff, "the barrel that fired them, nobody can match the bullets to the weapon." He smiled at Skean. "It would be a shame to dispose of such a fine firearm." He began to reassemble the gun with the new barrel. "As the only other person who knows the approximate location of the incriminating parts, Joseph, you will, of course, remain aware that you are an accessory before, during, and *after* the fact. Your culpability matches mine. Remember that while you are disposing of the evidence tied to your fencepost over there."

He patted Skean on the arm. "Do a good job." He unzipped his leather tunic and took out an inch-thick packet of bills. "A further payment on account, my friend. The balance due, as usual, upon delivery. Pay off those bumblers responsible for this mess. This project is terminated; we can't afford any more attention after this debacle." He put the weapon back under the seat of the motorcycle and straddled the machine. "Clean up, Joseph," he said, inclining his head toward the body by the barn. "I'll talk to you when the delivery is finalized." He thumbed the starter button and the engine rumbled to life. He fitted the black helmet back over his head and cinched the chin strap, then touched his forehead in a two-finger salute before roaring out the farm lane, standing on the footpegs as the motorcycle bounced over the rutted road.

"Amateurs and assholes," Skean said quietly as he turned to contemplate the remains of the driver. He was a linear thinker, slowly following one idea to its probable conclusion before taking up another. He stood in the farmyard for a long time, staring at the body, then slowly walked toward the tight board fence that formed a corral in front of the lower level of the barn.

The Pennsylvania bank barn was a creation of the German immigrants who settled the counties west of Philadelphia in the early eighteenth century. The bottom of the barn, invariably laid up of fieldstone and lime mortar, was dug into a south-facing slope; if forced to build on the flat, the farmer would berm up earth and stones until the north side of the second story was at ground level. This accomplished two things: The barn presented a low profile to the prevailing winter winds and allowed access to the second floor by horse and wagon. It was in high bays on either side of double doors that hay would be pitched in mows reaching to the eaves, and shocked grain was stored until threshed on the heavy plank floor. The livestock lived below, snug below ground on the north but with windows facing south, through which the low December sun penetrated to the deepest corners of the structure. The Palatine settlers intuitively knew the advantages of passive solar two hundred years before computer printouts told his descendants how to site their houses. The second floor jutted out over the lower one, forming the overshoot found on nearly every barn in eastern Pennsylvania. This shaded the animals from the high summer sun and kept wind-driven rain from penetrating into their stalls. A stone-fenced loafing yard sloped away from the building was a sure sign of a prosperous farmer.

The size and fertility of the farm, and hence the worth of its owner, could be judged by the size of the barn. The standard measurement of a bay was about fifteen feet by thirty or forty, wide enough for a load of hay and deep enough to accommodate the wagon and a team of horses. Three and four bay barns are most often seen, although in the more prosperous areas of Lancaster County fifty-by-one-hundred-foot structures are not uncommon.

The barn of Hunter's Game Farm spoke of no such prosperity, neither present, nor past, when the foundation was first laid in the second decade of the nineteenth century. Northern Berks County, nestled into the first slopes of the Appalachians that mark the transition from fertile lowlands to coal country, cannot compare with the rich soils to the south in the counties of Chester and Lancaster.

The roof was sagging and its slates were starting to slip, signs of terminal illness in a post-and-beam structure. Once the roof goes, the rest of the building is doomed to follow in a few short years.

The top floor housed a rudimentary butcher shop of the sort that never saw a government inspector. Rusty gambrels hung from the beams, and a pair of battered stainless-steel tables stood beneath a lone light bulb. Deer hides, salted and drying on lath and chicken wire racks, were scattered in the dim corners. A compressor cycled on and off spasmodically, pumping Freon through a five-by-eight-foot walk-in cooler box.

The bottom of the barn contained a dozen makeshift farrowing pens around a central area split into three larger pens for the boars, barrows, and gilts.

The Russian wild hogs came up out of the Great Smoky Mountains of Tennessee, crossbred with the indigenous razorbacks that had gone wild. An evil-tempered beast that would eat anything that moved slower than itself, the animal was one of the few true omnivores: it ate acorns, roots, reptiles, small mammals, birds, and amphibians. It stands high at the shoulders and slopes quickly away to the hindquarters, looking like the bison and the hyena in profile. Their short tail has a brush on the end and they are covered with coarse dark bristles over an undercoat of heavy wool, a legacy of fifty thousand years' evolution in the cold Russian steppes.

An awesome head, dominating the body, features a long, knobby snout with eight-inch tusks, the upper canines curved upward. They can disembowel an adversary with the effortless ease of the straight razor; their lower canines constantly grind against the uppers as they feed, honing the tusks to a razor sharpness. Like rats, as the teeth wear down, they grow fresh from the root.

They feast on rattlesnakes; kill them with their hooves. As the locals tell it, they'll "walk up to a rattler and plain eat him alive."

For all their ferocity and destructiveness to the indigenous flora and fauna of the area, they are looked upon as a valued resource by both the North Carolina Wildlife Resources Commission and the Tennessee Game and Fish Commission, who control the hunting of these beasts. The Great Smoky is the oldest but not the only population of European wild hogs in the country.

In 1924, a dozen of them were trapped and sent across the continent, to be released near Carmel on the San Francisquito Ranch. It wasn't long before a few escaped into the Los Padres National Forest and went native, forming the western branch of the family.

Half a century later another small band moved north, to a run-down farm in eastern Pennsylvania. Joe Skean discovered them; his partner Mobay brought the concept to fruition.

Skean chuckled and rolled over on the bunk above his cellmate. "Listen to this," he said, and using a finger as a pointer, followed the words. " 'As the beady-eyed tuskers whooshed from the crates, some of the mountaineers went shinnying up trees like scared squirrels. They had been used to wild mountain razorbacks and acorn-splitter hogs all their lives, but these wild pigs from abroad were something different.' Fucker got to be something to tree a mountain man!''

"What the hell you got there?''

"Book, I got it up the library. Animals that were brought to this country from someplace else. This part is about Russian wild boars.''

"Commie pigs.'' Mobay laughed a porcine grunt on the lower bunk. "What's this about men up in trees?''

"Wait, I'll start back at the beginning.'' There was a brief silence as Skean flipped pages. "Here. Wait a minute; here it is. It says that back in 1908, there was the Great Smoky Mountain Land and Timber Company; they sold a whole shitload of acreage to these two Englishmen. The Whites, the Whitings. Two brothers. Only they didn't have the money, so they got this American to get it for them. A two-million-dollar loan. Shit, I bet that was some deal back then, Mobes, 'cause they gave this guy, Moore, here he is, G. Gordon Moore, sixteen hundred acres of it for a game preserve. To have animals where you can go shoot them. Only you got to be one of his rich friends, or someone he's trying to snow. You see what I'm saying?'' Skean rolled over and looked down at the figure bowing the mattress below him.

"Yeah, I see,'' Mobay answered, thinking. "Like state game lands. Only nobody can hunt them, unless he says.''

"You got it. Except, the way this tells it, they're a son of a bitch to hunt. They band together, in a pack like, and mostly feed at night. 'Quiet, nervous, and always alert.' That's what it says. 'Never stand still for more that a couple seconds and can disappear in a flash.' ''

"Where these pigs at?'' Mobay sat up and swung his legs over the edge of his bunk.

"Down South somewhere. Wait a minute. The Snowbird mountains of western North Carolina. This place called Hooper Bald. On account of it don't have no trees on it. Moore guy built the hunting place up there. Fifteen hundred fenced acres. Christ! Five hundred just for the boars. Here it is; April, 1912, these foreign animals were brought in. That's what the book's about, Mobay, animals that were brought to America from someplace else. Anyway, there's a bunch of shit, bears and buffalos and elks and stuff, and fourteen of these Russian boars. This is where I read you the part about the pigs putting the mountain men up the trees!'' Skean laughed again at the thought.

''So, are the pigs still down there? Them rednecks still setting in the trees?''

''Naw! Hell, Mobes, the wild pigs escaped a long time ago. First this Moore guy hires this McGuire to run the place, and then I guess the idea doesn't pan out or what; anyway, he gives the whole thing to this local, this what-a-ya-call-him, this redneck, McGuire. And he figures, fuck it, we'll go shoot the goddamn pigs. Him and his friends. Here it is, it says by that time there's a hundred of them buggers in this five-hundred-acre pen. All fenced in, there. It says, 'He invited his friends up the mountain and they came leading their packs of hounds.' '' His finger followed the text across the page. '' 'When the men and their dogs entered the boar pen for the big hunt, all hell broke loose. When the hunt was over, and it did not last long, only two hogs had been killed. Assorted hunters clung to precarious perches in the trees and a half-dozen of the finest hounds in the Snowbird Range lay dead or dying because they approached too closely to those crippling tusks.' Shit! I'd like to of seen that! But, then, here's what it says, what you wanted to know. 'As for the hogs, the shooting and yelling had scarcely begun before they knocked the fence asunder and began escaping into the surrounding mountains. Their descendants roam there today.' Son of a bitch!''

Mobay stood up and reached for the book. ''Let me see that.'' He took the book and sat with it on his bunk, silently working his way through the entire chapter. Then he went back to the beginning, pointing out the salient parts. ''It says here they can reach up to four hundred pounds, but two and a quarter is a real big one. Lookit here, Joe,'' he said, standing up and pointing at a paragraph. ''Litters are four, five pigs, in the wild. Shit. It's twice that or better, in the farrowing barns I been around. I could do better'n that. And here, see this? They get their tushes when they's a year old, but they don't become sexually mature until they's a year and a half. Well, shit, I don't know about any wild boars, but I know pigs, and I know I can take a weaner to two and a quarter in six months time, on a feedlot. Figure, hell, these wild ones might take twice as long, you still got a two-hundred-pound porker inside a year. Them jackasses at them shooting clubs upstate, they could go for this. Goddamn, Joe, I think we're on to something. Damn, the way they'd go after the cockbirds I'd haul up there, I know we got us an idea to work on, once we get out. What do you say, you with me on this?''

Skean was with him and they were released from the Eastern State Penitentiary at Graterford and they moved into the game farm with the dying Hunter.

Skean made a few calls to customers in Hunter's notebook and found that he could get several hundred dollars apiece for mature wild boars; the shooting preserves would take every animal he could supply.

Mobay went south with the van and all the cash they could raise. Skean ripped out the exotic bird-housing in the bottom of the barn, built hog pens, and humored the dying old man.

Skean climbed up an oil drum and looked over the fence at the hogs that lay in the muddy barnyard. His eyes counted the numbers that his mind knew were there, twenty thousand for the mature barrows and gilts that were ready to move; he could have the cash in ten days if he wanted to run a couple of more trucks to deliver the pigs. It was late October and the blood lust was rising; small game season was under way and deer hunting would open in a few weeks. The desire for wild boar would peak when thousands of bear and deer hunters came back from the wilds empty-handed. That's when the shoot for pay preserves would be getting the frantic phone calls from sportsmen desperate for proof of their prowess.

He knew he and Mobay would sell a lot of deer, too, gutted, or dressed, or just the trophy head and rack, over the next few weeks. It was their busiest season of the year.

His thoughts were drawn back to the wild "Russian" pigs. Forty shooters ready to go. The boars at stud he could get a thousand apiece for, right now, fifteen hundred if he had the time. Say five thousand, conservatively. The sows were worth another five, and the younger stock, hell, say a nickel, too; maybe thirty thousand total, with a little luck. Eight separate loads over a three-, four-day period. It might come to that. Mobay would be pissed. He jumped down from the barrel. Mobay didn't have to know.

Skean walked toward the corpse of the IGT driver; his right hand went behind his ear, grasping the haft of the double-edged knife in the sheath between his shoulder blades. A local longhair farrier, part-time knifemaker, had forged the blade for him from a piece of half-inch wire rope. Somewhere the man had learned that the twisted steel cable used for cranes and ship hawsers was made up of soft, flexible, spring steel and hard, extremely brittle high-carbon metal. The two together, heated and forged into one, made the ideal blade. Tough and supple so as not to break when called upon to do some arduous task, but hard enough to take and hold a razor edge. The handle still held the shape and ridges of the cable that it had be born from while the double edges were sharp enough to shave a forearm. Skean reached behind the body and severed the twine that held him to the post.

He hooked the driver under the arms and dragged him to the fence.

Skean looked at his watch; Mobay'd be showing up to feed in an hour, he'd have to hurry. He loosened and removed the driver's boots, a nearly new pair of Wolverines. He boosted the body over the fence, heard it hit with a dull thump in the soft barnyard muck. There was a smear of blood on the boards where the corpse had gone over; Skean looked down at his shirt and saw another stain. He could hear the hogs moving, coming to investigate the newest presence. He picked up the boots and walked to the edge of the bluff, flung them after the pistol parts. Wet, smacking sounds, mixed with an occasional angry squeal, came from behind the fence. Skean went inside the house to change his shirt.

CHAPTER 6

Yearner Claxon poured coffee into a styrofoam cup, passed on the cream and sugar. He examined the cardboard box of doughnuts, picked out a pair of cinnamon-dusted crullers. Fuck it! An extra fifty sit-ups tonight would pay for the transgression. He dropped a dollar bill on the plate beside the Mr. Coffee machine. He had sculpted his twenty-eight-inch waist in boot camp and maintained it through the next eight years in the Corps with exercise, not diet. Four years of civilian life had not altered the hundred and seventy pounds he carried on his six-foot frame. "It takes a lean horse for a long race," the Biloxi Magnolia had once said, running an admiring hand over the washboard of his torso; stamina was becoming a matter of pride for a man who would turn thirty in a month.

Penelope Bucks looked up from her terminal and swiveled toward the front of her desk, throwing her shoulders back as he approached. "Hi, Yearner! Long time no see!" she squealed. She had the bright, open look of a recent hire and the eager enthusiasm of the unattached.

Nice smile, short frizzy hairdo, a pair of floaters he'd love to get into a hot tub with his sub and torpedo. He really had to spend more time in the office; paperwork could be fun.

"Hello, Penny. Yeah, I've been out around State College the last few months." His voice was soft and slow, with a faint remembrance of the South. "Still would be, but you know," he jerked his head toward the door to her right. "His master's voice."

On cue, a middle-aged man in two-thirds of a three-piece suit came through the door, glanced theatrically at his wristwatch, and said, "Claxon! About time you showed up; we start around here at eight. Ms. Bucks, coffee please, hold my calls." He turned and reentered his office, knowing Claxon would follow.

District Commissioner Harding leaned back in his chair, the springs

27

squeaking, and sipped from the ceramic cup that bore the inscription "World's Best Granddad." After a pause he said, "You look like shit, Claxon. You miss my directive on dress and deportment last quarter?"

Claxon looked down at his greasy jeans and sweatshirt, ran a hand over the four-day stubble and untrimmed ash-blond hair that could have qualified him for a *Miami Vice* walk-on. Out of the office he called his boss Commissioner Hard-on.

"Yeah, well, Warren, out there, in the field, the crewcut look of a Jedgar doesn't always hack it. Now you want me in here, shit-shined-and-shaved, in my go-to-court suit, I'll be glad to oblige, anytime. Just give me a little advance notice, so's I can make my excuses to the suspects out there in the field, give me time to find a shower and a dry cleaner, press my pants." He put his coffee on the edge of his supervisor's desk and bit a cruller, sprawled in the vinyl side chair. "I slept in the back of my truck last night, Warren, like I do about three nights a week. I was halfway between here and my motel out the other side of State College when your buzzer hit; and like the asshole I am, I figured it was *important*, so rather than head back there, change, get cleaned up, and report into the Eastern District Office of the Pennsylvania Game Commission tomorrow, I just snuck in this morning. Dumb old me." He stuck the other half of the doughnut in his mouth, slurped coffee, and swallowed.

Harding tilted forward in his chair, set the mug on his desk. "Yes, well, your punctuality is commendable. I'm sure it will be reflected in your annual proficiency rating." He picked up a manila folder, gestured with it. "I had you hustle your tail to Allentown because of this. Deer spotters have been decimating a tri-county area for a couple of years now and my office is right at the goddamn epicenter! Congressman Houer has passed numerous complaints from both the NRA and the damn Bambi-ists onto the Commissioner; it's an election year and he's all over my case." He paused, picked up his mug, and looked at his agent over the rim, favored him with a slight smile. "Like the good bureaucrat that I am, I'm now passing it along to you." He waved the folder in the air over his desk. "Get out there, Claxon, clean this shit up. Make me look good, son; I retire in three years. Get these sons of bitches that are harvesting product out of season. Pretty soon there won't be a damn deer left for the city boys to gut-shoot. I'm telling you straight out, Harrisburg is on my ass; pal, *mi* hemorrhoids *su* hemorrhoids, *comprende*?"

Claxon thought, digested the data, then talked around the second cruller in his mouth. "What the fuck's the rush? You said this has been going on for a couple of years; I'm three months living outta my truck like a goddamn scuzzball, out there at the university; I got jock itch and dingleberries on account of I can't go to the laundromat and risk my image; I can't make time with all those juicy coeds because I smell like a wild animal that's been rained on. And all of a sudden it's time to pull the plug on the project I been working since the middle of the summer, the experimental animal thing, with the research labs. Too *much*, Warren.'' He got up, tossed his empty cup toward the wastebasket, strode around the office with his hands in his jeans, looked out the window.

"Yeah, well cool down, Agent Claxon. I realize you lose track of time, out there in the field you're so fond of. But there's an election coming up, Tuesday next month, and a certain previously mentioned congressman sits on a committee that directly affects your ass. Those goddamn vouchers you turn in every week get passed along for approval, you know, and the money has to come from somewhere, out of a budget authorization. Now you want to go with the status quo, you get on this case and give the man some results for the six-o'clock news, handcuff shots for the minicam. Otherwise just maybe his opponent, a nice lady from Philadelphia, who has a bunch of cats I'm told, and they're all fixed probably, and who I know for a fact thinks that guns should be put into the crusher along with junked cars and has proposed *birth* control, for Christ's sake, for downsizing the herd, she could get elected and then where would we be?''

"Jeez, I don't know, Warren. Chasing around the woods, trying to put condoms on bucks?''

"Claxon, get the hell out of here, and stop thinking about sex.'' He tossed the file on his desk. "Absorb this data and effectuate a response. One that will reflect favorably on this department. I told you, I retire in three years. And election day looms, Claxon. It *looms!*''

CHAPTER 7

Defoe studied the new courthouse plans over a breakfast of tea and toast, activated the alarm system and locked up the barn, then put his two suitcases and the aluminum electronics case in the trunk. Sliding behind the wheel, he crossed his fingers and turned the key. The engine fired and he exhaled, sank back in the worn leather seat. The idiosyncratic electrical system could be annoying at times, but the walnut-and-leather interior balanced the occasionally unreliable English wiring. The car was nearly thirty years old and qualified for antique plates, but he thought them a silly vanity that only drew unwanted attention. Panache was anathematic to one with the self-assurance of Defoe.

He found the Coronary Care Unit on the fifth floor and Harold Askew on a heart monitor with an IV bottle dripping into his arm.

"Scared the bejesus out of me, Mr. Defoe, I don't mind telling you. Lucky for me I was at the State Police barracks; they started CPR and got me here in fifteen minutes. Turns out it wasn't all that serious, as heart attacks go, but swear to God, I'm changing my lifestyle. No more smokes, cut back on the booze. I gotta lose about forty pounds, too." He pointed at the bottom of the bed. "Crank me up, will ya? And get my case out of the closet over there. I made sure that stayed right on the gurney with me. I lose that and I might as well die, all the records I got in there." He opened the snaps and flipped up the lid of the briefcase. "What'd they tell you in Hartford about this?"

Defoe pulled a straight-back chair next to the bed. "Not much. A trucking company has had some loads hijacked. A million dollars' worth of French designer clothing. I got the impression you had the whole thing pretty well settled before you wound up in here; I gather that I'm supposed to tidy up your paperwork and ship it off to Hartford."

"That's about it; routine claim. Only thing that bothered me is all three loads of clothing were coming out of Kennedy. But after seeing the manifests I realized they were different consignees."

"All imported clothing? Doesn't that seem an unusual coincidence?"

"I forgot, you don't know this business; no, IGT, that's Interstate Garment Transport, all they haul is the rag trade. Mostly domestic goods, out of the Brooklyn knitting mills, the sewing contractors around Scranton, Wilkes Barre. But they do pick up container cargo coming into the port of Newark and JFK; haul directly to stores in the Midwest, down south."

"So you don't think there's a connection between these, what is it, three, hijackings?"

"Doesn't look that way, from what the police reports say, and I also talked to the head of IGT. I've dealt with him before, pretty straight-up guy. Been insured by us for a number of years. Ninety percent of these cases are walkaways, give-ups, as they say; driver is paid to go take a thousand-dollar leak, comes out, and his rig is gone. Swears up and down that he locked it. Recovery in this business is just about zero percent. Especially if the wise guys are involved. Then the load is already sold and someone is waiting for delivery even before the truck is stolen. That makes finding it impossible."

"What about the police?"

"Ha! Excuse my cynicism, Mr. Defoe. The cops deal with hard evidence and in cases like these all we have is hearsay; we got a driver who says he lost a truck, we got a trucking company with some papers that says a truck existed, and we got more paperwork that claims there was a few thousand pounds of merchandise on that truck. What are they gonna do? Besides, the police, what do they care about an insurance company losing a couple of dollars; they could give a shit. Now a citizen, a voter, comes in and shows them a busted head and says he was robbed, then they'll make the effort. They won't get the guy's wallet back, but they'll make the effort. But this case, it ever gets solved, we ever see a dime's worth of recovery, it'll be me who does it. Only I'm about a hundred percent satisfied that we have three separate incidents here. The one thing I didn't get a chance to do, before I got sidetracked into this bed, was go talk to the drivers, personal. But I read their statements to the police. And those three are dead ends; these were no walkaways, take my word for that." He turned toward the bedside table. "Hand me that glass with the funny straw, will you? This medication makes me dry as a dog in August."

"So you're saying the claims should be paid." Defoe held the glass for the adjuster.

"Well, yeah; at least this one the company is hearing all the noise about, the second load to get snatched. On the other two I'd ordinarily wait until I had all the loose ends tied up. Only with this thing here, I don't know how long I'll be out of work. But there is one lead that might amount to something." He sorted through the briefcase and extracted a Xerox of an eight-by-ten photograph. "A picture of a tireprint from the first truck that got hit. The second and third were grabbed at truck stops, but this first one happened at a pull-off on 22. Driver didn't like the way his trailer felt and pulled over to check his tires. A pickup came alongside and the next thing the driver knew he had a couple of cracked ribs and his load was gone. But he remembered the truck, one of those customized jobs, with the fat tires. That's what this photo is."

Defoe looked at the picture, sharp impressions in thick mud, an abstract of angles in black and white.

"State Police sent a plaster cast down to Washington. One of the cops who knows these trucks told me it's an unusual pattern, nothing he's seen. And the tires were new, see those little holes? They're made by those tits that you only find on new tires, where the rubber is injected into the mold. They break off, wear off, pretty quick. Anyway, this cop says there's a chance they can find out who made the tire and where they shipped any around here in the last six months. That's the kind of thing cops are good for. 'Course it don't mean that we'll find the owner of the tires with a load of dresses and a burning desire to confess. But it's all we got." He took the photo from Defoe and put it back in the briefcase.

"I say we make copies of all this and send it to Hartford with my recommendation to pay the claim. All three of them. It'll keep IGT happy, and they're a major account."

"If you're satisfied, then that's it. I'll take these down to the business office right now and run off the copies; I have a plane to catch, so time is, as they say, of the essence. I'll jot a note to Bill Pickering and mail the whole thing at the airport." Defoe held out his hand and Askew collated the relevant materials.

He stopped at the nurses' station and purloined a stethoscope and white jacket, then headed for the elevator.

"Yes, may I help you, Doctor, ah . . ." The secretary was a brook-no-nonsense type with iron-gray hair to match her will.

"Presume," Defoe said. "Livingstone, Livingstone I. The I. is for Irving." He tilted his head back and looked down his nose. "I need copies of these papers, but not to bother, I can run them off myself." He walked over to the copy machine.

"Certainly *not* Doctor Presume. This is my department, give them to me." She took the papers from Defoe and began to feed them through the machine, turning and collating the warm copies as they emerged. She paused as the tireprint came out. "What is this? This is not an insurance form!"

"Quite so; it is graphic evidence of why we had to rebuild both of the unfortunate man's feet. A toll-taker on the turnpike. Stood a bit too close, didn't he?" Defoe took the two sets of papers and smiled, turned toward the door. Another secretary came over to the first.

"What was that all about? Who was that man?"

"That," snorted the iron-willed woman, "is the sixty-four-dollar question."

Jesus Jorge Christobal cleared customs quickly with his diplomatic passport and went into the lavatory of the overseas terminal at Philadelphia International Airport. He wrinkled his nose at the pungent smell of the deodorant cakes in the urinals, locked himself in a stall, stripped off his suit coat and opened the sealed diplomatic pouch. He shrugged into the black Cordura nylon shoulder holster and picked up the Taurus PT-99 AF, a copy of the Beretta Model 92, official sidearm of the Brazilian military. Captain Cristobal loaded a fifteen-round magazine of 9mm Parabellum ammunition in the weapon, worked the slide and lowered the hammer on a live round, then put his jacket back on and tucked the envelope, containing twenty-five thousand American dollars, into the inside pocket where it rode just over the pistol. Such a lot of money! He tested the draw several times, his right hand sliding over his left breast; by moving his palm a few millimeters one way or the other he could grasp the envelope or the weapon. He smiled and left the toilet.

Defoe pulled into one of the long-term parking lots that hovered on the fringes of the airport complex. For a few extra dollars the vehicle would be stored inside during his absence and not subjected to the abuses of public parking at the terminal. The lot ran a shuttle van every half hour to the airport.

"Hey, slick wheels, mister; look like a old-timer."

Defoe opened the trunk, took out his bags. "Yeah, it's a Mark II."

"You jivin' me, that ain't no Lincoln!"

"No, it's a Jaguar, 1960. The Mark II was smaller than the Mark X. But then, so am I," he added with a smile.

The parking lot attendant chuckled, looking down at Defoe's five-and-a-half-foot frame. "You got that right. Keys in it?"

"Yes. Oh, and leave it in gear, the parking brake doesn't hold too well."

"Sixty a week, cash in advance unless you wanna put it on plastic. How long you gonna be?"

Defoe slipped a credit card from his wallet and dropped it on the counter. "Two weeks." The bald man did not even look up as he slid the card into an imprinter, entered the amount, and slapped the form back in front of Defoe for his signature.

Captain Cristobal wanted to catch Defoe as he arrived, before he got to the crowded terminal, wanted a little privacy to conduct his business. But that was impossible; he had no idea of where Defoe would park, assuming he didn't take a cab, and he was uncertain of his quarry's appearance. He dug once again into his trouser pocket and took out the coin.

"Take these papers and this five-centavo piece, Cristobal," his superior, General Rojas, chief of Secret Police, had said the day before. "The nickel, the North Americanos call it. You will find it a remarkable likeness of Senor Defoe. It will help you to identify him, before he boards the aircraft for our country. Which you will see that he does not do. Carry out this assignment and greater opportunities will be opened for you in the new regime."

Cristobal had saluted and spun on his heel, mentally packing his bags for Philadelphia as he left the general's office, round-trip ticket and travel documents in hand.

Defoe waited in line at the airline counter, his crocodile briefcase in his left hand, the aluminum electronics case in his right. He had checked his two suitcases in with the porter at the door to the terminal.

Cristobal looked at the coin, at the man with the bags, back at the coin. Both heads in profile. Sloping forehead, strong *anglo* nose, chin thrust forward. And that little smirk-smile; yes, this was the man.

"Senor Defoe?" His quarry turned toward him; Cristobal reached in his jacket, routinely scanning the crowd. He removed his passport, opened it for Defoe. "I am Captain Cristobal. I would have a word with you, senor, before you check in with the airline."

Defoe looked at the passport, the line ahead of him, noted the bulge beneath the suitcoat of the Latino. "Very well. Over there." Defoe motioned with his head toward a double row of plastic chairs fastened to the floor. "How did you get that weapon past airport security?" He smiled at Cristobal's raised eyebrows.

"I am sent from General Rojas, Senor Defoe. There has been a change in plans." He took the envelope from his pocket. "Recent developments in my country make it unwise for you to carry out the mission you have contracted with the, . . . ah,—*old* government.'' He paused, waiting for Defoe's reaction. When none was forthcoming, he continued, looking at his watch. ''In a few hours the announcement will be made; General Rojas is now preparing for the press conference. A new Democratic coalition is being formed even as we speak. It is felt that it would be inappropriate, an embarrassment, for a . . . a—''

''North Americano?'' Defoe smiled.

''*Gracias, señor*. Yes, it would be difficult if you were seen to be visiting all our embassies across the continent so soon after the . . . change. So I must ask you to turn over the equipment that you are delivering, and teach me here to use it.'' He handed the envelope to Defoe. ''Your fee, senor, as was agreed upon.''

Defoe turned the envelope, unopened, end for end in his hands. ''It's not quite that simple, Captain Cristobal. I planned to spend two weeks sweeping your embassies, and, believe me, that is not my idea of a vacation. There are many subtleties to be mastered, it is not a skill that can be taught in a few minutes, and a busy airport is hardly a suitable classroom.''

''Forgive me, Senor Defoe, but I hold a degree in electrical engineering from the University of Madrid. And I have been in charge of my ministry's clandestine communications for the past year. I am not exactly a neophyte in the field.''

Defoe sighed. ''Very well, Captain, let us find a more private location for your tutorial.'' He stood up and looked around, headed for an elevator that was used to bring handicapped individuals to the embarkation level. Defoe punched the emergency stop button and isolated them between floors. ''This should give us a few moments of uninterrupted quiet.'' He opened the aluminum case. ''This is a nonlinear junction detector,'' he said, fitting the head to the adjustable boom and connecting the wires to the receiver. ''The unit transmits microwaves and picks up semiconductors, both diodes and integrated circuits. They don't have to be transmitting to be detected; as an electrical engineer, you, of course, are aware that nonlinear devices allow current to flow more readily in one direction than the other.'' He turned on the battery-operated detector. ''It transmits at one gigahertz, and any semiconductor in the vicinity will generate harmonics in exact multiples of the original frequency.'' He swung the head around the elevator car, stopping at the control panel. ''There,'' he said, pointing to the meter on his equipment. ''It's picking up the circuit in the emergency call box. That's a drawback; it'll detect any semiconductor; your secretary's transistor radio in her desk drawer will respond the same way a burst transmitter wired to an electret microphone hidden beneath four inches of plaster will. You have to learn to separate the wheat from the chaff.'' And never mind finding the passive microphones, the fiber optic devices, the laser-activated transmitters that are snuggled with a TV signal, those damn band switchers that jump frequencies every few thousandths of a second. Defoe smiled and began packing the equipment back into its case. ''Good luck, Captain,'' he said, activating the elevator's control panel. ''Now let's go and retrieve my luggage before it ends up revolving endlessly on a carousel in Caracas.''

CHAPTER 8

"**H**ello-hello, anybody home?'' Defoe knocked on the kitchen door of the old farmhouse and walked in. The room was in cheerful disarray; sketches and fabric swatches littered the table, and a mannequin, dressed to the nines in Victorian formality, took endless tea at her place at the head of the table. A Siamese cat drowsing on the drainboard raised one suspicious eyelid, decided that Defoe passed muster, and went back to sleep.

"Back here!'' A muffled voice came from the hallway that led to the dining and living rooms, now studio space, toward the front of the plastered stone building. She came into the hall with an armload of silk dresses on hangers. "Chase! What a surprise, what are you doing here?'' She draped the clothing over the back of a kitchen chair and hugged him.

"I was in the neighborhood, on my way back from the airport, so I stopped in. How have you been, Leilani? Busy as always, I see.''

"Sure. I have a trunk show in Boston this weekend, and as usual I'm not nearly ready. You're coming from the airport; been away?''

"I was supposed to spend the next two weeks in South America, but the deal was canceled. So I've got a fortnight with nothing to do. Thought I'd start it off by taking you to dinner.''

She squeezed his hand, sadness in her smile. "Oh, I'd love to, Chase, but I've got to get out of here by six; I'm meeting a friend in New York, we're driving up together. And I've still got a load of skirts in the dryer, sweaters to steam and everything has to be labeled; I'm a mess. So what else is new?'' She laughed and went to the sink. "But I can certainly spare a few minutes for tea and thee.''

"Great. I did have an ulterior motive for dropping in; I'm going to use this unexpected free time to help out a friend. My godfather, actually. One of his insurance company's clients recently had several truckloads of imported clothing hijacked. I've decided to put my mind to the puzzle, and since I'm not up to date on the rag trade I thought I could pick your brains over dinner.''

"Sounds like you want someone with Seventh Avenue experience, anyway, Chase. Which leaves me out. But I *do* know someone, Caroline Graff. She's an artist, but she worked for *WWD* for about a year. She lives in Reading now; has a piece of a warehouse—what they call a *loft* up in New York, and charge a fortune for. Let me give her a buzz, see if she can help you.''

Defoe made the tea while Leilani went back down the hallway to call her friend.

"Not there," she said, coming back into the kitchen. "I left a message on her machine." Leilani picked up her cup of tea, warming her hands. "I explained that I'm on my way to Boston, gave her your phone number, told her to call you." She took a sip of tea and smiled. "I didn't tell her what it was about, 'cause I'm not sure that I know myself. So I just gave her a brief bio and told her she'd be sorry if she didn't call you." She winked at Defoe. "She's single.''

Defoe dropped his bags inside his front door, smiled, and made a small nasal noise that originated somewhere deep within his sinuses as he read the note from his lawyer. "Thanks for the gun. Will ret. it in 2 wks with moose steaks. Peter." He made a second trip to the car and brought two bags of groceries into the kitchen, then went up the cast-iron spiral stairs, an ornate double helix that he had rescued from an abandoned lighthouse on the Outer Banks, and unpacked his bags. He clattered back down the steps, passing the main floor, continuing to the bottom level where once the cows had reigned. Now the floor was brick, the plastered walls gleamed with a lime wash, and over-head fluorescent strips chased the evening shadows. At one end of the room a gym mat, weights, and a lifting bench sat, a still life on the herringbone floor; centered at the foot of the stairs was a billiard table, the cue and two object balls centered on the green felt. He punched a four-digit code on the steel firedoor and went into the office he had partitioned at the opposite end of the building. It was cool and dry, ideal for the computer that sat against the back wall, and a pleasant climate for the several dozen cases of wine that were stacked beside it. He opened the center drawer of the battered steel office desk and tossed the envelope of cash inside, then checked the telephone and fax machine for messages. All quiet on the western front. He was, after all, not expected back for two weeks. A shame that Leilani had to rush off to Boston. He looked at his cellar book and chose one of the last two bottles of '81 Sauvignon Blanc from the Mayacamas vineyards, past its prime but still drinkable, and having the added advantage of only needing half an hour's aeration; it would be ready by the time he whipped up something to eat.

He washed his dishes and inoculated the remainder of the wine with a little cider vinegar; in a few days it would be ready to marry with a bit of cold-pressed olive oil and finish out its career as a delightfully delicate salad dressing. He poured a measure of the Macallan single malt in his wineglass and swirled the Scotch; sniffed, sipped, and smiled. A whisky that could hold its own with the finest cognac France could offer.

He turned off the lights, carried his drink and his briefcase upstairs, showered and put on a terry-cloth robe, then shook out the futons on the raised sleeping platform and settled down with the insurance report.

Pages of data from the police of three states and a hatful of jurisdictions. Statements of the drivers. Witness interviews. Official forms filled out by Officer Responding. Follow-up Detective's Report. Physical Evidence Form: (A) Held in Evidence Room [State Police Barracks No ——](B) Evidence Located Elsewhere [Give Location]. Shipper's manifests, U.S. Customs declarations and duty paid tickets.

There had been three trucks hijacked in less than a week's time, all originating at the Kennedy Overseas Freight Terminal. The first load contained three thousand dozen woolen sweaters, country of origin Great Britain and insured for six hundred and fifty thousand dollars. Defoe scratched the figures on a legal pad and did the long division. About eighteen dollars apiece, including duty. Three thousand dozen. Three twelves are thirty-six. He took a pale-blue Shetland crewneck from his closet, hefted it. Maybe three-quarters of a pound. Figure fifteen tons for the load. He looked at the sweater. Roughly a foot square, folded, and two inches thick, but could be compressed to half that; the shipment was around thirty-five hundred cubic feet, a full trailer. It took more than one guy to handle the load. Had to have a secure place to transfer the stolen sweaters, a loading dock, fork lift. This was the one taken along Interstate 22, the one with the tireprint. Xerox of the police photograph in here someplace.

The second theft involved the French designer clothing. Lagerfeld, Yves Saint Laurent, Claude Montana, Sonia Rykiel; most were names he didn't recognize. Insured for two and a half million. This was the load the consignee was screaming about. Reade Industries. New York City. The truck had been heading for their Manhattan warehouse. Should have been a short haul from JFK, no stops. Defoe flipped the manifest shut, picked up the police report. New York City, 87th Precinct, Det. Corolla filed this one. Japanese? Wonder if his first name is Toyota! The driver, Francis Schaftmaster, had come out of the Queens Midtown Tunnel into the bright sunshine of Manhattan Island. A door on the passenger side of a parked car had opened and the IGT truck had torn it off. The driver stopped; as he got out, someone had hopped onto the running board behind him, clamped a hand on the driver's neck, propelled him with the other between parked cars. Driver sustained bruised temple from contact with bumper and cut on upper lip inflicted by rear license plate of aforesaid vehicle. Aforesaid? Refused treatment. Be interesting to hear the driver's first-person account. The car with the missing door had been stolen from a shopping center outside Easton, Pennsylvania, the same morning. How had Askew overlooked this: there seemed to be a common thread here. Easton, with Allentown and Bethlehem, was part of the Route 22 corridor that connected New York and New England through Pennsylvania to the Midwest. A heart attack could tend to concentrate the mind on the singular issue of self.

Where had the first load been going? Defoe picked up the Pennsylvania State Police report. Thirty-six thousand wool sweaters, heading for Dayton, Ohio. Consigned to Gleneagle Stores. Handwritten note in the margin, he assumed by Askew. "Gleneagle—dept. str. chain; Cincy, Chi, Dytn."

The third, the last, load was headed for Atlanta, the apparel distribution center, consigned to another small chain with stores in Birmingham, Chattanooga, Memphis, Nashville, and on up into Kentucky. Italian knitwear, average piece priced at forty dollars. Insured for a million seven. Hit in South Jersey, just before crossing the Delaware Memorial Bridge. Routine stop this time; diesel fuel, piss call, and coffee. Big guy had followed the driver into the men's room, a kidney punch, shoved into a stall. Didn't get a look at his face. A little rough for a give-up; the driver had bloody urine, was held overnight at Wilmington General for observation. Defoe didn't know just how professional the pros were; from the little he knew about organized crime they were anything but. JFK was the common denominator. Perhaps someone at the terminal, a clerk in the customs office, was passing manifest information to the hijackers. Defoe made a note on his yellow pad: "Call Sally."

He shrugged off his robe, pulled on a T-shirt and sweatpants, went barefoot to the lower level with the briefcase.

He keyed the modem, typed, and sent a message to his broker's office. THURS 9:40 PM: WALTER: DATA PLEASE READE IN-DUSTRIES NYC; GLENEAGLE STORES DAYTON OH; NOR-

TON & NORTON ATLANTA GA. FAX SOONEST. LOVE & XS, CHASE.

He shut down the computer and set up the two object balls on the billiard table, chalked the cue, and began making three cushion-bank shots, working the angles.

See the three drivers, hear their own words, look for the subtle body language that didn't come through in police reports. Even the most inexperienced detective would never put supposition into a written report; he'd hold back his hunches, follow them up, and if they panned out then commit the resulting hard evidence to paper. Defoe put the cue on the table, scrabbled through the papers, and wrote the three drivers' names and addresses on the legal pad, then circled all three and drew an arrow across the page. Back to the papers: IGT, Interstate Garment Transport. President: Calvin Bullfinch. He made a note under the arrow—See First. This trucking outfit was fully bonded; the three claims, totaling nearly five million dollars, would be paid in full.

The cueball clicked softly against the two object balls, kissed the cushions at the corner, and hit both balls a second time. He smiled at the shot. Great Britain, France, and Italy, three Common Market countries. A very tenuous thread. A better shot was this trucking company; maybe they were in trouble, needed quick cash. He went back to the computer, added IGT as an addendum to his query. Probably not even traded, but best to touch all bases. Talk to this friend of Leilani's, what was her name? Caroline. Caroline Graff. Maybe she could give him a fresh insight. He needed all the help he could get.

CHAPTER 9

The blue van passed the farmhouse and reversed into a cloud of dust; the dry fall had turned the barnyard to a soft powder. The springs squeaked and the shocks rose as Mobay got out; he had bulked up to over three hundred pounds after prison, and with his infrequent shaves below his close-cropped head he bore an ever closer resemblance to his charges, the Rooskies. He opened the back doors of the van and bent forward, flipping a sack of meal onto either shoulder. The soybean supplement, at nearly forty percent protein, made pigs grow as you looked at them. But too much soybean makes for soft pork, especially when you're finishing them out; got to cut the beans and put the corn to them the last ninety days if you want to do it right. Mobay did it right; he knew about pork, knew what made good meat, it didn't make a damn bit of difference if it was lard hogs like Poland Chinas and Durocs, or the long lean Landrace, or even these ornery sons of bitches, these cross-bred, ill-tempered, so-called Russian wild hogs, in reality a mixture of all the unwanted and previously bred-out characteristics of a thousand years of domesticated swine. Low birth weight, small litters, sloping hind quarters that produced hams better suited to a goddamned woodchuck, and a personality first cousin to a sore tooth in a sleetstorm. Son of a bitch, but he loved them anyway. Fourth generation now, from the ones that he had brought up from the Smokies, wild and fierce as they were, the animals responded to him, tolerated his presence in the yard, in the farrowing pens. He wanted them mean, and wild; wouldn't allow any other contact with man. Mobay figured with his size he looked different from what an ordinary hunter would present to his hogs, once they got out into the combat zone. He was protective of them, and a little jealous. He knew they were going forth to be slaughtered, shot and killed by assholes with more money than ambition, men who paid to shoot fish in a barrel. But it was good money, triple what he'd get for domestic hogs at auction, and by damn, he'd give the hunt-for-pay boys a show for their fee, whatever camp they went to. And if they missed, blew the whole thing, if they got into a situation where it was them, one-on-one with one of Mobay's pigs, no guide with a .44 Mag. to bail him out, well, the tusker would get the job done, and no doubt about it. He remembered the stories from down Hooper's Bald. And he saw those razor-sharp sabers every day, heard them clicking as he dumped the buckets of slop, watched the hunched, powerful shoulders as the beasts fought for their space at the trough.

"Hey, Skean!" His voice carried across the barnyard to the house. "Who the fuck'ths been messin' wi'f the pigths?" He waited in the dusty driveway, anticipating Skean's emergence from the house.

"Hey, Mobes; you're back. I didn't hear the van. What's the matter?" He walked up to his partner, slight smile on his lips, handed a cold can of Miller's to Mobay.

"Somebody fooling with the pigths again; they're off their feed."

"Nah, come on, I been here all day. It's the weather, hot for this time of year. Let 'em go an hour or two, cool down."

"Yeah, well." He ran a hand over his face. "I picked up a half ton of mash at the mill." He fished in his shirt pocket. "Here's the slip. We gonna cut tonight?" He popped the beer and took a swallow.

"Uh huh. I was fixing to head out to the Corners after I get washed. Hunchie, the Red, they put the word out, should be a good load tonight."

"Ith's about time! Them two hasn't brought nothin' in the last three weeks. Season opens next month, an' we're gonna have to shut down; we can't be jackin' no deer when all the city boys are running around the woods, shootin' each other, the game wardens working overtime." He paused and shook his head. "Ith's not like Hunchie, not to bring nothin'. He's good for eight, ten a week from his farmers. Fuckin' Gloeckner, now there's another story. He's about worthleth, you want my opinion." Mobay set his beer can on the stack of feed sacks inside the rear of the van and dug a foil pouch of Beechnut out of his overalls.

Skean sighed. "I been meaning to tell you; but the time never seemed right; either one of us was on the way in or out, or someone else was here. The thing is, Hunch and Red been doing a little sideline thing the past few weeks. It pays better than jackin' deer, and I guess they've been letting the regular business slide."

Mobay opened the pouch of chewing tobacco and scuffled his big fingers inside like a dog at a 'chuck hole, fluffing the moist flakes, then bent over the pouch and spooned a fistful into his mouth. His tongue settled the wad into his left cheek before he answered. "Maybe you better tell me now," he finally said.

"There's this guy, up in New York, in the city. I been selling him meat for a while yet. Venison, wild boar. Birds. Private; he pays twice what the clubs do. Well, shit, you remember last year, we sold all those pheasants up there in the Catskills, that's the man. He worked up this deal, Mobes, to take a couple of trucks out. Quick and easy. I knew you wouldn't want anything to do with it, so I didn't say nothing. Just a couple of trucks, in and out. I lined up the Hunch for the wheel and Big Red to help him out, like. This guy calls me with the details, I tell Hunchie and Gloeckner when, and where, to take the load. The guy slips me a few bills after the delivery is made. See, I'm not really even in it; our setup here, there's no connection." He watched the big man's eyes. "You pissed?"

Mobay worked his jaws, spat, and picked up the can of beer. "No, I'm not *pithed*, exactly, but I'd like you to tell me what the fuck ith going on. We still running a game farm here or are you a goddamn Jesse James now?" He rolled the chew into the pocket of his cheek and drank from the can, hovered over his smaller partner like a thundercloud. " 'Cuz I didn't like it down that place. And I ain't going back down, all them queers 'n' shines."

"Take it easy, Mobes. We're still raising deer and razorbacks for the sports. That part hasn't changed. This truck thing was a one time deal, a little sideline. It seemed like an easy couple of bucks; well, I can see by the way you're taking it, it was a bad idea. I should have talked to you about it first. It's all done with, anyway. It's over and done. No more. I told you, I'm going down to the Corners, tonight. We'll fill up the walk-in, partner, 'n' move some *meat* this week!" He laughed and smacked his friend on the arm. "Go get ready up top, and I'll be back, a couple hours, with a load for you to cut! You eat yet? You want me to bring you something?"

"Yeah, I don't care. Whatever." He turned and began to unload the remaining feed bags from the van.

Skean showered and shaved and talced his body. He put on clean underwear, fresh jeans, and a shirt. Something always developed on the nights they brought venison back to the farm. It was dark and a nip was in the October air as he left the farmhouse. The light was on in the upper barn, Mobay was getting ready to butcher. He stood in the barnyard and lit a cigarette, listened to the night noises of late summer. The incessant sound of the cicada, dominant chord of the summer's insect population, was diminishing with the approach of the first frost; it would taper to nothing by the end of the month. Stars began to appear in the twilight sky, unchallenged by the lights of any nearby cities that cast their polluting presence onto the horizon of the night sky. He ground his cigarette under the heel of his boot, turned toward his van, and exhaled a lungful of smoke that blended with the night air into a white cloud.

Unlike his partner's vehicle, stock except for heavy-duty shocks and a trailer hitch, Skean's van carried most options and a few accessories not available from the dealer. Like a heavily insulated rear section and a refrigeration unit that could keep a half ton of meat chilled during a four-hour delivery run. With venison bringing ten dollars a pound at the restaurant door, it paid to deliver the meat in top condition.

The Corners, as the intersection was informally called by the locals, was a conjunction of two country roads that had been important routes connecting several agricultural communities with the colonial cities of Philadelphia and Reading. Now the roads led to and from no place in particular, and only four buildings remained. The old Garville Hotel, last vestige of a town long gone from the rolls of the taxman and the census taker, stood on one corner; across the street was a general store of equal vintage. It catered to the residents of the back roads who did not have the means, wherewithal, or inclination to travel into the shopping center ten miles along the route and obliged its customers until payday or a government check arrived. The third available corner of the intersection was a used-car lot that sprawled across two acres of weedy gravel and featured ten-to-fifteen-year-old cars of unknown provenance and instant financing. The office was a prefab shack on skids with a kerosene heater and a closed sign in the lone window.

The final corner was occupied by Shorty's Garage, a three-bay cinderblock structure with a forty-year patina of grease on all observable surfaces. It had twin gas pumps in front and several thousand square feet of wrecked automobiles scattered around its perimeter. The only outstanding feature of the place was its specialization in building ''Bigfoot'' conversions; pickup trucks with thirty-six-inch tires and lift kits that jacked up the body until the vehicle resembled a gigantic child's toy. A heavy duty roll bar, mounted in the bed and sporting half a dozen spotlights, completed the look. De rigueur was a colored plastic strip bolted to the front of the hood and bearing the nom de guerre of the owner: Stomper, Eightball, Acey-Ducey. Occupying a slot somewhere between the Firebird/Camaro crowd in their polyester leisure suits and the Harley riders in black leather, the high-stepping pickups were the vehicular personification of the Hairy-chested Nutscratcher, a Levi and T-shirted bird whose genesis was in the southeastern United States but had spread to all parts of the country via the phenomenon of the special-interest magazine, available at your local drugstore for two ninety-five a copy. An instant hit with a target group that consisted of single males between the ages of eighteen and thirty-five living in a rural area with a density of less than five thousand per square mile and a per capita income of fifteen to twenty-five thousand dollars, these self-styled "good old boys" drove their trucks over the back roads of Berks county, and when extraordinary circumstances dictated, would even venture to take their shining chariots off the paved asphalt and deign to bounce across the hayfields if the possibility of illicit sex or game warranted it. They were far more frequently found, however, at the local car wash, putting a Simonize shine on their chrome-plated rollbars while listening to popular music on after-market cassette players mounted under the dash. Their taste in music was evenly split between rock and country, just as their headgear was a fifty-fifty spread between the tractor hat (John Deer green, International orange), and the straw Stetson with the rolled brim that said to the peonage, "I done been south of the Mason Dixon line." They smoked or chewed or sucked on toothpicks and drank warm beer out of no-deposit bottles that they threw beside the back roads as they roared along in the night, killing skunks, rabbits, and the occasional raccoon with their fat tires in the dark.

Shorty's Garage was one of the rotating locations where Skean bought illegal deer. He and Mobay had increased the demand for venison far beyond the ability to supply it from their captive herd and had turned to the local poachers for the bulk of their needs.

Hunting, in or out of season, with or without a license, is a tradition in rural America that predates the Constitution. They neither heed nor tithe the bureaucratic government in a distant city; these men shot game when hunger or the urge of the chase struck. The Pennsylvania Game Commission calculates that of the deer harvested in the Commonwealth each year one-third are legally taken by licensed hunters, an equal amount is killed on the highways by traffic, and the remainder are slaughtered by poachers. Most of this illegal meat winds up in the home freezer; some irate farmers will shotgun a dozen or more of the animals infesting their crops and orchards and leave the bodies to rot. Others hunt for the ready cash that men like Skean will pay for a delicacy cherished in restaurants far from the fields of slaughter.

Eight of the latter waited behind Shorty's, their trucks rusted-out farm vehicles with homemade plywood caps, rough, utilitarian four-wheel drives, and the macho conversions with custom paint, air shocks, and bodies jacked up so high they had an extra step welded to the rocker panel to facilitate entry.

Cigarettes glowed in the dark and the night sounds of locusts and passing traffic were punctuated with low laughter and the occasional crack of a tab top perforating a virgin beer.

The kid slowed his dad's truck as he approached the intersection. This looked like the place, he hadn't seen nothing else like it for the last five miles. Coast on through and make a U-ball through the used-car lot. Back there, behind the lighted garage and those big high-rises out front, he detected movement and vehicles different in silhouette from the wrecks and junkers surrounding them. He swung around in back and killed the engine.

Ahh, shit.

He leaned back in the seat for a moment and rubbed his eyes, his fists setting off sparks in his optic nerves. He had parked a little ways off from the other pickups and took his time getting out; shoved keys into his rear pocket and sauntered toward the others as they lounged around the tailgate of a Bronco with a coating of mud that covered the taillights and license plate.

"How ya doin'?" he said.

They looked him over, silent, checking the slim seventeen-year-old with the first tentative wisp of a mustache.

"How'm I doing' *what?*" a greasy-haired man in overalls asked.

The kid had gotten up at five; the school bus would stop for him a half mile down the road from the trailer at six-thirty, but he'd be long into the woods by then. He usually woke up at six, and fixed his own breakfast; his old man worked second shift and wouldn't let his mother set the alarm in their bedroom before eight when his little sister had to get ready for the nine-o'clock kindergarten bus. She was a surprise, coming a dozen years after the doctor told her she'd never have another.

Dollar a pound, a hundred, hundred and a quarter at least; he might get real lucky and get a pair. He knew where to look. Do this once a week and he'd have his own truck by Christmas. Get a lift kit, nothin' outrageous, four inches. Shit, he could put it in himself, he'd helped out with his cousins over the summer. He wanted breakfast but the noise would wake his ma. He slipped four slices of bread and a can of Coke into a pocket of the oversize surplus field jacket and carried his shoes outside.

The sky was bright with stars and a gibbous moon, and there was a crisp feel to the air; fall was around the corner. He'd never done this before, it wasn't until yesterday, after school, that the guys had been talking about the deer that Ronnie had shot the week before and sold to that man down in Berks County. The man that bought, buck a pound, fresh and gutted. All you could supply.

He sat on the metal front steps of the trailer and laced up his high-tops. He had chased up Ronnie, caught him at the DQ, and asked about the guy.

"Yeah, I got that fucker dead on. Blew him up at hunnert 'n' twenty yard with my little three-oh-eight. Dropped, I mean he didn't *move*. Nine points, I figure he went one sixty, maybe more. The man give me hunnert an' a half, but that's okay." He smirked and reached for his comb. Ronnie humped sacks at the Agway and had a three-year-old Chevy with four on the floor. The girls at the DQ giggled and poked one another when he drove in, went in peals of hysterical laughter when he sang, "Hey, sweethearts, is this the place to come git my money for nothin' and my chicks for free?"

"Yeah, but what I want to know about is the guy you sold him to."

"You want a piece of that action, do you?"

"Well, I been thinking about it, yeah. I hear from the talk he buys regular, but you got to know where he's at. Moves around."

"Oh, yeah, you got to know where he's at." Ronnie chuckled and looked at the little sophomore behind the window, leaning over the steamer and putting a hot dog in a bun, her ass twin orbs beneath the tight white nylon of her uniform. "Why, you thinking about doin' a little business?" He pronounced it "bidnezz." "Well, I can find out where the buy is goin' to be but not until a couple hours before. See, I call this guy I know, tell him I got one, and he calls me back, later, says where. Then I got to haul ass down there, 'cause the man is only there for maybe ten minutes; the man is careful. But first you got to shoot you a deer," he said and laughed.

"Hey, I done took enough to know how to go about it."

"You shot a deer before? I didn't know that!"

"Bull*shit*. I been out with my uncles, my old man, since I was twelve. Hey, you saw that ten-pointer I got last year. You come by our place." He looked at Ronnie, saw his smirk. "Aw, you're pullin' my chain." He smiled and dug into his pocket, brought out two quarters. "You want a root beer?" He tossed the coins on the ledge and the girl inside opened the sliding glass window.

"No, you go ahead. I got me some better kind of beer in my rig. Come on over when you get your soda pop." He turned and walked toward his truck with a rolling gait that he had picked up from a

Busch commercial. Damn cayuses and lonesome doggies better watch out when *this* old boy came by.

The sun crested the hill, an exploding yellow fireball; autumn colors burst into a symphony of reds and golds as the sharp line of daybreak crept down the ridge. Up here, at the higher elevations, the first frosts of fall had turned the leaves, a preview for the lowlands, colors to come in the following weeks. A dozen plumes of steam rose from springs on the hillside as the groundwater hit the colder air.

The first tentative sounds of the day began; squirrels stirred, chattering, talking of nuts to be gathered against the advance of winter. Birds clattered into the sky and called noisily, some to start the day's endless round of feeding, others anticipating their southern trek.

And a chorus of insects, from the cacaphonic cicada to the sonorous cricket, gave voice to the song that celebrated their conatus, a rhapsody anticipating the first hard freeze.

He came hesitantly forward along the trail, an interloper, down from the ridge, trespassing toward the water below, brushing aside the branches of laurel and rhododendron, their deep-green leaves coating his camel coat with dew. A rub was ahead; the big buck had rutted and torn the ground with hoof and the limbs with horn, marking his turf.

The kid had seen the scrape, knew a dominant buck had staked this territory for himself. It would be an oval, a mile and a half; with a hard forty acres at the center. And this rub had to be close to it. Breeding scrapes, what was it his uncle Ralph told him; head high. Yeah, under overhanging limbs, at the height of a buck's head. In September, they started to rub, but in October, the serious demarkation of territory began.

He eased around the tree and looked uphill; visibility improved by the minute. On the trail was a handful of deer droppings, he stooped and picked them up. Hard, gray, they rattled softly as he shook them. Yesterday. Not here yet. Fresh manure was softer, black. Shiny. He looked up at a sound off in the dim light below the canopy of the trees. There; forty yards, soft movement, the flash of amber hide and the outline of antlers against a bright patch of dawn.

He threw the rifle to his shoulder; son of a fuckin' *bitch*. The scope caps were still on, he wasn't ready. He ripped the plastic protectors off, sent the two covers and their connecting elastic strap spiraling into the brush behind him. The buck bolted at the sound with a snort, wheeling sideways. The kid fired, a snap shot. The recoil hit him with a surprise, the sound as much as the jolt to his shoulder causing his heart to skip, even as he tracked the movement of the deer to his left. He could hear it crash through the rhododendron, knew from the sound that the shiny leaves were smeared with fresh blood. Shit! He needed a clean kill, today.

He slung the rifle and forced himself to stop, listen. Downhill, heading toward the creek below. He ran to the spot where he knew it had turned; yes, the hooves had pivoted in the soft earth. Ten feet on through the thicket he found the bloodstains on the underbrush. Bright arterial smears on the dark leaves, branches torn in a desperate downhill rush toward salvation.

He tracked the buck for an hour, finally found it, exhausted, lying in a tangle of thorns, gut-shot, its eyes bright as he approached. Not the big one he had hoped for. Six points, one twenty.

He couldn't risk another shot; even up here a game warden was always a chance, you never knew where they'd show up. He figured he was at least two miles from the road. Do it? No . . . no. Guys that jacked deer, used lights, at night. Hit them with the spotlight, *pow*. Flip the carcass in the truck and—GO! The wardens and the game protectors liked to sit and listen for the shot, then home in on it. He waited, watching the deer die. The sun was higher now, he could feel the heat. Flies, where the fuck did they come from in the middle of nowheres? The flies lighted on the deer; he watched as they crawled across the tawny flanks, tested the dark wound.

With a whimper he cut its throat and gutted the carcass.

At two-fifteen he reached the road, hid the deer and the rifle under evergreen boughs. An hour later he went into the trailer. It had taken him six hours to get himself and the dead deer to the edge of the highway; he would never had thought that he was that far in when he shot the animal.

He made himself a bologna and butter sandwich and drank a quart of iced tea, then saw the note under the refrigerator magnet.

HON:

sis and I went to town with your aunt
Sar. well be back befor dinnertime i hope.
if not well bring somethin back for you.

MOM

Piece of luck; he didn't have to talk her out of the truck. The old man's other keys were by the door and he was out of the drive in five minutes. His daddy wouldn't be home from work before midnight; he always stopped for a couple with his friends. He could almost taste the money, his start on wheels of his own. That damn deer had to weigh in at a hundred and ten, at least. There were times this morning when it felt like three hundred and ten.

"I hear this is the place to come with deer." The kid fished a pack of smokes out of his pocket. Three left. He lit one and looked at the greasy-haired farmer.

"Where'd you hear that, sonny?"

"Around; at school. Guys say there's a man buying down here. You him?"

The farmer laughed, showing black, eroded teeth. "At *school*." He turned and spoke to the others. "At school! Damn kindygarden'll be in here next with dead mice. Shit!"

"Fuck off, Corey," another man said, coming forward. "You want a beer, young fella?" He leaned into the back of the truck without waiting for an answer and opened a cooler.

The kid smiled, eased his tired muscles off a bit. "Yeah, sure, you got one." He snapped the top on the can and took a sip.

"That'll be a buck, sonny." The man smiled.

"Buck! That's kind of steep, ain't it?" He dug into his jeans and looked at the five ones. He had to put gas in the truck before the old man saw the gauge.

The man held out his hand, snapping his fingers. "Bring your own next time, boy." He stuffed the bill in his shirt pocket, gestured with his chin toward the road. "Go on wait by your truck now. Here comes the man."

The kid turned and saw the van pull up at the gas pumps, saw its driver wave to someone inside the building as he headed for the line of trucks in back. Red Gloeckner came out of the garage and ran to catch up with Skean, then skipped a couple of paces, matching his gait to the smaller man's. "Hey, Joe! Me and Hunchie just got back. He's over the hotel, getting washed up. That dock foreman, that Willard guy? He was kind a pissed, on account of we were so late and he had to wait around. Spooky fucker, shaves his head and that earring and all. That leather shit, I figure him for some kind of fag."

Skean ignored the chatter, scanned the faces of the men who waited for him, making sure that he knew them all. He stopped by a battered blue Ford that looked as though it had been a finalist in a demolition derby.

"Corey," he said, throwing his glance in the direction of the kid who stood by his tailgate a dozen yards away, "who's the new face?"

"Dunno, pulled in a couple minutes ago." He sent a dark stream of tobacco juice between the trucks. "Axed me if I was the man what bought deer. Hey, Bobbie, he say anything to you?"

"Just that he thought a dollar was a little high for a cold one. Hi, Joe, Red."

"I'll check him out first. Come on, Red."

Skean stopped by the tailgate, stared into the kid's eyes saying nothing.

Finally the youth broke the silence with a nervous chuckle. With his build and his stance he could look cold in July. "I guess you must be the man that does the buying. I plan on being a reg'lar from now on."

"What makes you think I might be interested in buying anything?"

"Well, Ronnie says you buy off him; he brings you a couple a week; I figure—"

Skean turned his head over his shoulder. "Who the fuck's Ronnie?"

Gloeckner leaned forward, spoke softly. "That new kid from up over the mountain. Calls me pretty regular, last six, eight weeks. 'Bout six foot, blond, built good? Drives a cream Chevy with a four-inch lift."

"I don't know any Ronnie, kid. What you want?"

"Got a nice one here, fresh killed. Seven pointer." He turned toward the truck, dropped the tailgate. The carcass was concealed under a ragged sheet of black plastic held down by a pair of bald tires. "Nice, huh? Goes, I figure, hundred and ten, twenty pound. But I guess you can judge better'n me." He laughed nervously, took a sip from the can of beer. On his empty stomach it spread a warm glow in his gut.

Skean turned away. "I don't buy road kills."

"Road kills!" The kid jumped down from the tailgate, put his hand on Skean's arm. "Wait a minute, mister! This ain't no roady; I shot him two, three miles back in. Took me pretty near six hours to get him out. *Shit.* Road kill! I don't believe this!" He laughed without humor, looking at the other men who watched the scene in silence.

"Sonny, you'd better go on home and learn how to do it right, then. That carcass is a disgrace; you gut-shot this animal and then didn't field-dress it proper; look at that, you didn't even cut out his nuts or his asshole, I bet half his guts are still in there. Meat's probably sour. And then you drug it, looks like, behind a goddamn tractor for about forty miles. Meat's all bruised up, hide's no goddamn good for anything and you expect someone to buy this piece of shit off you, a snot-assed kid I never seen before? The *hell* you say.''

"Aw, man, I can't believe this! I been working this since five this morning; I cut school, drug, 'n' carried the deer until I was ready to drop, snuck my old man's truck to get it down here, and now you won't give me fair money!''

Skean pulled a ten off his roll, stuck it in the boy's shirt pocket. "Pull it the fuck out of your truck then, and get out of here. I'll feed it to my dogs.'' He started to turn away toward the others, who stood in a semicircle, grinning. Big Red giggled, looking first at the kid, then at the men.

"Ten fuckin' dollars! Fuck you, mister, and your ten!'' The boy hoisted his middle finger and pumped it up and down in Skean's face. His fingernail nicked Skean's nostril, the scratch drawing a drop of blood. "Here's what you can do with your ten dollars!''

Skean took a short step forward and bumped the boy back against the side of his truck. He reached up with his left hand and grabbed the offending finger as he went to the back of his neck with his right. The kid twisted in pain as his hand was bent backward over the side of the truck; he felt a sharp bite on the middle joint of his finger, then a cold numbness. Skean was walking away. A blinding stab of pain made him look down at his hand; he stared in disbelief. His middle finger was gone, blood spurted around the white knuckle bone. He looked up at the back of Skean, down at his hand, and cried out. Gloeckner grabbed his sleeve and turned him toward the cab of the truck. "Better get on out of here before he gets mad. Liable to cut your *nuts* off.'' He laughed and watched the kid bounce back out onto the highway and turn north. Then he stooped and picked up the pale finger.

I can have me some fun with this, he thought and stuck it in his back pocket.

"Hey, Jumbo; how's it goin'? Haven't seen you for a couple of weeks.''

"Yeah, shit, Joe; I been on third shift since Labor Day, makes it tough. Got a couple of nice doe tonight, though.''

Skean looked in the bed of the pickup, lifted the blue plastic tarp, ran his hand over the flanks of the dead deer, tugged on the hair. "When did you get them?'' He lifted a hind leg, pumped it up and down, feeling the rigor.

Jumbo laughed. "Shit, Joe, you know that as well as I do. Just like I don't bother to weigh them no more.''

"Night before last. About this time, if you're working third. Sixty apiece.'' He took a folded stack of bills from his jacket and peeled a twenty off the top and a pair of fifties from the bottom.

Jumbo took the money. "Aw, hell, Joe, I thought that bigger one went seventy-five.''

"Probably weighed closer to eighty, Jumbo. But that was before you tore off her shoulder with that damn twelve gauge. You use punkin' balls, you're gonna keep bringing me hamburger. The whole front quarters, both of them, are stew meat, Jumbo. Get yourself a nice little .243.'' He slapped the man on the arm and laughed. "It'd pay for itself, the way you been tearing up the bitches!'' He moved to the next truck, worked his way down the line, checking the condition of the meat by eye, smell, and feel. His regulars knew it was useless to bring along a deer more than three days dead, less than that if the weather was hot. Just as they knew not to ever bring a carcass out to the game farm, not if they expected to sell another deer to Joe Skean. That was a real good way to get set up by the Game Commission. This way nobody knew more than a few hours in advance where the buy was to be. With only two undercover agents in the entire state it was highly unlikely the wardens would waste the time and manpower to stake out all the locations that Skean used to do business.

"All right, Red, load 'em up. Any of you boys want, stop on out for a beer.'' He paused at Gloeckner's truck where the bodies of the deer were being stacked like cordwood and pulled Red aside. "Here's the payoff from the truck job.'' He handed his assistant five one-hundred dollar bills. "I'm going over the hotel, settle up with Hunchie. Pick up some eats to take on out. You want anything?''

"Yeah, shit, I could chew the asshole out of a dead skunk. The Hunch didn't want to stop with that load being as hot as it was, and by the time we got out of that New York and back to my rig we had to bust ass to get over here. That bus ride is for shit, Joe; next time we got to get a third person in on this, follow me and Hunchie and pick us up. Thelma'd do it, for the fun.''

"Hey, you keep your mouth shut about this, don't go telling your girlfriends any of your business. Unless you want cops to go along next time, keep you company. Half the guys in Graterford are in there because someone said something to somebody. You remember that; I ain't fooling you now. Besides, I don't think there's gonna be another truck job. The man was pretty well pissed about that driver today.''

"Yeah, I forgot. What's he, still out at the farm?''

"No, he ain't still out at the farm, asshole. Don't worry about it, that part's taken care of. Go on, get out of here, you got a job to do.

Take this load right on out to Mobay, and don't make no pussy stops on the way."

"Shit, Joe." Gloeckner grinned. "I don't need to do that. I already told a couple girls to come on out tonight!"

Skean drove across the highway and parked behind the hotel, went in through the kitchen. A fat, gray-haired woman in white sweated at the ancient eight-burner stove and the grill beside it. Soups and stews and grilled sandwiches were the choices at the Garville Hotel, it did not even have a dining room as such, just half a dozen tables along one side of the barroom. Liquid nutrition was favored by the majority of its patrons.

He came up behind the woman and cupped her massive buttocks with both hands, squeezed.

"Joe Skean!" she said, turning and swatting at his hands with a wooden spoon. "You'll do my heart with your sneaking around!"

"Hello, Queenie. What's to eat yet?"

She turned back to the stove and gestured toward the large stainless-steel pots along the back burners. "Corn chowder, potato soup, rivel soup, and there's still some chicken pot pie. But the beef and dumplings is all."

"Queenie, what the hell is rivel soup?"

"Rivel soup?! Aye aye-yie!, you don't know what rivel soup is! You're not Dutchie, then!"

"Hell, no; I'm from up over the mountain, coal country. Up there it's Polak food; pierogies and galumpkis."

"Rivel soup; well then, you mix up flour and eggs and baking soda and salt and pepper all at once, till it gets lumpy-like. Then you drop your rivels in boiling milk." She pulled one of the pots forward and dipped her spoon in. "Poor man's rice we called it when we were little."

"I'll pass on that. Your pot pie is always good; a few roast beef sandwiches, too. Be a love and make me up some platters to take with. One for me and Mobay, and that kid I got working for me, too." He went through the swinging door to the bar. Several of the men he had just bought deer from were already perched on stools; he recognized most of the other half dozen as regulars.

"Rye and a draft, Russ," he said, leaning on the end of the bar closest to the kitchen. "Hunchie around?"

The bartender, stout as Queenie and equally gray, wore wide red suspenders that held up his green work pants. He set a shot glass in front of Skean and poured, then looked down the bar. "Prolly in the can. How's it going, Joe?"

"Oh, I'm keepin' busy. Yourself?"

Russell put a pilsner glass beside the shot. "Ah! Can't complain, don't do no good, right?" He laughed.

Skean threw a twenty on the bar. "Take a case of Miller Lite out of that. And Queenie's making up a couple of platters."

"Joe! Hey, Joseph!"

Skean turned at the sound of his name, saw two women across the room, one waving at him. He raised his glass in salute. "Who's that with Verna Schmoyer over there?" Verna was in her late thirties, chubby, and carried most of her excess weight in her face and breasts; her companion was perhaps ten years younger and needed the twenty pounds that Verna could well afford to shed. She had a mass of blond hair that was her sole similarity to Dolly Parton, although she felt the resemblance went well beyond the shared coiffure. A cloud of cigarette smoke hovered above the table; Verna stood up and headed toward Skean.

"I dunno, some bar whore; comes in with Verna."

"Hello, Verna."

"Hey, Joe," Verna said in a tobacco baritone. "Come on over to the table; there's someone I want you to meet."

Skean rolled his eyes at the bartender, smiled, and got up.

"Joe, this here's Linda Rohrbach; she works with me down the mall."

Both women had the overt makeup and polyester dishabille of lonely and not terribly discriminating women; the key to their virtue was eighty proof and not much of it.

"Pleased to meetcha," Linda said, offering Skean a limp handshake, the palm damp from her beerglass.

"Likewise, Linda," he said, and turning to Verna, "You got company?" gesturing with his eyes at the two extra beer glasses at the table.

"Couple a guys, bought the pitcher. Hal?" Verna said, looking at Linda. "Hal and, and . . ."

"Ronnie," Linda offered.

"Yeah, Ronnie," Verna agreed. "They're taking a piss. Great guys, right, Linda?"

"No, Robby, not Ronnie. Robby. Robby and Hal from Scranton. The studs from Scranton, that right? Who said that, Verna, you say that or did they? Don't matter. How 'bout a beer, Joe?" Linda gestured toward the pitcher with her cigarette.

Skean lifted his glass and smiled. "Thanks. I'm okay. How you been, Verna, haven't seen you in a while."

"I was down the shore, all of August and September. Ocean City.

I miss any good parties, Joe?'' Her eyes were glazed; he guessed she had been drinking since the afternoon.

"We're partying tonight. We missed you, the guys been asking about you, where's Verna.''

"Yeah, shit, I bet they have!''

"No, really, I wouldn't hand you a line. How 'bout it; Linda, you want to party?''

Linda looked at her friend, then at Joe. "I don't know; what about Harry and Ronnie?'' She looked back at Verna.

"Hell,'' Joe said, "bring 'em along, big party. Be a bunch of guys out there, right, Verna? This them?'' He looked up at the two men approaching the table, stood up and smiled, transferred his beer to his left hand. Both were in their forties, wore greasy wide ties and sportscoats by Sears, courtesy of Goodwill Industries. Siding salesman, Skean decided. Or timeshare in a Pocono resort, lifetime stainless-steel cookwear. All the same shit, just the product changed. A hundred years ago it was lightning rods and Lydia Pinkham's tonic.

"Joe Skean,'' he said, offering his hand. "Own the game farm up the road. We're having a little party tonight; Verna and her friend are coming out. 'Course you're welcome to come along, fellas. Right, Verna? You girls want to get your coats, freshen up? The thing is, boys,'' he said, coming around the table and putting his left arm, the one with the beer glass, around the shoulder of the bigger one, tilting it at a dangerous angle, "the boys, well, they all chip in twenty, for the beer, so I wouldn't feel right, not telling you that up front. You men want to join in, well feel free. How about it?'' He smiled and stood close.

"Well, Jeez, I don't know,'' the one said. "Hal?''

"Well, hey, we'd like to, friend, only we're supposed to meet our sales manager in the morning, real early . . .''

"I understand, boys,'' Skean said, smiling. "Some other time, perhaps. Pleasure talking to you.''

"Who're them two?'' Hunchie asked, watching the departing backs as he regained his seat at the bar. "Fuckers tried to sell me books! In the can.'' He looked up and smiled. "Went like a dream, Joe! Wheeled in, unloaded, and wheeled out. Except Borzillo had a hair up his ass. About having to wait for us. You'd think he was partners with your guy or something, 'stead of a goddamn dock foreman. We left the rig over by the West Side Highway, along with about six hundred others. She'll sit there for a week. I don't like that bus part, Joe.'' He lit a cigarette and waved his glass at Russell for a fresh beer. "Sitting on them fuckin' benches, the Port Authority, waiting, then we got to get back to wherever we left Red's truck; it's a hassle.''

"Yeah, I know, I already hear that song from Gloeckner. Here, this will cheer you up." Skean took the bills from his pants pocket, fifteen new and sequential hundreds. He put the slim stack under Hunchie's package of cigarettes. "Make you feel better?"

"Jesus Christ, Joe, don't flash that out here!" Hunchie stuffed the bills and smokes in his pants pocket. "You want to get my head cracked open?"

Skean laughed. "Come on, I'm heading out to the farm; Mobes is cutting and there's gonna be a bunch of assholes loose; we got to keep them in line. Verna's coming out, got a girlfriend. Hey, Russ! Can you spare a bottle of Southern Comfort?"

"Oh, Jesus." Hunchie swallowed beer or smoke or both down the wrong way and began to cough, his face turning red. "Not the choo choo again, Joe!"

"It's been a big day, friend, a real big one. A whole lot has happened and I feel like cuttin' loose tonight, throw the bones. We crap out, well then, that's the way they fall. But, damn! Something's in the air, Hunch, I can't, like, I don't know." He finished his beer and put the glass on the bar. "It's like you hit the number and got a phone call that your ma died. You don't know how to feel."

Queenie had three styrofoam plates wrapped in aluminum foil on the warming shelf over the stove. She stacked and handed them to Skean, along with a large brown paper bag. "There's corn pudding and sauerkraut relish in here and some red beet eggs. And a bottle of horseradish for the roast beef."

Cars and trucks were parked at haphazard angles in the farmyard; someone had a cassette player bouncing CCR off the stone farmhouse.

Skean waved to the casual coterie of partiers and headed for the top of the barn. By fiat it was off limits to all but a functional few. Mobay and Gloeckner were finishing the last of the deer. Skean set the foil-wrapped dinners on the top of the air compressor, hot from near constant use. Mobay looked up from the cutting table, wiped sweat from his eyes.

"Hey, Joe. Nice bunch tonight. Not too much stew meat."

" 'Cept for the one got hit by the howitzer, right? That was Jumbo again, how 'bout it, Red?"

"Yeah; Joe told him to buy a two forty-three. Still and all, it's the buckshot that puts the meat on the table. Does for me." Red could drop a deer at two hundred and fifty yards with his scoped '.06, but that meant a long walk to retrieve the prize with an out-of-season rifle report echoing around the hills. Far quicker, and far more profitable, was his shotgun surprise method of hunting. He knew the good locations, remote. Logging roads, fire trails, away from chance traffic. He knew where the deer crossed, knew the spots to set up his ambush. Aim that truck at dusk, point the roll bar and its eight lights at the trail where it emerged from the woods. A twenty-five-foot wire and remote switch allowed him to sit against a tree, rock-still, waiting for darkness, waiting for the herd.

The deer, six, eight, ten, would be frozen in the middle of the crossing, heads turned toward the blinding explosion of light. Red emptied the autoloader into the mass of venison, firing five rounds of buckshot, a tearing cloud of .32 caliber balls. A thousand pounds of meat harvested in a killing fury of ten seconds. He'd load the carcasses and be gone in less than a minute.

Red went back to work with the air hose, shirt off, shoving the sharpened football needle under the skin at the base of a leg and squeezing the valve. A ripping sound preceded the bubble of inflation that swelled upward toward the flank, separating the hide from the flesh as the compressed air tore the skin and subcutaneous tissue apart. He spread the hides, flesh side up, on wire racks, and sprinkled them with salt.

Mobay sawed the deer carcasses into hind and fore quarters, cut out damaged portions, tossed them into plastic pails destined for the grinder or the hogs. Heads and hooves and bits of internal organ missed by the hunters in the field were thrown directly down the hay chute to the pens below, where appreciative noises signaled their arrival.

Skean lifted the cuts of meat, slipped sharpened hooks through tendons, and began to hang them in the cooler box. He slammed the door; the compressor cycled, the fuse blew.

"Oh, shit. Not again."

"I been tellin' you, Joe, the box and the air compressor draws too much. We need another line out here."

"Yeah, yeah, I hear you. I'll pick up some thirty amp fuses; that'll fix it up. Hey, Red! Go down cellar and put a new one in, will you? Is there a flashlight up here, Mobes?"

"Down cellar? You mean out here or in the house?"

"In the house, you asshole, there's no cellar hole in the barn!"

"Well, I don't know where the fuck's the fuse box is at!"

"No, there ain't no flashlight."

Skean flicked his Zippo and edged toward the door. He screwed the last of the fuses, a twenty amp, in the blown circuit and they finished dressing the meat and they ate their dinners and drank half of the case of beer between them.

Gloeckner and Mobay cleaned the butchering equipment while Skean wrote an inventory of cuts and weights on a sheet of notepaper that he folded and tucked in his wallet. Then they headed for the house, nearly ten thousand dollars worth of venison chilling in the walk-in box.

An eclectic dozen was evenly split between the outside, hovering about the vehicles, and in the farmhouse, coagulated in the kitchen, ranged around a freshly lighted Franklin stove, hunks of slabwood pushing back the descending October chill. Drunks, farmers, thieves and poachers, blue-collar workers and the terminally under-employed; most of the people assembled at the farm could claim allegiance to more than one of the classifications.

He sipped beer and looked at her chest, breasts, stretching the polyester, doing their impression of the front end of a '57 Caddy. Shit. She's got them double D's cinched tighter than a saddle bronc at Cowtown. Pop her bra strap an' her nipples and navel'd form a triangle you could span with your hand. "Hey, Verna," Gloeckner said with an eye toward impressing the two high school girls he had invited to the party, "pull my finger." He held out his hands, the left wrapped around the right. "Go ahead."

"Sure, Red, and you'll fart for us, right?" Verna drew on her cigarette. "Why'nt you grow up?"

He laughed. "No, really, pull it, I'll show you a trick. Not too hard, though." He held out his hands, put them close to her face.

"Oh, Jesus Christ." She put her cigarette between her lips and pulled the proffered digit. "What's the tri— O! Jesus Mary and Joseph!" The finger came away and Gloeckner was yelling in pain. The cigarette fell from her lips, covering the front of her blouse with hot coals and ashes; she threw the severed digit on the floor, looked at it, then back to Gloeckner, who giggled and retrieved the finger.

The men laughed and, encouraged, Gloeckner approached the teenagers, poking at their crotches. "How about it, hey? Want to finger-fuck?" He laughed as they backed away, spilling beer, squealing.

"Hey, Red."

He turned, looking across the kitchen where Skean sat. "Get rid of that thing."

"Aw, Joe, I was only foolin' around; wasn't doing no harm."

"Get rid of it." Gloeckner knew by the tone and the look that it was time to obey. "Come over here, Red."

Skean looked up at the young man sheepishly standing in front of him. "You want to have some fun," he said in a low voice, "go on out to my van, 'n' bring in that bottle of Southern Comfort under the seat. See if Verna wants a drink." He smiled a sly grin and took a sip

of beer. Gloeckner laughed again and stuck the finger in his pocket.

Gloeckner set the bottle of liquor on the table in front of Verna. "Here you go, girls, some real sippin' whiskey. Right, Choo, Choo?" He snickered and turned back to the crowd for approval.

Verna had once consumed nearly an entire bottle of the sweet liquor and in a moment of amorous unconsciousness had pulled a six-car train that began with Skean and ended with Mobay as her three-hundred pound caboose.

"That's not very nice, Red," she said, eyeing the bottle. "Just because one time I drank a little too much and forgot myself, is no reason to call me that!"

Skean got up and took a handful of shot glasses from a cupboard. "Come on, Verna, he's just kidding." He filled four and gestured toward them, saying, "Drink up, ladies. It's partytime!"

CHAPTER **10**

Yearner went to the outer office and found a desk where he couldn't see the distracting torso of Miss Penelope Bucks without major contortions and opened the folder. He spilled eighteen months' worth of field reports from half a dozen different game protectors across the desk and began to read, occasionally writing on a yellow legal pad.

An hour later he closed the folder and stared at the single sheet of notes. Someone was moving a lot of venison, that was apparent. A couple of dozen animals a week, maybe more. That much meat had to be going into some legitimate pipeline, but damn, there were enough leads here to keep a dozen agents busy for a year. Well, nothing to do but start with the freshest data and work backward. He leaned back in his chair, rubbed his eyes with the heels of his hands.

But first he was going to check into the Allentown Hilton, have his laundry and dry cleaning done, take a long hot shower and catch a couple of hours sleep. Maybe he'd get a suite; flog the old vouchers a bit. Live it up a little after that fleabag in State College. Yep, the Hilton. They had a pool, and a sauna, too, if he remembered correctly. And a decent restaurant. Might as well enjoy himself for a few days; as soon as Warren saw the chits coming through he'd find his ass out at one of the twenty-buck-a-night motels near the airport. Hmm. Perhaps Ms. Penny Bucks would have dinner with him at the hotel, then a cognac in the lounge. Maybe a nightcap up in his suite.

He called the hotel and made a reservation for himself; he knew better than to walk in off the street cold, looking the way he did. And his truck would have to stay here, in the lot. He'd pack up his clothes and dirty laundry and take a cab to the Hilton. They'd think he just got in from the airport. Yeah, that's the game plan for this morning. Then he'd look into the latest entry in the file, go see this kid who just lost his finger.

CHAPTER 11

Caroline Graff called Chase Defoe at nine on Friday morning. She told him she'd gotten her phone messages shortly before midnight. "Leilani said it was important, Mr. Defoe, but not urgent, so I figured it could wait until morning. Did you really spend a hundred and fifty bucks taking her to breakfast in San Francisco?"

Defoe wondered what else Lelani had told her about him. "Yes, but there were three of us, Leilani's friend was there, too."

Caroline laughed. "Oh, well, that makes all the difference! How about buying me lunch?"

"Certainly. Actually, what I had in mind, though, was dinner."

"Hey, I was kidding, Mr. Defoe. What's this all about? From Leilani's description you don't sound like the kind of guy who needs to get fixed up with blind dates."

He laughed and said, "Call me Chase. I sure wish I'd listened in when she left that message on your machine. What I wanted, Caroline, was to talk to someone about the clothing business. I'm investigating a series of truck hijackings, and Lelani said that you worked in New York for a year or so, something to do with fashion."

"Yeah, *WWD*. I was an illustrator."

"Yes, she said that; what is it?"

"*Women's Wear Daily*. You know, the newspaper of the rag trade? I did sketches of the collections. Until I got the boot. You're working on hijackings, you said. What, you a reporter? No, wait a sec, with that name, you got to be a cop, right?"

Defoe laughed. "No; it's a long story, but you're wrong on both counts. What do you mean you got the boot?"

"Canned. Fired. I forgot that I was an employee first and an artist second, started making demands that labeled me temperamental. What do you want to know?"

Defoe carried the telephone over to the windows on the southwest side of the barn and looked across the corn stubble of the fresh-cut field. The morning sun was burning through the haze and the shades of autumn glowed tan and gold. "I've got a lot of raw data here, police reports, information from the insurance company. I'm out of touch when it comes to Seventh Avenue; I stopped at Leilani's yesterday, hoping she would look this stuff over, maybe come up with an idea or two. I haven't seen her for a couple of months, and to be perfectly honest, Caroline, my first thought was just to touch base with her, have a pleasant dinner."

" 'Touch base.' Yeah she said you were . . . *different*. Well, listen, sport, I've got about eight hours free today and I really need to fill them up with a distraction, so let's get together and see what happens."

"Fine; I can gather up my data here and meet you; how about I bring it to your place? Leilani said you lived in Reading?"

"No way, this place is a fuckin' dump; besides, I got to get out of here today, that's what this whole operation is about. 'Lani said you lived up toward Allentown, out in the boonies. Give me directions."

Leilani has some unusual friends, he thought, and told Caroline how to find her way to his farm. If she left now she'd be here in half an hour, forty minutes. Of course a friend of Leilani's could have a Porsche, be here in ten.

He cleaned up the few bits of breakfast evidence and started a fresh pot of coffee; if she hadn't gotten in until midnight she would probably appreciate a cup. He went down the grassy ramp on the north side of the barn and strolled across the gravel, hands in his trouser pockets. The October sun hit the back of his neck as he came out of the shadow cast by the building; he felt its warmth and was reminded that the days were growing shorter as Indian summer yielded to the approaching chill of winter.

The distant caulk-ta-caulk of a male pheasant carried across the hayfield and was quickly answered by the challenge of a closer cock, unseen in the third cutting stubble a dozen yards away. At the fence, the measured chirp of a cricket sounded counterpoint against the steady background whir of cicadas in the woods that bordered the field, their cry so all-pervasive that it disappeared into the surrounding white noise of the country.

Defoe went around the far side of the barn to his small kitchen garden, picked up a hoe, and began to scuffle at the purslane and lambsquarters among the tomatoes.

*   *   *

The barn was easy enough to find; she only had to glance a couple of times at Defoe's directions on the seat beside her. She remembered his admonition to slow down after crossing the small stream, otherwise she would have missed the lane and the rural mailbox with the faded numbers neatly lettered on its door. A rolling hayfield ran right up to the verge on the left; corn stubble, separated from the lane by a pair of hot wires strung on temporary metal posts, flanked her on the right. The driveway ended in a turn around on the north side of the barn where slate flags were let into the close-clipped turf of the ramp, forming a walk that led to a door.

She knocked, found it unlocked, and walked in, said "hello?" And caught her breath.

Centered in the doorway, she stood between two walls that rose twelve feet and ran for thirty-five to the south; one plastered white, the other brick, both punctuated with the deep amber of two-hundred-year-old oak beams, intersecting occasionally at a pegged mortise, their color an echoing counterpoint to the honey-hued pine planks underfoot, thick boards scarred by the shoes of half-ton horses as they stamped impatiently, a floor marked by the steel-shod wagon wheels, but at the same time smooth, polished by the countless scourings of flails on the threshing floor.

The Sarouk, fifteen by twenty-two feet, picked up the creamy warmth of the beams, echoed the deep pink of the brick end wall on her right.

The south wall, floor-to-ceiling glass, was a gigantic Rubens canvas of a sky, clear blue, dotted with white clouds so sharply delineated that they seemed stenciled on a backdrop. She looked at the walls, floor, beams, the intricate carpet against the Shaker-simple building, the lone buff-colored leather sofa and low table the only apparent furnishings, the total scene overwhelmed by the skyscape. In the recesses of her memory images flashed, calling up long-forgotten data from art school. A bird flew across the static scene, and she had the sudden absurd image of a man in a bowler hat outside the window, plastered against that incredible blue sky. Of course, Magritte. The whole place was a surreal still life; the measured order of the interior and the brilliant sky beyond were two environments merging at the wall of glass.

She walked slowly toward the windows and realized she was elevated above a landscape that only began to reveal itself as she approached the glass. First the distant hills, a pointilist composition dominated by the hues of autumn, next the bent and twisted stalks of a yellow cornfield under the open sun, marked by the shadows of scudding clouds, darker shades that hinted at the coming winter.

Then, closer to the panes, she saw the crumbling walls of an old building overcome by Virginia creeper, and finally she looked down on the forecourt of the barn itself: a low stone wall, plastered and whitewashed like the interior, enclosing a graveled yard, the stones raked into a rippling pattern, surrounding an island in its center; three sedimentary rocks, their striations upthrusting from the earth, mirrors of the Triassic tremors that were the culmination of the quarter-billion-year-old Pennsylvanian period. Nestled in the groin of these rocks was a single pine; twisted, stunted, bending west. She wondered at the sort of man who would think to put such a tree in the placid landscape of eastern Pennsylvania.

"Hello, Caroline?" Defoe came into the barn with half a dozen ripe tomatoes cradled in his left arm. "I'm Chase Defoe. Would you like a cup of coffee?" He smiled and went into the kitchen, arranged the tomatoes on the counter.

"No thanks. You have any soda? Tab?"

"Afraid not. I could squeeze you some orange juice."

"Nah, forget it. This is some place. You do it yourself or use an architect?"

Defoe looked at her and smiled. She was petite, with dark hair and fine features, wore baggy white cotton pants with a drawstring waist and an electric blue satin warm-up jacket with "Dodgers" in flowing script across the front. Her short hair was gelled and teased into spikes and had a fuscia streak sprayed above her left ear. Sunglasses hung from her neck on a black plastic strap. Twenty-five, he guessed, certainly not over thirty. "No, it's mostly my plan and execution." He nodded toward the south windows. "I used to live in that vine-covered folly over there. The house burned a few years back, and rather than rebuild I just moved over here. I like the space."

"Looks like it was totaled." She waved at the lone sofa and low table. "Couldn't save anything, huh? Bummer."

Defoe laughed. "Yes, I thought so at the time. However, possessions can be a curse; I look at something very carefully now before I acquire it. We all ought to have a good purifying fire every couple of decades."

"Yeah. What's the scoop on this clothing deal?"

"Right. As I mentioned to you on the phone, there have been a series of truck hijackings; the total to date is around five million dollars. I'm looking into it for the insurance company. I thought that someone familiar with the clothing industry might see something in the data that I'm overlooking. It's a long shot, I realize, certainly not something worth dragging you out here for. That's why I offered to bring the paperwork to your place."

"Nah, nah, I had to get out of there anyway. This is a whole lot more fun than spending the day at the movies."

"Okay. Well, let's take a look at what I have so far." He opened his briefcase and took the police reports over to the sofa, spread them on the table in front of it. "I think I'll have another cup of coffee; are you sure you don't want one?"

"No, I'm okay. You got any beer?"

Defoe raised his eyebrows. "Sure."

She followed him into the kitchen, watched him get a bottle out of the old glass-doored dairy case. "Pretty funky refrigerator."

He laughed and opened the beer. "I guess it is a little weird. It was in the top of the barn here, with a lot of other junk, when I bought the place. It works, so I never bothered with a real refrigerator. Must be forty years old. Let me get you a glass for that."

"No, I'm fine. Let's go check the papers."

She sat on the sofa and scanned the police reports, settled back against the cushions, and put her feet on the table when she got to the listing of the designer imports.

"Whoo, some heavy stuff here. Montana and Rykiel are both pretty avant-garde, you got to have the market for them. Not that YSL or the Chanel are exactly easy to sell." She looked up at Defoe. "What I'm saying is that your average gal looking for an outfit is not gonna drop four or five thousand bucks for a jacket and skirt. Whoever stole this either doesn't know what the fuck they're doing, or they have a customer all lined up." She waved at the other reports. "I mean, those sweaters, yeah, hell, you could sell them easy enough. But this French stuff, nuh uh." She took a long swallow of beer. "I bet Montana's not in more than a couple of dozen stores in the whole country. And they're mostly places like Saks, Neiman Marcus. No way is a store like that going to buy hot merchandise, you see what I'm saying?"

"Sure. Maybe this will make more sense after I talk to the people at the trucking company."

"Yeah. Can I use your phone?"

"Certainly. It's right over there, by the stairs."

Caroline dialed a number, then took a beeper from her jacket pocket and aimed it at the receiver. "Shit!" she said after a moment, and then laughed. "I swore I wasn't going to do this, sit by the phone all day. That's why the hell I came out here. And what's the first thing I do? Check for messages!" She walked back to the sofa and flopped down, picked up her beer. "I got this major career move going on, Chase. I've got a chance to do a book, and the decision is going down today."

"Sounds interesting. What do you mean, do a book? Something involving your artwork?"

"Yeah, this publisher, in New York. Tom Wolfe, the writer? He's writing a book for them, profiles of celebrities. People like Brando, Liz Taylor, I don't know who all. I think they mentioned Kissinger. Anyway, there's about a dozen. And each one gets a full-page portrait. It's about fifty-fifty whether they go with photography or line drawings. That's where I was last night when Leilani called. This editor came down to look at my work, schmooze me with a fancy dinner, and then haul a bunch of my drawings back to New York. Anyway, they're supposed to get back to me today, before five, with their decision. You can see why I didn't want to sit in my place waiting for the phone to ring. I'd go nuts!" She finished her beer and stood up, took the empty bottle to the kitchen. "Hey, I'm going outside for a smoke. What a *super* day. All that sunshine and air and stuff."

Defoe read the intensity of her emotions in the break of her voice and beneath the punk hairdo and makeup and the swagger of the oversize baseball jacket he thought he saw a scared kid playing out of her league. It made him want to peel away the layers and see what was underneath. He put the empty bottle under the sink and rinsed his coffee cup and walked down the barn ramp toward Caroline. She leaned on the fence, staring out over the hayfield.

The distinctive smell of marijuana mingled with the subtler aromas of alfalfa leaf and corn stalk.

Defoe stood beside her for a moment before speaking. "I have to go down to Philadelphia for a couple of hours, Caroline. How would you like to meet someone who is, as they say, 'connected'?"

CHAPTER 12

"**H**e ain't a bad kid, I know his father. The emergency room, well, a thing like this, they report it, it's like a gunshot. I mean the boy's mother brought him in, without the finger or an explanation of how he'd lost it. So they got to cover themselves, file a report with us.'' The policeman was in his fifties, beefy and balding. He leaned against the side of the squad car, blue and gold, like his uniform. "This is a big township, Claxon, and a poor one. No tax base to speak of, most of the residents work down the line.'' He pointed with his jaw in the general direction of the strip that was Allentown-Bethlehem-Easton, thirty miles of industrial park that sprawled along either side of Route 22. "The people up here lead a hard life, a rough life. Boy loses a finger in some brawl and we don't pay too much attention. But like I said, I know his daddy, he belongs to the Legion. So I stopped out there the next day. Hell, that was yesterday morning! You got up here quick. I guess I did the right thing, sending a report along to the Game Commission.''

"I won't know that until I talk to this boy. I just got assigned the file on this today, figured to take a look at the freshest information first. What can you tell me about the incident?''

"I tried to put it all in the report. Seems like the kid was straight with me, but today, who knows? He shot an illegal deer, he admits that. I think his old man put the fear of God in him. Kid heard a rumor, at school he says. No names of course. A rumor that some guy down the line, west of Allentown, buys fresh-killed venison. The man tried to cheat him and cut off his finger. Off the record I say it serves him right. I don't hold with this selling game. Oh, I look the other way, someone pops a buck out of season. That's *your* job, right? None of my business. Besides, a man's got to feed his family.

69

But I don't hold with selling it, nosir. Then it's a different story. You're nothing but a goddamn thief, you do that. And we've got 'em around here, I know that, spotlighting deer, shoot three or four a night and haul them off. I catch one of them and you'll know it, and so will the District Justice. So when I heard about this man buying, well, I reported it.'' The policeman snorted a laugh. "Got his old man a little miffed with me, too. But I worked with you boys enough to know you ain't interested in the kid. It's this other buzzard you'd like to talk to. Am I right?''

" 'Bout a hundred and ten percent. There's a file down the office thicker 'n' a Wendy's Hot and Juicy, and I got a boss who wants results before election day, so if you'll point me toward this boy's place, I'll go have a little chat with him.''

"I don't give a good goddamn if you shoot a deer every damn day, that's between you and the local game protector, kid. I could give a shit, ain't my job. But you don't tell me how to find this guy, how to set up a buy, I can double damn guarantee you six months in the county jail, getting your asshole stretched by them Puerto Rican dope dealers.'' Claxon spat a stream of tobacco juice on the front tire of his battered Powerwagon and brushed back his suede jacket so the kid could see the stainless-steel .357 Smith in the belt clip.

"I don't know how to get ahold of him, honest to Christ, you got to believe me! This was the first time I ever done it, I told Chief Waters that.''

"Yeah, and you told that nice old man some half-ass story about hearing it at school. Bullshit. Names, sonny. I want to hear names and places.''

"Yeah. An' then I get the shit kicked out of me for talking to you.''

"Hey, asshole. You don't watch the TV? Now you know us cops always protect our snitches. Besides, you don't tell me, you gonna have a whole lot more to worry about, trying to keep your back to the wall in that jailhouse shower room.''

"Ronnie. Ronnie Harwood, works down the Agway.'' The kid looked down at his hand, the stump of his finger wrapped in gauze and adhesive tape, still fresh and clean from the intern's work. "He's the one who told me about it. But he says the guy moves around, Ronnie has to call some other dude to find out where the man's gonna be. Then the dude calls him back, says where the place is. Honest to God, that's all I know about it. Don't tell him I told you.''

"Son,'' Yearner said, smacking his arm, "you can count on it.''

He jumped into his truck and made a U turn, heading back toward town. A hundred yards down the road he stopped, leaned out the window and extracted the chaw from his cheek, then reached into the cooler on the passenger seat and popped a cold beer. He rinsed his mouth, spat, and took a long swallow. "Damn," he said, pulling back onto the highway, "how can they put that stuff in their mouth?"

"*Harwood?* I fired *his* ass at seven this morning, when he finally dragged it in here. After three days without calling in. What, he owe you money?"

He was a dry little man, wrinkled and dressed in gray poplin that went with his hair, skin, and soul. Red embroidery spelled "Agway" on one shirt pocket, "Ralph" on the other. "I put up with that boy coming and going as he pleased for three years now, and I finally had it, had it a while back, only until this week I didn't have anyone big enough and dumb enough to replace him. Now I do and he's gone. Go talk to the men on the loading dock, maybe they can tell you where to find him. I know I never could!" He put his head down and went back to the invoices spread across his desk.

Yearner thanked the manager and went down the aisle between the shelves of livestock paraphernalia; green tins of bag balm, strip cups, and cow towels, udder infusions, teat dilators, and cases of black rubber inflators for milking machines on one side, the cartons across the way containing hog rings, chicken bands, and fly tape, cardboard boxes printed in type styles dating from the thirties and forties advertising products that had not changed in a century.

He went through the swinging door into the big old mill, stepping around skids stacked high with hundred-weight burlap sacks labeled twelve, fourteen, sixteen percent dairy feed, smaller tiers of fifty-pound double-walled paper bags containing 40% Hog Supplement, Hi-Pro Calf Starter, Big Red, A Balanced Blend.

The atmosphere was a haze of dust that had the dry smell of cracked grain, and a throbbing din enveloped the structure, the steady, overwhelming roar of a fifty-horsepower hammer mill turning ear corn into screenings that rattled through a galvanized mixer the size of a compact car where they were blended with soybean meal and molasses and showered from an iron pipe into the sack held by a shirtless youth, his sweat-stained torso and face powdered with the cornmeal. He hit the valve with his wrist and swung the sack away in one fluid movement, then pinched the top of the brown bag and ran a portable sewing head across the mouth, closing the top with a chain stitch of cotton thread. He dropped the sack onto a slow running rubber conveyor belt and grabbed an empty burlap bag, flipped the mouth open under the hopper, and looked up at Yearner.

"Lookin' for my nephew. Ronnie Harwood," Yearner shouted in the boy's ear.

The ghostly apparition shook his head and pointed with his chin toward the back of the building where a square of daylight announced the loading dock. Yearner stepped onto the conveyor, rode a feed bag for a dozen yards, and stepped off to watch another young man flip sacks of meal onto a hand truck, piled them up until he had eight hundred pounds balanced on the rubber tires, then tilted the load back over the wheels and pushed it into the dark cavern of a dual-axle truck. A faded sign lithographed in block letters was tacked to a ten-by-twelve beam; it announced in red ink "Please Don't Smoke Here. Use our Office. We would like to be able to do business with you tomorrow."

Yearner had on his straw Stetson and point-toed boots: the Marlboro Man always got results around places like this; the smell of sweet feed and alfalfa made his speech slow to a cadence recalled from his childhood in rural Maryland, a mellifluous rhythm that inspired trust and confidences. He said, "Hey, son, you know whereabouts I can find my nephew Ronnie? I hear he just got his ass fired from this here job, and shit, I drove all the way over from the Lancaster stockyards to see him."

The boy lifted his T-shirt and wiped sweat from his face, spat. "That a fact?"

"Yip; I hauled a load of heifers up the sale, and I promised my sister down Balmer I get the chance I'd go see the boy." He reached in his pocket and pulled out a sheet of notebook paper, squinted at it. "He's working at this Agway place, she says, only that old fucker out front told me he fired Ronnie this morning. I can't go back down to Merlin, tell her I got this close and didn't say hey."

"Merlin? Oh, Maryland. Yeah, well, Ron got fired all right. He's been out partyin' last couple of days and I guess he pushed it too far. Anyhow, he's gone. He ain't out at Eaby's I don't know where the fuck he is." He tilted the handtruck back and leaned into the load.

"Well, I'll try 'er then. Where's *he* at, this Eaby?" Yearner waited by the conveyor while the young man ran his load into the truck, swung around, dropped a fresh pallet over the bottom of the cart, and positioned it at the foot of the conveyor just as a feed sack fell onto the waiting skid.

"Eaby's? Shit, out of town, on three-oh-nine. Eaby's Tavern. Can't miss it, sets by itself out where Five Mile Run comes in there. Ron ain't at Eaby's, he's out chasin' pussy someplace, I don't know where. You catch up with him, mister, you tell him I ain't forgot he still owes me a hundred on the sled.''

"Sled?''

"Snowmobile. You don't have 'em down there? A Yamaha, had a nearly new track and I sold him a towalong with it, too. He's . . . ah—gonna haul firewoood out in the wintertime.''

I just bet he is, Yearner thought. "Yeah, I'll do her. Say, what's that boy driving these days?; so's I don't waste my time lookin' in every beer hall 'tween here and there.''

"A off-white C-10. Jacked up, bugscreen says 'Harwood's Hauler.' ''

"Appreciate it, I'm sure. And I'll mention that snowmobile, I catch up with him. What's your name again, so's I get it right when I tell him about the sled.''

"Josh. You don't have to make no big deal about it, mister; I'll catch him Friday, he shows for his paycheck.''

"No, that's all right.'' Yearner shook his head and looked down, then into the boy's eyes. "I don't hold with owing other folks money; I'll see that Ronnie makes good by you. Oh, there a lunchroom around here, Josh? I'm about ready to chew my boots!''

"Mmm, that's *fine.*'' Yearner crumpled the Coors can and tossed it on the floor of the passenger side of the pickup. He unwrapped the burger with one hand, spreading the paper on his lap as he drove. Beef juice, sauce, and bits of lettuce dribbled from his mouth as he chewed. He swallowed, skinned another silver belly, and took a long draw. Then he cradled the cellular receiver on his shoulder and punched in the familiar number.

"JoAnne. Heading north on Route 309 for a place called Eaby's Tavern. Still lookin' to contact Ronald Harwood. Update: he drives a three-year-old Chevy C-10, cream, one of those jacked-up asshole mobiles. You running tape on this?''

JoAnne: twenty years old, living in an electric wheelchair since a stray shot had severed her spine as she shivered in a tree stand on opening day two years ago. Yearner had picked up the call on the police band, been the first one there, ahead of the local ambulance, his four-wheel drive churning up the wet logging trail, her father running toward him in his florescent orange bib overalls, yelling about his teenage daughter, shot and hanging in the tree. Yearner got her down, eased her into the back of the Powerwagon, and met the ambulance at the hardtop.

She spent a year in therapy, three months physical and nine psychiatric; the emotional scars ran deep in the pretty Bloomsburg State freshman who knew she'd never have children, never walk.

Yearner suggested the business, knew the constant contact with people on the outside was what she needed to crack the shell of self-pity she had built around herself. He set up the answering service with a little help from friends in state government. A WATS line was installed in her bedroom and a hundred foot FM mast stood beside the house. Yearner was her first and, for several months, her only customer, then others began to sign on until she had a dozen regulars, becoming a clearing house and call-forwarding service for those who needed more than an answering machine with a canned message. For Yearner she was his insurance policy; he checked in regularly with her, updating his moves, scheduling his next contact. There were times when he knew he'd be deep in the woods, far from official backup and on the trail of men who carried guns and were not averse to using them. Fifteen minutes late and JoAnne would be on the radio to the nearest State Police barracks with the report that an agent of the Game Commission was overdue to call in and map coordinates of his last position. He had not needed her, and hoped he never would. The warm sound of her voice in the night made the cost worthwhile.

"Yearner, you know you got your own separate cassette here. Didn't find him at the Agway, then?"

"Got fired this morning. I'm looking to catch him drowning his sorrows at this bar. Anything for me?" Yearner's police and FM radios, along with the cellular telephone, were well concealed in the disheveled cab of the road-weary Dodge; only the CB was in sight, and he routinely kept them all shut down during any undercover work, using JoAnne instead as his contact with officialdom.

"You got a buzz from your boss at twelve-thirty-two, wants you to call in. And about five minutes ago a call went out on the police radio, any game protector in the area. Staties are down on the Interstate, mile marker twenty-nine, lady hit one and is raising a fuss."

"Shoot! Hold a sec, let me see where I am." He pulled to the side of the road and rooted through the many maps in the glovebox, pawed one open to the section he was in. "Yeah; JoAnne, I'm about ten minutes from there, I guess I better give it a shot, keep on the good side of those boys. Check with you in two hours, sweetheart."

"Two hours, Yearner. I'm logging it. G'bye."

He turned on the police band and in his best standard radio procedure voice told the trooper at the scene of the accident he was proceeding to their location.

The deer had almost made it. The right fender of the Mercedes 190 had clipped its hind leg, breaking the headlight and creasing the sheet metal. The lower half of the leg hung by skin and tendons and the doe was in shock, lying beside the road, not moving, eye staring, heart pounding.

The driver of the Mercedes was standing, her back to the animal that lay on the berm, arms folded across her chest, talking rapidly to a state trooper with corporal's stripes. His partner sat behind the wheel of the patrol car, working on a clipboard. Yearner parked behind their unit and pulled a woolen necktie from the pocket of his suede sports coat, then walked to the patrol car and showed his ID.

"She looks a little worked up. What's going on?"

The officer glanced over at the woman and the corporal. "Yeah, we got a real live one here. She whacked the deer and almost got taken out herself by a tractor trailer in the passing lane." He pointed to thick black stripes angling off the highway. "Guy laid down about three hundred dollars worth of rubber getting out of her way. He's the one called us; was going to put the animal down with a tire spoon and she flipped out. Says the deer can be saved." He shook his head. "You want to handle it? She talks like she's got some clout, that's why Johnny radioed for someone from the Game Commission. More to cover his ass than anything; we didn't figure any of you guys were in the area."

Didn't figure anybody would be dumb enough to answer your call, you mean. "I'll go talk to her, see if I can get you guys back on the road." Yearner went over to the deer, squatted, put his hand on its neck. Cold, coat clammy-damp. He looked at the shattered leg. Had to be doing seventy-five. Nice car, black and shiny new.

He flipped open his ID for the state trooper, made eye contact, winked, turned to the woman, but still held the ID for the policeman to inspect. "Yearner Claxon, Pennsylvania Game Commission. You want to tell me what happened, ma'am?" Defer to the power source, it always made them feel good. This particular one was about five five, trim, expensive suit, dark hair with little flecks of gray, a face he read as a well-preserved forty. Eyes that flashed anger as she swiveled from the cop to Claxon.

"This poor animal was trying to cross the highway and darted right in front of me, and then was almost hit by a truck. The driver stopped and wanted to kill it! Look at it, besides its leg there's not a mark on it, except the little thing's scared to death. Our setter was hit once, and reacted the same way. Well, we rushed her to the vet and he put a cast on the leg. She's recovered completely!" She turned back to face the corporal. "But this storm trooper here wants to shoot it. He claims that's standard procedure! I can't believe it, in this day and age, treating a wounded animal like that. My husband is a vice president of Mellon bank and very active in Pennsylvania politics.

I'm sure he knows the head of the Game Commission quite well."
She turned back to Yearner, daring him to concur with the trooper's
monstrous solution to the situation.

Yearner smiled. Good-looking woman, and the kind that was used
to getting her own way. The kind that could get real active between
the sheets. He reached in his jacket pocket and handed her one of his
cards. "No, ma'am, that's not official policy, not at all. I can
promise you this doe won't be shot. But this deer's in shock, and
prognosis for recovery in a wild animal is never very high."

"Nonsense. I told you that a vet could easily repair the damage. If
it's *cost* that bothers you, I'll be happy to pay the bill."

"No, ma'am, it's not that at all, the state has facilities available.
In fact, I was about to say I think this animal needs to be taken to the
New Bolton Center. Are you familiar with it? Outside of Philadelphia, it's the finest veterinary research facility on the East Coast."
He leaned forward, earnest. "University of Pennsylvania," he said
quietly. "Let me go and radio for the Vetivac helicopter, they'll have
this poor animal down there and in an operating room inside the
hour. Fit her up with a prosthetic leg, she'll be back in the woods in
two weeks, good as new." He took a three-by-five card and a pen
from his jacket. "Let me have your name and address and telephone
number, ma'am, and I'll keep you posted on her condition."

What a tight little ass, he thought as she slid behind the wheel of
the Mercedes and accelerated into traffic.

"You serious about not shooting this deer?" The corporal looked
puzzled. "I never heard of a Vetivac unit. That something new with
you guys?"

"Pretty new; I just now came up with it. And yes, I'm dead
serious about shooting the deer. You got to file a report every time
you fire your service weapon, right? Not to mention the noise; and if
someone drives past and sees you with your revolver out, no telling
what might happen, could cause an accident. Another woman like
that could stop, and then where would we be?" He walked slowly
over to the deer, took out his pocket knife, opened the bigger of the
two blades. "No, corporal, no shooting." He knelt, stroked the
animal's neck, feeling for the pulse of a carotid, drew the blade
swiftly across it. The bright arterial blood ran onto the gravel,
staining it dark. The deer's breathing slowed and its eye glazed.
Yearner held his breath as he watched it die.

"One of the lucky ones," he finally said, wiping his blade on the
dead animal's flank. "Usually, get nicked like this, they made it into
the woods, live for two weeks before infection and the maggots kill
them. Good meat here, you boys want it?"

CHAPTER 13

"**T**his makes me nervous as hell, riding along on the left-hand side with no steering wheel to grab onto. Where'd you get this thing, anyway?"

Defoe was navigating the Schuylkill Expressway and the right-hand drive Jaguar had Caroline twitching and stamping on the floorboards as he threaded the dark-green saloon through the heavy traffic like a skier cutting gates in the fog. "I found it in Carmel. An English stage actor, big name in the fifties, brought it over when he deigned to do a Hollywood picture. After six months of farting around the project was canceled and he had to sell her for airfare back home. It kicked around from dealer to dealer for a couple of years before I came along. Drophead XKE's were all the rage back then. And of course the right-hand drive tended to put people off, so I picked it up rather cheaply. She's got the three point eight engine, same as the E Jag that won Le Mans that year. Pretty peppy." As if to punctuate his statement, he floored the accelerator and the four-door sedan, lithe compared to the luxury automobiles of the late fifties and early sixties, but a behemoth beside the downscaled ciphers of the fuel-efficient eighties, shot forward, the dual overhead camshaft six voicing a throaty growl.

"Far out. How about some tunes?" Caroline reached for the radio.

"Sorry. Radio doesn't work. Wires seem to be screwed up somewhere. There's a Walkman in the glovebox, though. Help yourself."

She opened the burled walnut door and took out the cassette player, read the titles of the stack of tapes behind it. *Polovetsian Dances, Goldberg Variations, Eine Kleine Nachtmusik.* A whole bunch of Beethoven. Classical shit. She closed the compartment.

"Not your taste in music, eh?" Defoe looked over at her and smiled.

"Nothing personal; my idea of the classics are Jimi Hendrix; early Doors. Where we headed, anyway?"

"South Philadelphia, near the Food Distribution Center. The Italian part of the city." As they took the right split at Thirtieth Street Station, heading for the airport and the Jersey bridges through the perennial construction, the traffic began to thicken and slow, more trucks and cabs competed with the passenger cars for space in the three lanes. The Schuylkill River ran beside them, ten feet to their left and fifteen below. On the opposite side of the highway sweat-suited University of Pennsylvania students ran around an athletic field, oblivious to the stream of traffic. The highway rose above the river, crossed it, snaked past the sprawling Gulf Oil refinery, and widened to six lanes, picked up speed. Defoe ignored the airport exit this time, continued east toward the bridge, then took the Broad Street ramp and approached Veterans Stadium.

"Hey, Chase," she said, pointing across his right front fender, "how about hitting that Mickey D's? Burger and a shake would go good about now, right?"

He looked at the fast food restaurant, cars and pickups queued at the drive-by window. "Not my style. Besides, Sally will surely have some real food for us to sample." Defoe plunged into the shadow of the Walt Whitman Bridge, turned down one of the narrow side streets that was a mixture of commercial and residential, row houses punctuated by the occasional loading dock and galvanized roll-up door. The facades of the buildings were a hodgepodge of the original brick, often painted a deadly pastel; aluminum or vinyl siding, and a painfully artificial stone veneer, complete with protruding grout at the joints; one could almost see the waves of salesmen washing through the neighborhood with the latest decorator camouflage, pitting neighbor against neighbor to be the fastest with the mostest.

"Jesus, look at that." Caroline pointed to an expanse of wall clad in artificial redbrick shingles and windows sporting aluminum triple track storm sash overhung by green-and-white enameled awnings. The cement steps that led to the door were flanked by wrought-iron railings painted gold.

"Yeah, kind of Christmas-y, isn't it? That's where we're going." Defoe found a gap by a fire hydrant in the solidly parked street and drove onto the sidewalk, stopped in front of an overhead door. They got out, she looked up at the sign on the door in black vinyl stick-on letters.

"Scarface Imports? You weren't kidding about the Italian influence! Where's the guys with the tommy guns?"

"Hey, Caroline; listen. This is important. The punk hairdo they can handle, what the hell, it's the twentieth century, MTV is in every house on the block. But I have to give you a brief lesson in Italian pronunciation." He took her arm and turned her toward him. "Listen carefully; it's Scar-FAH-chi, not Scarface; forget Al Capone. ScarFAHchi. Northern Italian, Milanese, the family predates the Scarlattis. I know you aren't into classical music, but you must have heard of Scarlatti, right? Harpsichord? Anyway, don't call him Mr. Scarface."

"Hey, the fuck you doin'? You can't park there!" A dark-haired youth in a sleeveless undershirt ducked under the roll-up door and swaggered toward them, hips rolling in low-slung jeans. A silver goat's horn on a leather thong was tight against his throat.

Defoe tightened his eyes, drawing the corners of his mouth into a smile. Kids spent all their time in the movies, looking for a style, instead of living and developing their own. Who the hell was this supposed to be? He gave up; *West Side Story* was the last hoodlum flick he'd seen. "Sorry," he said. "We're friends of Mushroom Sally's; I thought it was okay to park here, but if you want us to move . . ."

The young man backed down at the mention of Sally's name, more important, the use of a nickname that only a few cognoscenti were permitted. "Whynt cha sayso, yer friends a Sally's? I'll keep an eye on ya wheels." He looked over the Jaguar sedan, an automobile that was five years old before he was born. "Nice; old-timer, ain't it?"

"Mark II, nineteen sixty." Defoe tossed the keys to the youth, who caught them with a flourish. "In case you got to move it."

"Lincoln. Yeah, they don't make them like they used ta." He tucked the leather key case into his front pocket. "Don't worry, mister, I'll watch it like it was mine."

Defoe locked eyes for a dramatic heartbeat, finally said, "No. Watch it like it was Sally's," and went up the steps.

"Whoo, the real thing, huh?" Caroline said, following. "Bring on Mustache Pete!" She rolled her eyes, muttered to herself, "*Mushroom Sally?*"

CHAPTER 14

The jacket lay on the seat; he pulled the dirty sweatshirt over his head and reset the green-and-yellow "Nothing runs like a Deere" cap. Swapped the cowboy boots for a pair of worn high-top work shoes, popped a Coors, and waited. Ronnie's truck was parked with a couple of dozen other vehicles on the gravel lot that surrounded Eaby's, but it wasn't the sort of place you could just walk into without drawing attention. A place like this, every time the door opened twenty barstools squealed as their occupants swiveled to see who the latest player was. A stranger brought conversation to a halt, the regulars waiting until he ordered a six-pack to go, worked the cigarette machine, asked directions; only after the newcomer was looked over and classified would the atmosphere return to normal. A place like Eaby's was as much a members-only club as was Boodles or the New York Athletic. Yearner needed to ride in on a regular.

He didn't have to wait long. A red pickup with ladder racks and half a dozen yellow plastic buckets of Gold Bond joint compound in the back pulled into the parking area. A white vinyl sign on the door said "Cuthbert Smith General Contracting" and a local phone number. Yearner gambled.

"Yo, Smitty! Wait up." Anybody named Cuthbert would sure as hell call himself something else. He slammed the door of his truck and walked toward the bearded contractor. "Yeah, it *is* you! How you doing? Been, hell, a year since I seen you. Still hanging sheetrock?"

The man looked at Yearner, puzzled. "Yeah. I know you?"

"Randy. Randy Krotch. You drywalled that warehouse, where was it? Down around Bethlehem someplace, right? I was on that job. Shit, we went out and caught a few beers a couple of times."

"Sorry, friend, can't say's I remember."

"Oh, well, shit, then I guess you don't remember the ten I owe you, either. Must have been some other guy."

"Oh, *that* Randy, yeah, I remember you now. You got the ten?"

"Sure do; let's go in and break this twenty, I'm buying. Interest like, on the loan. Say, ain't that Ronnie Harwood's Chevy?"

Eaby's had a commercial steel door stolen from a job site and installed by a patron to settle an outstanding bar bill and a red neon Stroh's sign in the lone window punctuating the otherwise blank cement block front wall of the thirty-by-forty-foot single-story structure.

The bar ran along the right-hand side of the room; chrome-and-red leatherette stools, spilling their upholstery from cuts and cracks, were screwed to the floor and occupied by men in denim pants and blue or gray sweatshirts, the uniform of men in the trades. Through the haze of cigarette smoke Yearner quickly inventoried the place; ten mismatched dinette tables, fugitives from the fifties, ringed the room. An equally eclectic collection of chairs were casually arranged around the tables. A shuffleboard machine stood against the wall between the doors to the rest rooms and a coin-operated pool table sat center stage on the unfinished wooden floor. About half of the tables were in use; men and a few women leaned their elbows on the worn Formica surfaces and drank from brown or clear bottles, the occasional green of a Rolling Rock breaking the monotony. There was no draft beer, no juke box, no kitchen. The only food available was sealed in plastic and stapled to cardboard displays along the back bar: beef jerky, pepperoni sticks, blind robins.

Yearner glanced at the styrene Budweiser clock over the register: a few minutes after two. If the noise level was any indication of alcoholic consumption, the patrons had been busy for several hours. The young lions in the building trades like to start early, at first light, but they run out of gas a couple of hours after lunch and head for the bars to get a jump on the evening's drinking. On a payday like today a healthy percentage cash their checks at lunchtime and never make it back to the job.

"Hey, Tessy! How about a refill here. An' a pack of Winstons."

"Tess! Do me again."

"Yo, Bobo; couple a Miller Lites."

"Keep your shirt on, fellas." Tessy was twenty-five, blonde with dark roots, and a forty-four-inch bust.

"You haven't paid for the last round yet, Husker. I ain't running no tab for you." Bobo was forty-five, built like a fire plug and owned the building.

"How about a shot with your beer, to start things off, Smitty?"

"Yeah, I don't care." Smitty lit a Salem and leaned on the bar.

Yearner held the twenty between two fingers, made it tremble like a swallowtail on a trumpet vine and caught the barmaid's eye. "Tessy, sweetheart, couple of Buds and a rye on the side." He winked at her. "When you can get to it."

He tilted the neck of his bottle toward Smitty and said, "Here's to cold beer and hot pussy," then swung around, resting his elbows on the bar. "Shame about old Harwood, ain't it?"

Smitty downed the shot and shivered, chased it with a long swallow of beer. "What do you mean?"

"Well, him gettin' fired, like that."

"Fired? From down the mill? You're shittin' me."

Yearner held up his hand. "God's truth. Go ask him." He turned back to the bar and dropped a five on it as Smitty headed across the room. "Three more of the same, and keep the change, honey." He slipped the necks of the bottles between his fingers, two in each hand, and followed Smitty to the table where Ronnie sat, surrounded by empty bottles and a full ashtray.

"This guy Randy here says you got canned."

"What? Hey, Smitty, how's it goin'? Who's Randy?"

Yearner smiled, setting the bottles on the table. "Hey, Ronnie. Randy Krotch, you remember, last year. I was asking you about putting a lift kit on my truck, like you did yours." He pushed a fresh beer across the table, pulled up a chair, and sat. "Buy you a beer."

"How'd you know I got fired?"

"Stopped in the Agway, see Josh about that sled of his. I was fixing to make him an offer, I find out you bought it out from under me. That peckerhead Ralph said you was through. I'd of popped that sucker, I was you."

"Yeah, shit, I *could*. After I get my pay. You maybe get your chance at that sled yet, me out of a job. Josh gonna be all over me for the rest of the money." He took a long swallow, smacked the bottle heavily on the table, and fumbled in his shirt for cigarettes.

"What you worryin' about, Ron? You'll find a way to come up with the money." Yearner turned to Smitty. "Ain't that right? Old Harwood always got a way to hunt up a few dollars, am I right?"

Smitty chuckled. "Seems to."

"Yeah, what you got in that Chevy of yours? About six, eight thou? Shit, they don't pay *that* good down the Agway, else I'd be workin' there." Yearner laughed and finished his first beer. "Can I bum a smoke, Ron? I left mine in the truck."

"Jack, you know the guy sittin' with that Harwood kid?"

Jack eased his chair around ninety degrees and peered across the room. "Yeah, the Smith boy. Marlon's oldest. All these young guys grown beards, it's a wonder you can recognize any of them anymore."

"No, not him, the other fucker. He looks damn familiar, but I can't place him. Shit, it's gonna eat at me until I get it figured."

"Hell, Jumbo, go ask him."

"No, something's telling me I don't want to do that. Hey, Darlene. Get your butt over here."

The waitress was thin, had lived a hard thirty-five years, and was loaded down with a tray of empty bottles. "Cool it, Jumbo, I only got two arms and two legs. You want another round, you'll just have to wait."

"Don't get all pissy on me, young lady, else I ain't gonna give you this ten spot. Set here for a minute now."

Darlene put her tray on the table and eased gratefully onto a chair. One leg was slightly bent so the chair rocked back and forth, teetering from side to side. He offered her a cigarette, lit it. "You know that Harwood kid over there?"

Darlene blew out a plume of smoke, picked a bit of tobacco from her lip, and looked across the room. "I guess I ought to, he tries to get into my pants every time he comes in here. Thinks he's a real lover boy."

"Don't they all. What I want is, I want you to go over there and see if you can find out who that feller is with him, the good-lookin' one, see what they're talking about. Do that for old Jumbo and this ten might wind up in your pants."

"I can't be settin' with the customers, I ain't on break. Bobo'll be all over me."

"Never you mind about Bobo, I'll go square it with him. Won't take you but a couple of minutes anyhow." Jumbo stood up and lifted her tray. "Go on, Darlene, I'll take these back to the bar."

"I could, too, don't say I couldn't, you young fucks don't know nothing about it!"

"Aw, Hayman, you're so full of shit your eyes are brown."

"Yeah, Hayman, and your eyes are bigger than your mouth." He laughed and pounded his neighbor at the bar on the shoulder, tickled by his own joke.

Tessy stopped at the end of the bar where the old man, his red face bristling with white stubble, was sandwiched between two men in bib overalls. "What's all the noise down here, boys? Hayman, what kind of devilment you starting up now?"

The two farmers laughed and nudged Hayman. "Yeah, Hayman. What kind of devilment you up to. Go on, tell Tessy!"

Hayman Moyer had a stake truck with a fourteen-foot body and had made his living for the past forty years buying hay by the ton at the farm and hauling it to local livestock auctions, where the load would be sold, along with twenty or thirty other lots of hay and straw, to the highest bidder. That morning he had sold five tons of second-cutting alfalfa for a hundred and ten dollars a ton, netting him two hundred dollars for the day. In the last hour, thirty of those dollars had disappeared in drinks and crazy wagers with the regulars.

"Yeah, Hayman, go ahead, tell her what's on your mind."

"Damn right I will, you assholes set there and see if I don't." Hayman picked up his near-empty bottle, licked his lips, and drained it. "These two here got to talking about your bubbies, how big they was." He swung from one side to the other on his stool, looking at the two farmers who smirked in mild embarrassment. "And I said they wasn't all *that* big, I could get one of them in my mouth!" He laughed and smacked his palm on the bar. "There, you two jackasses, how about it?"

Tessy laughed and picked up his bottle. "Old man, you're crazy, you know that?" She took the empty and walked away, shaking her head. Half a dozen of the men at the bar burst out laughing, taunting and toasting Hayman.

Darlene stopped beside Ronnie's chair and put her hand on his shoulder. "Hi, Ronnie; you fellas okay here?"

"Hey, Darlene. Yeah; buy you a beer?"

"Now you know I can't drink while I'm workin'. I can sit a minute, though, cool of my feet." She pulled an empty chair from an adjacent table and turned it backward, straddling it, her black nylon skirt hiking up and exposing her thighs. "Hello, Smitty. I don't know you, do I?" She looked across the table and smiled at Yearner.

"Randy Krotch, ma'am. I ain't been up this way for a while. I'd surely remember you, so I guess we haven't had the pleasure of an introduction." He reached across the table and squeezed her hand, held it a flicker longer than necessary.

More laughter burst from the end of the bar and Hayman stood up, reaching into his pants pocket. He was scowling at his tormentors as he brought a fistfull of cash out and peeled off a fifty, waving it across the bar. "There it is, then. Tessy, c'mere, dammit; I got fifty dollars says I can get one of them things in my mouth. Now you want to pick up on the bet or don't you?"

Tessy stopped and smiled at the old man for a moment, thinking it over. She didn't see any way he could do it. "You're on, you crazy old fool!" She smiled and folded her arms across her chest.

$*$ $*$ $*$

"What's going on over there?" Smitty looked at the commotion at the bar.

"Just Hayman up to his usual nonsense," Darlene answered. "He's in here every Thursday, after the sale. Carryin' on."

"So, Ron, you're telling me how I can pick up a quick hundred, couple times a week. Just who is this guy, buys all this venison you say you shoot?"

"Say I shoot? Damn, I shoot it, all right, right Smitty? Say I shoot? I bet I took more deer out of these woods than most anybody, even the old-timers."

"All right, okay, Ron. How do I go about delivering the deer. Where do I take it?"

"I can't tell you that. Don't know, nobody does, till a couple hours beforehand. I got this guy I call, see, let him know I got one, got something for the man. And then I sit tight, 'cause he calls me back, between five and six, tells me which place to go. The man shows up around seven, eight o'clock. Looks at what you got, drops the cash on you right there. Only it's got to be good stuff; fresh, field-dressed nice, and all. He's a picky sucker." He picked up an empty and looked at it. "Damn. All this talking is making me dry."

Yearner pushed a five across the table to Darlene. "Sweetheart, you want to bring us another round? How about a shot to go with yours, Ron?"

"Yeah, don't mind if I do."

"You see, Ron, what I'm thinking about, is I know this guy, got him a pen with about eight, ten deer in it, tame like. Feeds them up and all. Raises them for fun, y'know. Well, I know where he works, him and his old lady; ain't nobody around home during the day. So I figure you and me, we drop by some afternoon and pop them. But we got to be certain we got a buyer. I mean, what we going to do with ten deer in the back of my truck, hey?"

Ronnie looked at Yearner and laughed. "Ten! Hot damn, we get ten of them buggers, don't worry about what we do with them. I'll take care of that part. I call him with ten, he'll probably set us up a buy of our own."

"Wait a minute, wait a minute!" The bigger of the two farmers held up his hands for silence. "How we gonna decide if Hayman gets it all in or not? We got to have us a judge."

"Yeah! Hey, Bobo, we need your valued judgment down here, you're sober, right?"

Bobo wiped his hands on a towel, looked at the crowd that had coagulated at the end of the bar. "Don't get me involved in your bullshit." He turned away, chuckled to the several patrons still on their stools. "That Hayman's crazy, ain't he?"

"A'right, a'right, here's what we do then." The smaller farmer waved his arms over his head, searching for a semblance of order from the crowd. "We got to get something to make a mark with, like, I got it, yeah, a lipstick, that's perfect, right? We draw a line all the way around her tit, where it stops being tit and commences to be, to be—*not* tit. And then, if Hayman finishes up with lipstick on his face, he wins, he got it all in. If his lips ain't red, Tessy gets the fifty."

That drew a roar of approval from the crowd and a deep discussion as to who would apply the marker.

"It's only fitting since it was my idea, I should do the job, right, boys?"

"Bullshit. I can do it myself," Tessy said, fished a tube of bright red lip gloss from her purse and pulled her sweater over her head.

"Says his name's Randy something. He just bought a round for the three of them, gave me a buck tip. Ronnie's telling him about some guy buys deer meat, how Ronnie has to call someone, then wait for them to call back. How about it, Jumbo? I get that ten?"

"Son of a bitch. I remember, Jack. Yeah, yeah, you did good, Darlene." He handed her the bill and waited until she was out of earshot. "That son of a bitch is with the Game Commission. Couple years ago, I did ninety days 'cause of him. A thousand-dollar fine, too. Bastard testified against me in court. And that goddamn Harwood's settin' over there spillin' his guts about Skean and his operation." He wiped beer from his lips with the back of his hand and stood up. "Watch them, Jack. I'm gonna make me a phone call."

Tessy reached behind her back and opened the four hooks of her bra as a shout of approval, punctuated with whistles, went up from the crowd.

"Damn, I'd like to slobber her mushies," Ronnie said, tilting the bottle to his lips, unconsciously running his tongue around the neck.

Tessy drew a thick red line around her right breast as Hayman removed his full set of false teeth, doubling the capacity of his mouth. He set them on the bar, licked his lips, and grabbed the breast with both hands, coming up under it with his jaws spread wide, inhaling the nipple.

He stuffed and crammed and pawed and halfway choked himself

and got a little more than a third of the ample mammary gland past his lips.

Tessy wiped her breast with a bar towel and flipped herself back into her bra, saying, "Easiest fifty dollars *I* ever made."

"Damnation, I thought I could just squeeze that baby in."

"They ain't filled with *air,* you know, Hayman. They ain't like a goddamn *balloon.*"

"Joe?"

"Red."

"Red, Jumbo. He there?"

"Somewheres, yeah."

"Lemme talk to him. It's important."

"Hold on, then."

Jumbo stood by the door to the men's room, the pay phone's receiver in his fist. Two younger men went through the door, trailing the aroma of cannabis. "Joe; hey, listen up. I seen this guy, he's a game agent, and he's talking to that Harwood kid, been down with deer a few times, you remember him?"

"When?"

"I don't know, last week, couple weeks ago, shit, I don't remember when. But you bought off him, I know that."

"I don't mean him, I mean when did you see this state guy."

"*Now,* for Christ's sakes. I'm lookin' at him."

"Where?"

"Where I'm at. Eaby's."

"I don't know it."

"Schnecksville, outside of Schnecksville. On 309."

"Yeah, well, I don't get up that way too much. So what do you want me to do about it?"

"For shit's sake! This guy, this Game Commission guy, he's trying to set up a buy; it's your ass he's after, what do you mean what do I want you to *do* about it?"

"Okay, Jumbo, calm down. You heard him trying to set me up?"

"No, not me. I spotted the guy, remembered him. See, I had a run-in with this fucker once. So I got this barmaid to go listen in, find out who he was, on account of I couldn't remember."

"I thought you just said you recognized him, Jumbo. You got a fucking load on?"

"No! Well, yeah, I had a couple beers. What I mean is, I knew I seen him from someplace, but I couldn't place him. You know? So I sent Darlene over to check him out. When she told me they were talking about selling deer I remembered."

"Remembered what?"

"Remembered who the fuck he was!"

"Yeah? So who is he?"

"I don't know, Randy something. But he's the one got me ninety days. I remember that real good."

"And he sat there and told Dorine about jacking deer."

"Darlene. Yeah."

"And then she ran over and told you. And the guy still sits there."

"No! It wasn't that way. He didn't pay her no mind, at all. Besides, everybody was watching this old guy trying to swallow a tit."

"The Game Commission guy?"

"No! Hayman, Hayman Moyer. It's that fuckin' Harwood kid, shootin' his mouth off about the business. He's the one told that boy the other day, the one with the finger, about you, Red said. What you want me to do?"

"Don't do anything, Jumbo. I'll take care of it. Stay away from him. Better yet, leave, go on home."

"Shit. I spent ten bucks getting this for you and this is how you treat me."

"Hey, Jumbo. You got it wrong. I appreciate what you did, I really do. And you'll get your ten back. It's just that I'm afraid you'll spook this dude, he'll pull back. And next time I won't be so lucky, having a sharp operator to spot him for me. Now go on home, leave us handle it. This Ronnie Harwood calls in, ol' Red's gonna set up your game dude. Have a little private party, just for him, teach him not to go messing where he shouldn't.''

"Yeah? Well, I want in on it, then. Fucker got me ninety days, Joe."

"I'll let you know, Jumbo. Soon as I set something up." Skean hung up and turned to Red. "That goddamn Ronnie friend of yours is causing me problems. We got some official, State business kind of trouble."

Gloeckner held up his hands in a defensive gesture. "Whoa, wait a minute, he ain't a friend of mine."

"No? You're the one brought him around. You're the one he calls, find out where the buy is. The way I look at it, he ain't your friend, at least he's your problem. He calls, you set it up for Saturday night."

"Saturday night? That's the next buy?" Ronnie watched Randy and Smitty shooting pool, ran his fingers up and down the armored cable of the pay phone. "Nothin' tonight? How come?"

"You ask too many questions. The man's out of town, that's why. Call me same time you always do, Saturday, and I'll have the place for you then." He hung up and turned to Joe. "I do that okay?"

"I don't want any more calls coming in on this number. I got to change it." Skean shook his head, muttered to himself. "Too many people got the number, this state prick gets ahold of it, he can trace me right here." He chewed his lip, looked at Gloeckner. "We got to have a new procedure. You got to be home, your place, every day, a certain time for them to call. Then you call them back from there. Or better yet, a pay phone someplace. But I got to get this number changed. Yeah, I'm going into the telephone office in the morning, get a new number. And don't give it to nobody."

"No, I can't give you the number; man would bust my balls I do. Besides, he don't know your voice. Red don't know you, he won't say shit. See, that's the beauty part, Randy. Only a few guys, like me, he trusts. And with just a couple hours, ain't no way anyone gonna go get drunk, let on where the buy is set up for, shoot off their mouth. 'Cause there must be ten places he buys, all different, spread around. We gonna do these deer you're talking about, just got to wait until Saturday night, my friend."

CHAPTER 15

The front parlor was an uneasy amalgamation of residence and commercial reception area and consequently suited neither. The house was a typical Philadelphia Father-Son-and-Holy ghost dwelling dating from the early nineteenth century; three single rooms stacked one atop the other and repeated endlessly along the street: solid housing for the immigrant hordes who descended on Philadelphia in ceaseless waves from Ireland, Italy, Eastern Europe in the 1840's, '50's, and '60's.

Wall-to-wall shag carpeting in bright rust formed a base for the Mediterranean furniture: a dark and ponderous fruitwood sofa with royal-blue velvet upholstery encased in a clear vinyl slipcover was flanked by matching end tables that supported blown-glass lamps with tasseled shades and three-way bulbs. A shin-threatening coffee table guarded the sofa; a half inch of plate glass on a black iron base with a five-pound freeform ashtray and a brandy snifter full of matchbooks centered on its immaculate surface. Opposite the sofa, a painting on black velvet, three by five feet, enormous in the small room, dominated the wall. A scene of Venice by an artist who had never been east of Seville; an assembly-line piece with mustachioed gondoliers and their boats against a doge's palace that never was.

Between the sofa and the painting and guarding the alcove that led to the kitchen and the stairway to the second floor stood a receptionist's desk with the standard six-button telephone, calendar, and dish of mints, all presided over by a blond and bosomy tootsie who touched the intercom with a scarlet nail. She announced Defoe and ignored Caroline; in her world women shared a level with seeing eye dogs and briefcases.

Caroline was expecting the swarthy bulk of either Marlon Brando's Godfather or Anthony Quinn's Zorba and got neither; Salvatore

Scarface was a tall, thin, immaculately tailored blue-eyed northern Italian in his late seventies. He embraced Defoe briefly in the doorway of his second-floor office and bowed slightly at the waist when introduced to Caroline; she felt his eye scan and assess her teased and tinted hairdo, the Dodgers jacket.

"Chase, my boy, you don't get down here often enough."

"And you don't get out to the country anymore. The morels were magnificent this year."

"Yes, I know. The UPS driver brought me a lovely box of them in the spring. Of course I am old and becoming terribly forgetful, but I seem to recall that your return address was on the carton." He smiled at Caroline and his left eyelid fluttered in what, if it were not for his age, she would have certainly interpreted as a wink. "Speaking of food," he continued, taking them each by an arm and turning them down the narrow hallway, "we have several new items that I would like to have graced with your opinion."

Scarface Imports owned four adjoining houses on the block and had gutted their interiors, breaking through party walls and creating new office space out of cramped bedrooms; Caroline peeked in doorways as they walked along, seeing busy young women hunched over computer terminals or talking to customers on the WATS line. At the end of the hall they entered a room with a plate-glass window that overlooked the warehouse next door, twenty thousand square feet of crates and cartons stacked in tiers on steel shelving that rose three stories from the concrete floor where yellow, propane powered forklift trucks backed and filled, shifting and shuttling their loads. Caroline went to the window and looked down, saw Defoe's car parked inside by the overhead door. The glass was thick enough and they were high enough above the bustle that no sound penetrated the room, but Sally pulled the curtains, shutting out the distracting movement below.

The room evidently took up the entire second and third floor of the last dwelling that abutted the warehouse; the ceiling was eleven feet high and the walls ran the full length of the building from front to back, thirty feet from curb to rear yard. A conference table, flanked by a dozen substantial chairs, dominated the room, but off to one side, near a doorway, a square table under white linen was set for four. Crystal shone and full course sterling tableware paraded on either side of white china.

Defoe smiled and Sally held a chair for Caroline. A waiter, schooled in service but ignorant of English, materialized and placed a wicker basket of fresh bread, sliced thin, on the table and cleared the fourth setting, then retreated through the doorway to the service area. In addition to a commercial bain marie and a refrigeration unit there was a video camera mounted on a ventilation grill, its 16mm wide angle lens focused on the conference table. Microphones could pick up the slightest whisper uttered in the room. Both were turned off. He reappeared with a bottle of '82 Barbaresco and poured a healthy splash into three wineglasses. He did not bother with the formality of offering the host a first taste; both he and Signore Scarface knew it was a fine vintage and the waiter had sniffed the cork and tasted a spoonful when he had opened the bottle six hours earlier to allow it to breathe.

Defoe held his glass to the light that shimmered from the crystal chandelier and sipped, smelled, swished the wine in his mouth.

Sally watched Defoe, then took a small sip from his own glass, enjoyed the vibrant, plumlike flavor. "Gaja," he said, swallowing. "Has a good decade ahead of it."

Defoe looked down at his plate. "Vibrant," he said, putting his glass beside his plate.

Caroline drank her small portion and thought it tasted like Italian red wine.

The waiter brought a second bottle to the table and filled fresh glasses.

"Also a Gaja Barbaresco, same vintage, Chase, 1982. This one's a Sori San Lorenzo, and poor old Alfred had to set his alarm to aerate this lovely young lady. We contracted for a thousand cases and I wish I could get more. Wholesaling for three hundred a case, it's bringing sixty dollars a bottle right now, more than that in New York. Should have a good quarter century ahead of it; no less a light than Martin Gersh called it a 'peerless, titanic Barbaresco.' "

Defoe tested the wine and found it a remarkably overpowering red, redolent of black cherries. He picked up a slice of bread and cleared his palate, went again to the wine. "Titanic is the word, Sally. Can I have a couple of cases? I promise not to touch them until the mid-nineties!"

Caroline drank her wine, picked up a piece of bread, looked for butter, ate. Boozers picnic, she thought.

The waiter returned with a wheeled serving cart, lifted two small platters heaped with black olives and placed them on the table. He touched one with the fingertips of both hands, repositioning it slightly toward his employer, saying to Sally, "*Catanese*," and turned back to his serving table, then put larger plates in front of the diners, each containing olives prepared as antipasti.

"*Olive farcite alla catanese*," Sally said, pointing to the larger plate in front of him. He picked up the smaller dish and offered it to Caroline. "These are ripe black olives from Catania, from Sicily.

You know, where the Mafia comes from." He laughed gently, eyes crinkled as he glanced at Defoe. "Please try one, unadorned, savor the sunshine of the Mediterranean. Then compare, see how they differ from the Umbrian Olive, there, on the other small platter."

She picked up one, popped the pitted fruit into her mouth and chewed, swallowed, reached for her wineglass. Then the other.

"Yeah, I can see the difference; the one, the first is . . . olive-ier?"

Sally laughed again. "Yes, well said, Miss Graff."

"Hey, call me Caroline, everybody does. Hoo, they're salty. Think I could get another shot of wine?"

Sally raised his gaze toward the waiter who stood discreetly out of earshot; he read the rapid, angular movement of his employer's eyes as they dropped to Caroline, then to the table before her, and knew to refill the young lady's glass.

"Now try them, *farcite,* stuffed with capers and anchovies. They're marinated with fennel and salt, then stuffed and marinated again in olive oil. Nice, eh?"

"What's the other one? I like it; not so . . . olive-y." Defoe popped a wrinkled black fruit in his mouth.

Sally looked at his friend, smiled, said, "Umbrian olives. Garlic, bay leaf, orange peel, all marinated for a few days in virgin cold-pressed."

"What's the difference?" Caroline rested her elbows on the table and tore a piece of bread in half, dipped it in the marinade. "I mean between the two olives?"

"Sicily is the big island off the toe of the boot, Caroline," Defoe answered. "Out in the Mediterranean; sun-drenched, home of Syracuse. And Umbria is what, Sally? Seventy-five, a hundred miles north of Rome? Up the Tiber, inland, about the only province without a coastline, except for those pissy little landlocked ones snuggled up against Switzerland, right, Sal?" Defoe smiled and rolled an olive over his tongue. Lombardy, with its capital Milano, was the birthplace of Salvatore Scarface and the most densely populated of Italy's twenty regions. It is completely landlocked.

"Exactly, my friend," Sally replied. "That is why, as a small boy in the twenties, I ran away to Tuscany, to make my fortune."

Defoe turned to Caroline. "He lived with an uncle and spent his days in the Tuscan hills, collecting wild mushrooms to sell to the restaurants in Firenze."

Sally nodded toward the waiter. "Speaking of mushrooms, we've prepared a *funghi alla trasteverina* for you with a new oil from Cordoba; a very nice cold-pressed, and with the dollar the way it is against the peseta a real bargain."

The waiter placed a carafe of oil on the table and Defoe poured a teaspoonful on a slice of bread, tasted.

Sally waited, watching.

"Very nice; clear. I think I'd rather cook with it than use it in a salad, though."

Sally nodded enthusiastically. "Yes, yes, you're right." He touched the lip of the cruet to a piece of bread, offered it to Caroline.

"Hey, oil's oil, Sal," she said, but took the offered sample. "Heat it up and throw in the fries, know what I mean?" She ate the bread and waved her wineglass at Alfred.

The Mushrooms Trastevere were generic button rather than an esoteric wild, but nonetheless were delicious; even Caroline helped herself to another spoonfull of the cold hors d'oeuvres. "More like it," she said, sucking tomato sauce from her finger. "Made with your new oil, huh?"

Sally touched his lips with his napkin. "Yes. The mushroom caps are sauteed in the oil; in a separate pan garlic and onion are also sauteed, then simmered with white vinegar before combining with the tomato pulp and a bouquet garni. Combine, chill—eh!" He smiled and gestured at the platter. "Lovely, yes?"

"Lovely," Caroline reached for a slice of bread. "Sort of like a mushroom pizza without the pizza. Think I could get another glass of red?"

"You have a marvelous appetite, my young friend. Finish the funghi; we'll sample the final vintage for the day. Chase, I think you'll find this an extraordinary wine." He caught Alfred's eye and nodded once.

"Biondi-Santi," Defoe said, reading the label as Alfred poured. "Oh, well, I know it's going to be a treat, Sally. You seem to be specializing in their Brunellos lately; buy a piece of the vineyards?"

Sally chuckled. "I should. This is a '77 Montalcino Riserva; absolutely monumental, don't you think? One wine critic called it a colossus."

Defoe swished and swirled and closed his eyes, then opened one and looked at Caroline. "Perfectly structured," he said. "What's your prognostication for its life expectancy?"

"Should go out to forty years. Lay down a few cases, Chase. This one will be at two hundred a bottle by the turn of the century. It's at ninety now."

Defoe tapped his index finger on the side of his glass, calculated that the wholesale was around six hundred a case. "Bit salty, Sal. Still, I did have a windfall recently." He leaned back, gazing at the glass before him. "What the hell, send me a couple of cases. Carpe diem, eh?'' He laughed. ''More like having my cake and eating it, too, right? I assume Alfred will make us up the usual doggie bag. Can we talk? I have to get Caroline back to her place for a very important meeting.''

She had been listening to the two men, turning her head from side to side, her lips pursed and eyes wide like Richard Pryor trapped in a white man's movie, trying to make sense of hundred-dollar-a-bottle wine and lunches that consisted of black olives and cold mushroom caps.

''Forgive me, my friend. At my age, time tends to slide by unnoticed. Come, let us go into my office.'' They went back down the hallway and the old man placed Defoe and Caroline in comfortable leather armchairs, then sat behind his ornately carved Romanesque desk, it's surface a pristine expanse of ebony and ivory, unblemished by the trappings of modern business; no telephone, appointment calendar, in and out basket intruded on its perfect lines. Sally leaned forward, elbows resting on the desk. ''What can this poor old importer do for you?''

''Sally, I'm trying to do a small favor for an old friend in the insurance business. A trucking company in the Allentown area recently had several substantial losses, losses that will have to be covered by my friend's company. He wants to be sure that the claims are legitimate.'' Defoe paused, looked at the bookcases that covered the walls of the small office, their shelves filled with leather-bound editions in English and Italian, Latin and Greek, the expanse of books occasionally broken by Etruscan and Hellenic artifacts, and regretted the commercial intrusion into his friend's world; this was not the room where Sally conducted business. ''As a man with such a long career behind you, you have met many people. I thought that perhaps you might know someone who might have an associate who may have heard something about these losses. You understand of course that I am not terribly interested in a recovery; merely being assured of the legitimacy of these losses will be enough for my friend.''

Sally drummed his fingers on the desk for a moment, then stood, looked at Defoe and then Caroline, saying, ''Will you excuse me for a moment?'' before leaving the room.

She did not answer, or even notice that he was speaking to her; she stared at the wall behind his desk, her attention completely captivated by a small painting, no more than a foot and a half by two, mounted in a large and ornate gilt frame. It was a portrait of a young man in a red cap, his features sharp, angular, but with full, sensual lips and eyes that fixed the viewer from beneath lowered lids. It was a face that reminded her of John Travolta, but stronger somehow, more dynamic and immediate in its presence. "My God, Chase, that *painting*. If I didn't know better, I'd say it was a Botticelli. It's absolutely magnificent; I wonder where he got it?"

"Well, why don't you ask him?" Defoe smiled. "I'm sure he'll have a wonderful story about it."

Sally reappeared at the doorway and motioned to Defoe. "Come, there is someone I have on the telephone who may be able to provide you with the information you seek. I believe the line to be a secure one, Chase, but these days one never knows, eh? Be discreet." He led Defoe to an empty office and gestured toward a telephone, its handset resting on a desk littered with piles of invoices.

Defoe, more than anyone, knew just how insecure a telephone line could be; it had seemed to him during his career in Naval Intelligence that the likelihood of electronic eavesdropping rose in direct proportion to the desired confidentiality of a conversation. He picked up the receiver. "Hello?"

"Yeah; Sally says you got some questions. What can I do for ya?"

"A trucking company, IGT, Interstate Garment Transport, recently lost three loads. I'd like to know if the losses are connected to each other and if it was an inside job, either involvement by the drivers or higher up, management level."

"You're askin' a lot, pal. You must know Sally pretty good. Leave me make a coupla calls, I'll get back to you."

"Where, here? You want this number? It's—"

"I know the number. Sit tight."

The connection broke abruptly and Defoe sat behind the desk, riffling the stacks of invoices, idly reading the manifest lists of Mediterranean foodstuffs that were the life blood of Scarface Imports.

The thought of secure lines brought a smile to Defoe's lips as he recalled a bright spring day several years earlier when he had met Sally in Franklin D. Roosevelt Park, across from JFK Stadium in South Philadelphia. They sat on a bench and watched the traffic heading down Broad Street toward the Navy Yard. The sycamores had shed their bark from the previous year and the trunks were beginning to show patches of pale green, their smooth skins mottled like a snake.

"Won't be long before the first puffballs, Sally. I cut some pokeweed the other day; first tentative shoots on the south slope."

"Where does the time go; seems only yesterday that fall was in the air and now we are speaking of hunting wild mushrooms. As I grow older the calender has replaced the clock. But that's not why you asked to meet me here, my friend. We could be discussing *boletus edulis* and *morchella esculenta* in my office.''

Defoe paused, chewed his lip. ''Sally, I have to ask you a question; you don't have to answer it. We've known each other for . . . I guess four or five years now, isn't it? Had some pretty deep philosophical discussions along the way. I hope you aren't offended by my asking, but it's not idle curiosity.'' He drew a deep breath. ''What, if any, ties do you have to organized crime?''

Sally stared across the highway at the dirty concrete monolith that was JFK Stadium. ''That's quite a question, my young friend, quite a question. May I ask the reason for it? You say it is more than idle curiosity.''

Defoe shifted on the bench. ''Fair enough. I was in Washington the other day and I stopped in at the Justice Department; one of my college roommates has achieved a fairly high position there. I haven't seen him for a couple of years, thought I'd touch base, see if he could get away for lunch. He heads up some sort of task force on organized crime. Anyway, I was in his office, standing in front of his desk, both of us going through the old long-time-no-see ritual, and, well, Sally, when I was in the Navy I developed this trick of being able to read upside down. Came in rather handy, dealing with government contractors the way I did. You'd be surprised at what people have scattered across their desks. Anyway, old habits die hard and as a matter of course I scanned my roommate's papers. There was a list of names, addresses, telephone numbers. Lots of numbers. It was a wiretap authorization. I don't follow this stuff, just what I read in the papers, but I recognized a couple of the names; big fish, very big indeed. And then, of course, there was your name, too.''

Sally stood up, put his hands in his trouser pockets, jingled the keys to the black Lincoln parked a hundred feet away beside the strip of asphalt that meandered through the park. Two kids on bicycles rode by, baseball gloves hanging from their handlebars. ''Chase, ever since we met that day, both hiking toward that overgrown hayfield full of morels that we were each convinced was unknown by the other, I have never lied to you, never misled you. Not my style. I am an importer; you don't need to know all the details, any more than I need to hear the specifics of what you did during your time in the Navy. Some secrets are best kept.

''To answer your question directly, no, I am not involved with organized crime, not in this country nor back in Italy. Sure, I know a some of the 'wise guys,' I believe the expression is; even have business dealings with a few. That is probably why my name was on that list. I supply a lot of restaurants, all over the country. Some are owned by pretty heavy hitters. It hasn't been easy, staying out of bed with them. I bring in a lot of tonnage through the Port of Philadelphia each year. You can imagine the pressures I get to slip a few unauthorized kilos of this or that onto a load coming out of Genoa or Palermo. They are a disgusting lot; uneducated, stupid, violent men, a generation removed, at most, from their peasant ancestry, and they cost me a fortune each year, a fortune in lost goods, union deals, overcharges, nonexistent men on my payroll. But I would rather write it off as a necessary cost of doing business than become involved with them. One may lie down with the tiger, Mr. Defoe, if one wishes. But then can he ever sleep?

"Let me ask you a question, now, my young friend. Our relationship has been along the lines of good food and drink, discussing the classics and hunting wild mushrooms. If I were a *mafiosi* how would it affect this relationship?"

"An interesting question, Sally. One that I gave some thought before calling you for this meeting. If the answer hadn't been a positive one, I wouldn't be here." He bent and plucked a blade of grass, a new, pale shoot, and bit a quarter inch from the stem, chewed. He stood up and faced his friend.

"You're right, our friendship has been that of casual acquaintances with several things in common. Good friends, however, have achieved a closer level of rapport, that of mutual assistance when the need arises. What I have to propose to you today is a partnership along those lines."

Sally looked at Defoe, puzzled. "I don't think I see what you are getting at. Evidently we Italians aren't the only ones who can be Byzantine."

"Sally, in my business, setting up security systems for companies doing sensitive work, information is my sole commodity. Generally it's information on what type of hardware to use and how to install it. But sometimes, especially when things go wrong, and a company calls on me to set it right, there arises a need for a different type of information. Information such as who did what and who paid them to do it? At present I don't have access to a network that can supply me with that sort of data. That's where you might be able to help me."

"Chase, I thought I made it clear to you that I am not connected. Sure, I know a few guys, as I said. I could make some calls, find out who broke into this hypothetical company of yours. And where would that put me? Squarely in their debt. No thank you, my friend; and I am bewildered that you would suggest such a thing. I thought I knew you, Chase; evidently I was mistaken!" He turned toward his car.

Defoe went after him. "Sally, you haven't thought this thing through. I don't for a moment expect you to put yourself in their debt; you haven't done it for your own gain, why in God's name would you do it for mine? No, what I had in mind was the exact opposite. Why not put these people, some of them, ones that you think will be able to honor a commitment, the ones bound by that code of conduct so popular in Godfather fiction, put these men deeply and irrevocably in your debt?

"A lot of unpleasant and dangerous men are going to prison when this thing is over. You can be the one who decides which one goes, which doesn't. A word from you to the chosen few to avoid the telephone like the plague will do wonders. Even when it's on the hook the speaker can be activated by new technology. Any room with a phone is already bugged. Not many people know that, Sally. Tell them. Also tell them who you are not going to inform of the wiretaps. This is perhaps the most important point, for this is what will make you a kingmaker. But read the character of these men carefully, it's a two-edged sword I offer you. This undertaking will not be without its downside risk, as my stockbroker loves to say."

"That is an understatement. But, Chase, I am still confused. I told you, I'm not involved with the world of organized crime. Except for maybe half a dozen people, I don't have the slightest idea of who is slated for this federal wiretap. I wouldn't know who to contact."

"You will, Sally," Defoe said, reaching inside his jacket. "While my roommate was in the washroom I memorized the list."

The telephone rang and Defoe picked it up.

"Hey, pal, on that truck thing; this IGT is a union shop, you know what I'm saying? I mean, certain people look out for the Teamsters. And the guy what runs it, guy name of C. Bullfinch, he's a regular contributor to the pension fund. Now I can't speak for every little piece a personal business goes on inside this outfit, pal, but the buzz I got is some new talent was involved in this operation you're concerned about. Some country boys up that way. That's all I got. Oh, one more item for youse. None of the goods went into any of the regular pipelines. And hey, it's four, not three trucks got snatched. You got that?"

"I got that. Thanks a lot, friend."

"Yeah." Defoe could hear the receiver clatter onto the hook at the other end, then a dial tone. None of the goods went into the regular pipelines. A whole network out there, running parallel to the legitimate world. And ninety-nine percent of the time we aren't even aware of its existence, let alone its everyday influence on our lives.

If I were a Mafia don, how would that affect our relationship?
That question of Sally's in the park Defoe had asked himself as he sat
in a stall in the ninth-floor men's room at the Justice Department,
copying the memorized list of twenty-three names onto a three-by-
five card. Tell Sally? Flush the list, pretend I never saw it? Just
leaving the building with it could get me five years. If Sally is not
connected he has nothing to fear. Bullshit. A fishing expedition like
this catches the innocent with the guilty. During his active duty days,
tracking down fraud and corruption in the military procurement system had been his first taste of reality, a harsh jolt after the ivory
towers of the Ivy League. Truth, Justice, and the American Way
were the stuff of comic book heroes; in the real world, political
payoffs, plea bargains, and career advancement were the watch-
words. He had stumbled across some inside information that day at
Justice; how, or even if, he was to use it depended upon the results of
his actions measuring up to his own personal code of ethics. Scratch
a pragmatist and find a realist.

Sally came back into his office, found Caroline still staring at the
painting. "So," he said, "how is my friend Tommy?"

"Tommy who?"

"Lasorda, your manager." He gestured toward the jacket, smiled.

"Oh, him, yeah. I haven't seen him in a couple of years to tell the
truth. He's a friend of yours you said?"

Sally eased behind the desk. "He has a restaurant in the area, buys
from us. An acquaintance really, not a friend."

"Can I have a closer look at that painting?"

"Certainly. Let me put the overhead light on for you."

She stood a foot from the picture, peering intently at its surface. "Incredible. I'd *swear* it's a Botticelli." She reached out to touch it,
drew her hand back.

Sally chuckled. "Alessandro Filipepi. Painted in Firenze, late
quattrocento."

She turned on him, eyes flashing. "Better known as Sandro Botticelli, died 1510. Born in Florence in the mid-fourteen forties. A
student of Filippo Lippi. Son of a *bitch*. I *know* this painting;
I mean, I've seen slides of it. It was destroyed in 1966 when the
Arno flooded the Uffizi."

"Ah, a historian, then."

"No, I mean, yes. Hell; I did a paper in art school on Botticelli.
How did you—"

"You mean what's a painting like this doing in the south Philly
office of a dago importer?"

"No, yes; that's exactly what I mean. I'd have phrased it a little more politely, but you got it, Sal."

"Ha Ha! The directness of youth. Yes, it is what you think it is. It is on loan from the Uffizi. On loan only because I intend to return it when I am finished with it. Not too many more years from now, either. There is a provision in my will for its return. It will be discovered in a warehouse that my company owns near Florence, high above the River Arno. My grandniece, a research assistant at the Metropolitan in New York, a specialist in the Medicis, will receive a letter, make the discovery, and be assured of a glorious career in the all-too-often boring world of museum art."

"It sounds like a TV show; how the hell did you manage to steal a Botticelli from the Uffizi? And why; here, in this—"

"In this row house in Little Italy? Why didn't I sell it for a million bucks? I think you watch too much of the TV. Why did I take a Botticelli? Simple. Because the Uffizi has so many and I had none. What's one painting, more or less, for a museum like the Uffizi. How did I do it? Again, simple. I happened to be there, that November in 1966, when the Arno burst its banks. So many rallied to save the museum. My people worked around the clock, loading the contents of the galleries into our vans, storing them in the warehouse. We used the forklift trucks to shove the pallets of olive oil, pasta, cases of wine outside, to make room for the paintings. The rain was unbelievable! A deluge. But we, our small part in the salvage operation, lost not a single piece of art. One or two might have been *mislaid,* temporarily, in the hurly-burly of the moment. The Botticelli. A Durer print; it's still in the building, by the way; my European manager has it hanging in his office lavatory!"

"Aren't you afraid that this might be stolen?"

"Here? You have to be pulling my leg. This building is occupied twenty-four hours a day by my employees; up here, secretaries are talking on the telephone to Europe at three in the morning—over there, the business day has started, you realize. In the warehouse, strapping young men are loading trucks around the clock. Besides, Chase must have told you, I'm what the movies call a connected guy; who would dare break into this place? No, I think that Sandro's painting—it's thought to be a self-portrait, by the way—is as safe here as it would be back in the Uffizi." He laughed, winked at Caroline. "Safer—the Delaware River rarely floods." He sat and swiveled his chair around, facing the painting as he had countless times before.

"And, my God, Caroline. Isn't that the most fantastic thing you have ever seen?" He put out his hand without looking and knew she would take it and they looked at the small tempera on wood painting in silence until Defoe came back into the office.

"Ah," he said, looking at the two lovers holding hands, "putting the squeeze on my date, eh?"

"Hey, Ace, how about hitting those Golden Arches before we get back on the thruway? I mean, lunch was interesting, what there was of it. Only see, that's the problem. You and Sally back there seem to survive just fine, talking about the food. But some of us mere mortals like to actually eat the stuff from time to time. We don't have to go inside, just make a flying stop at the drive-thru window, Chase. Please?"

He followed the white arrows through the parking lot and stopped at the menu board, looked at Caroline.

"Big Mac, medium fries, and a choc shake. No, make that a large diet soda. What do you want; my treat." She pulled a handful of crumpled bills from her jacket pocket.

He touched the button on the intercom. "I think I'll pass, Caroline. I don't much care for prefabricated food."

"What do you mean, prefabricated food? This is good stuff, fresh. You can see 'em cooking it inside."

"That's all for show. See, I have the inside story; the food is really made in a forty-acre factory, out in Kansas someplace, and trucked to the stores in heated trailers. Then they stick it under those infrared light bulbs to keep it hot. Six weeks old by the time you buy it."

She unwrapped the burger and took a bite, hunched over the yellow plastic container to keep the dripping sauce from the upholstery. "Pro'lly why they taste so good! Wanna bite?" She smiled at him around a mouthful of food and he laughed quickly, gunning the car up the entrance ramp to the expressway.

Traffic was building even at the mid-afternoon hour of three o'clock, for it was Friday, and on any given Friday twenty percent of the employable population had snuck, ducked, or just plain front-door left early, getting a jump on the weekend. Add to that half of the housewives in the country heading to the bank and the supermarket for the week's grocery shopping, all trying to make a left-hand turn from the right lane, and stir in a laid-off redneck asshole recently self-employed at working his way through a six-pack (and doing a damn fine job of it, too, thank you, ma'am), who thought that yellow meant "gun the sucker"! put him up against an eighteen-wheeler that needed a mite more highway than the recommended three car lengths to go from thirty to zero, and you have the situation on Hamilton

Boulevard, east of Allentown, across from Dorney Amusement Park, home of Wild Water Kingdom, where Yearner Claxon sat, drumming his fingers on the steering wheel and goosing the gas of the four-forty V-8, making voom voom noises that did nothing for the overheated tempers of the adjacent motoring public on that warm and sunny October day.

"Well, shit, piss and corruption," he said aloud, too loud, startling the woman in the Rabbit beside him who sat idling, all four windows cranked down and beads of sweat glistening on her chest, and he pulled off the road and punched up the office number on the cellular as he rooted in the icy water of his cooler for the last can of Strohs.

"Hey, Penny," he said, swallowing cold beer. "Glad I caught you before you left for the weekend. Listen, I'm staked out up here, way the hell and gone, and there's two good old boys just may spook and try to blow me away with buckshot, I try to move out right now. So how about you relay this to the bossman and chivvy my paycheck for me? I'll stop by your place later for it, we'll turn that little piece of paper into a nice dinner someplace. You make us a reservation? Oh, and tell me where you live, so's I can pick you up; 'bout eight. I should be out of this dangerous damn situation by then, have time for a quick shower before we get together."

He listened to her response, then reassured her. "Yes, I'll be careful, sweetheart. But you know, situations like this come with the territory, and, well, a man's gotta do what a man's gotta do." He cut the connection, looked at his watch, and searched his mind for the nearest beer distributor. Time to refuel.

"Time to refuel. One of the minor drawbacks of this car is that it only runs well on hi-test leaded; a rather rare commodity nowadays. And the gas gauge is erratic, have to cross-reference it with the odometer and mentally calculate via miles per gallon. The price of luxury, eh?" Defoe downshifted, double clutching through the synchronized gearbox, babying it; the older Jaguars have notoriously weak transmissions. Drop a cluster and wait six months for replacement parts.

She wriggled in the seat as he pulled into the gas station. "Yeah, but the luxury part's nice, all this crinkly old leather and walnut. That kid at Sally's didn't know how much he hit the truth with his remark about how they don't make them like they used to. You said you got this car in California; what were you doing out there?"

"Yes, I was in the Navy, stationed in San Diego. Married one of the natives; blond, blue-eyed surfer girl."

"So you're not gay; I kind of wondered, no sign of a significant other at your place." She looked at him. "What happened? Divorce?"

"Yeah." Defoe turned, threw his arm over the seat, looked back through the rear window at the kid pumping gas.

"Kids?"

"Uhm, one." Defoe turned back, dug out his wallet, fished for a credit card, then decided on speed, cash.

"And?"

"Uh, I'd rather not get into it right now, Caroline. Here, give the pump jockey this, they always come up on the wrong side for payment." He handed her a twenty, leaned down to look out her window at the pimply-faced boy in the greasy jacket. "Keep the change, son," he said, hitting the starter, praying that the ignition would catch; *don't make me open the bonnet this time and whack the voltage regulator.*

They rode in catatonic silence on the divided highway, separated by some unspoken median strip until he finally said, five miles closer to home, "I'm sorry, Caroline, I didn't mean to be rude; I'm . . . I have a hang-up about my . . . I mean, it's not your fault."

"No, hey, I . . . I don't have any right to pry—"

"No, you weren't, it was a simple question—"

"No, really—"

"Hey, let's start over. Me first, my question. You married?" He looked over at her and smiled.

"No, never; no time, desire. Few potential possibles along the line, but . . ." She shook her head. "Just never hooked in with the right guy at the right time. Too much career hang-up, I guess."

Defoe laughed quietly. "Me, too, at least that's what my wife said. The Navy job kept me away from home for months; I was halfway around the world when . . . when we finally split up; doing under-cover work; I shouldn't have even been there, I was a captain, for Christ's sake, should have been back in San Diego, running the project instead of posing as a French expatriot— LOOK OUT, YOU JERK!" Defoe hit the brakes and locked all four wheels, threw the sedan into a slide that avoided the fifteen-year-old Buick wagon drifting across his bows, cretin unseeing, slumped low in the driver's seat, sliding off the exit to their right. They finished the trip in silence, the last few miles a stew of anger, fear, and self-examination.

He parked below the barn and they entered the building by the bottom door that opened directly into the lower level and went to the office that was segregated from the rest of the building. She watched him punch in the code that unlocked the door.

"Why all the security, Chase? I mean, let's face it, there ain't much in the place to steal."

"No? You wouldn't think so, would you? But then, you haven't been in here." He opened the office door and stood back, letting her go inside first. "Oh, wow, yeah, I see. All that wine."

Defoe laughed. "Sure, the hundred-dollar-a-bottle talk at lunch. No, Caroline, the valuable stuff is in the computer there." He pointed at the squat IBM box beside the cases of wine. "That's the value; business data, security designs on a couple of hundred companies' systems. Any one of which could be worth a million or so to the right person, someone who wanted to get inside." He checked the phone for messages, tore a sheet off the fax machine.

Nasdaq National Market

52 Week high low	stock div	Yld O/O	PE Ratio	Sales 100s	High	Low	Last	Chg.
3⅝ 1½	Rdindus . . .	. . .	9	12	2	11/2	1½	-½

Gleneagle Stores: No longer traded (LBO last Aug)
Norton & Norton: No longer traded (LBO last Dec)
Interstate Garment Transfer: Privately held co.
Chase: I do not recommend Reade Industries at this time. Walter.

Defoe tossed the paper on the desk. "Not what I wanted, Walter, not what I wanted at all." He spun the Rolodex and dialed his broker's office. Left for the day. Sure; it's Friday afternoon. Redial. Catch him at home, just came in the door.

"Walter; on that data you sent me. I'm not interested in buying stock in those companies, just looking for any connection between them."

"Sorry about that, Chase. I'll look it up for you first thing Monday morning. I should have known you weren't interested in penny stocks for their investment potential."

"Distill the data, Walter. Use that analytical brain of yours, give me the raw essence of these oufits. Talk to you Monday." He hung up, turned toward the door.

"What's this all about?"

"My stockbroker. I asked him for background information on the principal players in the hijacking. Interstate Garment was the hauler, these three companies owned the loads. I learned from Sally's contacts that it wasn't a professional heist, now I'm trying to eliminate insurance fraud." He locked the office and said, "Let's go topside."

At the top of the stairs they met Magnificat, seventeen pounds of black feline who arched his back and rubbed against Caroline's leg. "Hello, puss," she said, scratching his head. "You're a big one."

"Ought to be, all he does is eat and sleep. He's been neutered, that tends to put on weight. The other one now, she's a different story. Still as scrawny as the day she showed up. Both are strays; city people bring their unwanted livestock out to the country and drop them off along the roads. Charming behavior, what?" He looked around the room, called, "Hey, No Name! Where are you?"

In answer a small female three-color cat with a shredded ear and a crooked tail padded down from the second level, sat and quietly watched them from the third step.

"No Name?"

"Yes, nothing ever seemed to fit her, at least not yet, only been here a few months. She's the hunter of the two, drags dead animals back here as big as she is."

"Yeah. The female of the species." She reached out and grabbed Defoe's wrist, looked at his watch. "Hey! It's sneakin' up on five. Use your phone?"

"Go ahead." He smiled. "I gather that you'd forgotten all about your book thing over the last few hours?"

She winked at him, picked up the phone. "Well, once or twice it did cross my mind . . ." She dialed the number and listened to the message, put the phone down, and yelped. "Yahoo!" She threw her arms around Defoe's neck. "I *got* it! Listen, can I make a long-distance call? He said he'd be there until five, up in New York. I want to see what the details are, I can't wait until Monday."

"Sure." Defoe busied himself with putting the cats outside with their dinner, came back in as Caroline hung up the phone. She threw her arms around his neck again, and kissed him. "Oh, wow! You won't believe this. A ten-thousand-dollar advance, and another ten when the final artwork is approved. Plus they're going to fly me all over, doing the drawings of these people. I can't believe it!" She kissed him again. Success can be a powerful aphrodisiac.

"Well," Defoe said, pulling away from her embrace, "this calls for a celebration. You really will have to let me take you out to dinner now."

"Yeah, sure. Only it's my treat. Listen, you're the gourmet, figure out someplace good. I'm gonna zap back to my place and get changed. I do own a dress, no kidding. See you here in a couple of hours." She went out to her car; Defoe heard her give a happy shout outside and he laughed aloud.

He went back to his office, called Askew at the hospital, told him of the canceled South American trip. Related to the insurance adjuster what he had learned in South Philadelphia, his feelers out to his broker for a connection between the companies.

"You've been a busy man, Mr. Defoe."

"Not really, just a few phone calls so far. I thought I'd have a chat with those drivers tomorrow, hear it from the horse's mouth. I believe that's what you said your next step would have been."

"Right. An exercise in futility, though. Chances of recovering anything are zilch. If you're thinking about the twenty percent, forget it, my friend."

"I suppose you're right. Oh, say, my source told me that there were four trucks taken; you know anything about that?"

"First I've heard of it. Let me try to get ahold of somebody at IGT. Can I get back to you if I find anything out?"

"Sure. Let me give you my number here. Talk to my machine; there's no time limit on the message; use twenty minutes if you need to. I'll check in with you tomorrow after I see the drivers. And I may run up to IGT, nose around there a bit."

"You don't have to do this, you know."

"Sure I do. Bill Pickering is my godfather and a friend. Besides, this is fun; I got a reprieve from South America and have a couple of weeks before my next project."

Defoe changed into his sweats and worked out with the weights for an hour, then went upstairs, showered and put on a chalk-stripe three-piece suit. He got downstairs as Caroline parked her car in front of the barn.

She had washed her hair, removing all traces of styling gel and florescent decoration. Beneath the baggy clothing she had worn earlier was a concupiscent body, and she had fitted it into a black sheath that commanded Defoe's attention. Her skin was very white, stark against the shiny black of her hair and dress. She either didn't care, or she had learned the lesson from Marilyn Monroe that jewelry is an unnecessary distraction.

"Where am I taking you to dinner?" Caroline asked as Defoe locked the front door.

"Joe's," Defoe replied. "In Reading; you probably know it."

" 'Fraid not. Denny's and Hardee's and Gino's I know, but no Joe's."

"It's a small place on a back street, but people drive all the way from New York to eat there. Dinner at Joe's is always an adventure." In answer to her puzzled look, he said with a smile, "They specialize in dishes made with wild mushrooms."

* * *

It was nearly eleven when they left the restaurant, and Caroline hooked her arm through his as they walked along the uneven brick sidewalk toward the Jaguar. In addition to the Bordeaux Defoe had selected, she'd insisted on buying a bottle of champagne, to celebrate her book contract, and her eyes had a bemused sparkle under the glow of the streetlights. "I think you'd better take me back to your barn, Chase," she said, looking up at him.

He gave her a quizzical look. "Sure; you want to pick up your car."

"No, Mr. Defoe. I want to get laid."

She was still asleep when he left the barn at eight. It had been a shock to wake up and find a naked woman curled against him, and it took him a moment to sort out the previous evening. Her ardency had been as memorable as her inebriation; it was not until nearly three that she had finally succumbed to exhaustion and allowed him to slip beneath the surf of sleep that washed over him.

He let the shower run hot, filling the space with steam that drained his sinuses and sweated the sparkling wine from his pores. When they had reached the barn Caroline had miraculously produced a carrier of cold duck from the trunk of her car. It was not a drink that he much cared for, but she had seemed determined that they finish the six-pack, punctuating the pop of each fresh bottle with another orgasm achieved with increasingly creative gymnastics.

Between rounds they had talked; first intellectually serious like two cautious college kids probing the other's psyche while covering their own metaphoric nakedness with a kaross of knowledge. He told her of the fire that had destroyed the farmhouse and his decision to convert the barn into a dwelling.

"All I really had in mind was living space. People seem to think it was some cerebral exercise in design, conceived as an architectural statement." He laughed. "All I did was put plate-glass windows in a wall and clean the place up a bit. The spiral staircase was serendipity."

"Yes," she countered. "But I watched you, listened to you at Sally's today, saw the way the two of you interacted. Both of you are connoisseurs, have an eye for beauty. And you've lived, traveled in the Far East. Maybe it was subconscious, but you designed this interior with harmony and balance ahead of access and utility. That the four came together as one is a measure of your success. Wright wouldn't have done it better, bucko."

And then, alternately, silly; playing Just Desserts: What do you serve a lawyer? Tortes, of course.

How about Jack the Ripper? Tarts!

A poet? Pound cake.

With Frost-ing!

Gene Autry? Angel food cake.

Aleister Crowley? She missed that one.

And finally, getting down to the soul-bearing stage that came with the last of the sparkling wine, their glasses long lost among the bed covers, drinking from the heavy green bottle.

Defoe looked up at the skylight over the sleeping platform, took in the sweep of the night, the panoply of stars spread across the October sky. Arcturus was bright in Boötes, luminous off the handle of the Big Dipper.

"My son. Andy. That's what I couldn't tell you about today— yesterday?—at the gas station." Defoe wiped tingling froth from his upper lip. "He was killed; hit by a car as he rode his bicycle home from a friend's house. By a drunk. Well, that was the end of my marriage; hell, it wasn't any too firmly founded before his death, but Andy; Andy was the coup de grace. When it happened, I was on the other side of the world on an undercover project that I had no business being physically involved with, playing macho man super spy. Captain Defoe as Captain Marvel. You're too young to remember him. A second stringer to Superman. Like me and James Bond. You remember *him*. Ol' Jack Kennedy made him famous, you know that? An offhand mention that he enjoyed the Fleming novels and bang. Overnight the bookstalls were flooded with James Bond paperback reprints. Nineteen sixty-two it was, I remember, because I was a young Ivy League ROTC Lieutenant JG, wet behind the ears, but connected, you know? Like Sally. Only my connection was through friends of my father at the State Department, senior officers in the Pentagon, his Yale cronies in the CIA. So here was this know-nothing pipsqueak sailor in the White House, smack in the middle of the Cuban missile crisis. Having five A.M. breakfasts with the President, briefing the Man from Harvard with the latest distillations of recon photos, pointing out the missile launchers, the Russian trucks camouflaged beside the warhead bunkers." Her head nestled against his shoulder, his fingers traced a meandering pattern around the areola of her right breast. "I was twenty-two and it was a tough act to follow. But Khruschev backed down, Kennedy got shot, and I was absorbed by the Pentagon's internal investigative system. Looking for crooked contractors. The ones who hadn't hired former administration officials as thousand-dollar-an-hour consultants. Fifteen years later I was chasing computer thieves off the east coast of Africa.

"I should have been back home with my wife and kid, running the program during a nine-to-five workday, like the others in my section."

The strobe of a jet winked red as it headed west across their field of vision.

She rose in the silence that followed, went to the bath at the far end of the room; toilet, sink, and shower clustered behind the translucent shoji. The rill of her pee triggered his bladder and he rolled off the tatami mats that upholstered the sleeping platform, went to wait his turn.

Curious, he thought, *how comfortable I am with her, after a few short hours,* then wrote it off to the champagne and nakedness. The moon was a day or two away from full. It flooded the bedroom with a soft white glow, made her skin shine like alabaster in its cold light. Her ablutions finished, she stood, flowed across the tiles to him, and grasped his arm with surprising strength. "It's not your fault," she said. "Where you were at the time was not a part of the equation." She released her grip, went back to the bed, fluffed the futons, snuggled under the warmth of their bulk. She was asleep by the time he rejoined her.

He knew she'd sleep most of the morning and he wanted to visit IGT, see the three drivers. The trucking company was located in a new industrial park off the Interstate exit for the ABE airport. A twelve-foot-high fence, topped by concertina wire, enclosed five acres of tractor trailers and garages. A guard at the gate referred Defoe to the office, a single-story brick building with its front door located outside the fenced-in complex. The chain link was lit by mercury lamps every fifty feet, and Defoe noticed a steel water dish beside the guard shack; at least one dog was on duty at night. Adequate security.

Inside the offices he found a middle-aged woman at an adding machine and a thirtyish man in shirtsleeves drinking coffee and dictating figures from a green-and-white computer printout.

"Help you, sir?"

"Yes, I'm Defoe, from the insurance company. Mr. Askew's my boss; asked me to stop out here. About the hijacked trucks?"

"Oh, yeah, Jeez," the man said, getting up, extending his hand. "Dave Oates, Mr. Defoe. The boss will want to talk to you, Mr Bullfinch; he's out in the garage, usually is Saturdays. Likes to get dirty once a week! Come on, I'll take you out there."

Calvin Bullfinch was more bull than finch, and had a voice that overrode the Mack diesel he bent over. He squirted the grease cutter on his hands, wiped them on a rag, and offered Defoe a firm grip, saying, "I talked to Harold this morning, first time since his heart attack. He told me the paperwork was about finished, the claims would be paid; but then said he'd heard we lost another rig. *God-damnit.*'' He threw the rag in a red safety can with more force than necessary. "I didn't want to say anything to Harold when it happened, not the shape he's in. I was planning on dropping by the hospital this afternoon, break it to him in person. Guess the cops told him. Yeah, we lost another truck last week. Same as the others, jumped the driver at a truck stop. Only this time there was a relief man on board. And he's missing. José, the driver, has a concussion, and now all bets are going to be off, right? On the insurance. One small, bright spot, though, my tractors are showing up. First one we lost my own men spotted at a truck stop on the Interstate. Probably been there since the day it was grabbed. And the New York police found another under the West Side Highway. At least they aren't getting chopped.''

"Chopped?''

"Yeah, parted out; usually, the pros heist a rig, they have a place to strip the tractor, sell off the parts. If it's a random snatch, sometimes they can get more for the rig than the load it was carrying. Ten tires at a hundred or two each. A good motor is worth ten thousand, no questions asked. These tractors of mine showing up tells me it's amateur night. Only the alarms were bypassed; somebody knows what they're doing.''

"You have alarms on your trucks?''

Bullfinch looked at Defoe. "You don't know much about the trucking business, do you? Sure we have alarms; come on, I'll show you.'' He led Defoe to one of the half dozen trucks aligned in the shop, mechanics under and in them, doing routine maintenance. They climbed into the cab and Bullfinch pointed to a panel of buttons under the dash. "Alarm control. The driver has to punch in the code to deactivate it. Engine won't start; he can't even open the doors to get out without the alarm going off. Of course they aren't that tough to bypass, someone knows the business. Your average guy, no, but someone, a driver familiar with the systems, can jump them. Hell, sometimes my own guys bypass the alarm. Or they write the damn code on the dash in case they forget it.''

"Did the police examine the two trucks that were recovered?''

"Pennsy did, the one my people found. I went out there, to the truck stop. They went over it pretty good. Found a lot of prints, but they sent a guy over here, fingerprinted all my mechanics, drivers that had been on that rig the last couple months. Nothing.

"And the one in New York; well. Cops towed it to their impound garage on account of it was illegally parked. Sent me a registered letter, cost me two hundred bucks to get the truck released.'' The owner of IGT shoved his hands in his trouser pockets, then scratched the back of his neck as he pointed toward a vending machine with his right. "C'mon, I'll buy you a coffee." He fed quarters into the slot and water heated the day before dropped into a plastic cup, splashing over coffee crystals dried a year before. "Mr. Defoe, nobody really gives a rat's ass about hijack losses, I mean, it's just part of doing business. You cover yourself as best you can; I carry your insurance because nobody would ship with me if I didn't. But my real insurance, the kind that counts, is paying off the wiseguys, the families controlling the ports; JFK, the garment center. See, those places are like a franchise, snatching loads from the different areas, I mean. You want to grab a truckload of fabric, just off the boat from Hong Kong, at Newark? Gambone's gonna want twenty percent of what you get for it, just to let you do business. Luchese's got JFK. Nobody steals nothing from the air cargo terminal without the okay. And for a price, they put the nixie on my logo. That's why my rates with you are so low, I don't have claims. Until now."

"So you're saying that organized crime is not responsible for your losses. That's exactly what I heard from another source."

Bullfinch looked at Defoe, a glimmer of respect in his gaze. "Yeah. Besides, like I said, the trucks weren't cut up."

"What about a walkaway?"

"You mean a give-up. No way, not the guys got hit. Two of 'em been with me twenty years. Don't get me wrong, we're no different than any of the others. I know I got drivers that would jump at the chance for a quick couple a C's. But not these particular boys. Besides, they were all roughed up by this big monkey. Cracked a couple of ribs, the concussion I told you about. I had a driver in the hospital, down Delaware, pissing blood. And another thing. The goods just flat out disappeared. I guess Askew told you that before he got laid up he talked to his contacts, and nobody has seen any of the stuff. Type of high-class threads we lost, there's only so many places they're going to show up, know what I mean? You don't retail three-thousand-dollar dresses off the tailgate of a truck in Queens. Askew's been an adjuster long enough to know his way around. He'd buy the stuff back if he could. It's new talent, Mr. Defoe. But they know the rigs, and they got someplace to unload the merchandise. And they're getting inside information from the other end. These cargos, the ones snatched, have been valued at two to three times what my normal load is. All high-end goods."

"You say the other end. You mean the shipper? Why not someone in your office?"

"Because we don't normally have the manifest before we pick up the load. No reason to; we're hauling freight: pounds, cubic feet. Doesn't matter to us if it's three-dollar sweaters or C-note suits, it's the weight, the bulk we're interested in. But the other part of your question. Not necessarily the shipper is feeding the info to the hijackers. I mean, in these particular cases, the shippers are European, leastwise the French designer stuff that was grabbed. Now if it was a professional heist I'd say it was possible that someone in the shipper's organization was in on it. A Sicilian stud romancing a squiff in Paris, Genoa. But in the case we got here, more likely it's somebody has a girlfriend who works in the Air France or Pan Am freight section at Kennedy. Or a customs clerk with a brother-in-law; that type of thing.'' Bullfinch put his coffee cup on a bright red Snap-On toolbox, leaned against the workbench.

"See, there are a bunch of steps between the original shipper and the consignee we deliver to. Freight forwarders, transshippers, the customs I mentioned. Then there's bonded warehouses at JFK, there's customs brokers, agents. You're new at this, aren't you? How come you don't know any of this shit?''

"Because, as you said, I'm new at it. But I'm learning. And now I want to go and see your drivers, see what else I can learn.''

Bullfinch shook his head. "Be my guest. Two are still out on partial disability, Frank I got on light duty; they should all be home today. But the men can't tell you anything they haven't already told me, told the cops. Waste of time. You got to understand, Mr. Defoe. The loads are gone, we'll never see a single thread of the stuff that was stolen. But do what you have to, get this thing cleared up. I want those claims settled.''

"So do I, Mr. Bullfinch, so do I.''

The subdivision was overlaid with the suburban sounds of chain saws, weed whackers, lawn mowers, and leaf blowers, interspersed with the higher whine of dirt bikes and AVT's piloted by prepubescent boys, so that Saturday and Sunday was a weekend-long steel cicada thrum, blending McCullough and Rupp, Honda and Stihl into a continuous, dawn till dusk background whine.

"Why they moved to the country,'' Defoe asked under his breath as he rang the bell. "Bet they got up a petition to get that dairy farm up the road to stop stinking up the neighborhood.'' He stepped back as the inside door opened in, and he pulled the storm sash out, said to the woman, late forties, her bowling pin legs a step above him on the Harvest Gold Nylon wall-to-wall, "Hello, I'm Chase Defoe; like to talk to Mr. Abelweis, Arnold? From the insurance company.'' He scraped nonexistent dirt from his feet and came into the living room of the split level, its picture window cantilevered over the garage and rec room below them, the gauzy curtains swagged back, framing a view of the neighbor's blue-and-white vinyl pool.

"Arnold," she said to the man who sat on the sofa, a newspaper in front of his face. "Man's from the *in*surance," putting heavy emphasis on the first syllable.

Arnold looked up, crumpled the paper with a flourish, picked up a coffee mug, and sipped. He had white socks on his feet, wore tan slacks and a blue T-shirt with a pocket. He could lose fifty pounds.

"Pardon me, I don't get up," he said, motioning toward a chair. "Ribs still hurt like a son of a gun. Martha, get the man a coffee."

"No, thanks, just had one."

"Oh, go ahead, once. It's fresh made. Cream and sugar?"

"Black, thanks."

"Well, all right, then," she said, rolling her bulk toward the kitchen.

"So, you brought my check already. Didn't think you people worked that quick."

"Not that kind of insurance, I'm afraid; I represent the company that insures IGT. We cover the hijacking losses. I'll need to get a statement from you; what happened." Defoe pulled out a copy of the driver's police report from the manila folder.

"Ah, Jesus, I already told the Staties all about it; Mr. Bullfinch, too. We got to go through this again?"

"Afraid so, you know how it is with insurance companies. I'll be as quick as I can." Defoe looked at his paper, picked up the thread. "You picked up your load at Kennedy, the overseas terminal, on the ninth? A forty-foot . . . 'igloo'—what's that?"

"Steel shipping container; there's twenties and forties. Loaded at the factory, over in England, sealed right there. No boxes, cartons, or nothing to hump. Just slide in on a lowboy and haul ass to wherever. Only I never made it to . . . Jesus—where was it? Someplace in Ohio, I think."

"Dayton?" Defoe looked up from the papers.

"Yeah." Arnold sighed, touched his torso. "Cracked a couple of ribs. Gleneagle. I hit them pretty regular, every six, eight weeks. Knitwear outfit, nice people. Gimme one of them English sweaters last trip. Didn't fit, though; the old lady has it. Pure wool. Can't stand it myself, itches, y'know?"

Defoe looked down at his own sweater. "Right. The report says you got hijacked on 22, you stopped to check your tires?"

"Yeah. Back end felt kind of funny; thought I was about to lose a skin. Sometimes they put shitty retreads on the shuttle trailers, you know? Anyhow, I was under the ass end and this son of a bitch hit me with something; two-by-four, piece of angle iron, I don't know. I didn't even hear him stop. Next thing, I'm under the rig, fucking fire in my ribs, beg your pardon, and the trailer's moving, rolling right over me. You want my personal opinion, I don't think this guy gave two shits if he ran atop me or not.''

"The police report says that you got a look at the hijacker's vehicle.''

"Just the tires; well, the bottom part. On account of I'm rolling around under the trailer with my busted ribs. Big, fat tires, chrome wheels. Kind of a bronze, burnt-orange truck. Running boards, I seen that. Not the same color; aluminum or stainless. Happened pretty quick, it drove out right alongside my truck. It's all in the report there. You're not from the disability, hey?''

Very little of it was in the report there; the cop who had interviewed Mr. Abelweis had not pushed and probed, and the victim, at the time, had been more concerned over the pain in his ribs than the details of the crime. He still appeared to be. Unless Defoe was losing his touch, this man lacked the élan for a give-up.

The second driver was half hidden behind a rampant hedge of forsythia, spectacular perhaps in early spring, but a straggly mare's nest in mid-October. Cement paving squares formed a tenuous path through a muddy yard; a mongrel on a chain inhibited the growth of grass and the passage of strangers. The sign, in two-inch aluminum stick-on letters, peeling from the side of a rusting file cabinet, its empty drawers agape, said "B WARE THE JABBERW CK.''

Defoe looked at the dog, sized to be intimidating but possessing enough blue tick genes to give it the floppy jowls and bloodshot gaze of the amiable goof. "Hey, dog, you a killer?''

In answer the animal whimpered and skidded its ass across the sparse grass for several yards before collapsing in front of Defoe, its tail thumping, rubbery black nose between protruding paws.

"Worms, eh?'' Defoe asked, leaning to scratch an ear. He was rewarded by moans and the flash of a bright red lipstick of a penis as the dog rolled on its back in spasms of pleasure at the attention. "Hold the fort, pal,'' he said, and stepped up on the single cinder block that was front porch to a trailer built long before the advent of the Double Wide and the Bi-Level, a roadweary aluminum structure that seemed to drape itself in tired abandon over the cement blocks that supported its rusty axles.

He tapped at the door, an assemblage of cracked jalousie slats, mended haphazardly with strips of duct tape.

"It's as open as my mind, friend. Enter, enter at thy will."

He sat at the dinette, eyes as sad as the dog's with a long, bony hand wrapped around a green Rolling Rock pony.

"Name's Defoe, I'm from the insurance company."

"Schaftmaster. I'm from the Andromeda galaxy." He waved the bottle in the vicinity of the refrigerator. "Pull up a beer and sit down."

Defoe glanced at the plastic sunburst clock, then at his watch for corroboration. "Little early for me, thanks."

"As long as you're up, then, I'll take another."

"I'd like to ask you a few questions about the truck you lost in New York."

"Fire away. While you're getting me that beer, toss me the pack of smokes on the drainboard."

"I read the police report; now I'd like to hear what happened, in your own words." Defoe sat on a chrome-legged chair upholstered in green plastic and strips of red vinyl patching tape.

Schaftmaster lit a Lucky and exhaled slowly, watching the smoke curl up in a lazy air current. " 'Twas a hazy dawn and the sky was rift with salmon-colored clouds. The diesel growled and tore the quiet morn asunder, thunder under . . . my girded loins that roared New York way . . . to JFK that fateful day. I plucked the load and hit the road and, and . . ." He took a long swallow from the green bottle. "Plunged into the Midtown Tunnel, delved deep 'neath the polluted privy misname-ed River East. It's bounded on the north by Long Island Sound, and south by the Upper Bay. Call it gulf, bight, estuary, or fiord; frith, firth, ostiary, or road. Strait or narrows, but, by Jesus, follow the straight and narrow and use the bountiful nomen-clature of the language. It is *not* a goddamn *river!*"

"Yes. What happened after you came out of the tunnel?"

"The tunnel. Ah! Shot from the Stygian gloom to the blinding flash of noon; my eyes surprised. And in that faltering instant the feral jackal leapt, seized the prize, and I, felled by the colossal hand of Timur, slunk away to lick my wounds. As even now I sit, good sir."

"Slunk?"

"Past participle of slink. Would you rather sneaked, snuck, skulked, retired?"

"They're all so apt, how dare I chose?"

"Indeed. All this talk has driven my thirst to the sticking point. Another green lovely, sir, if you would. I swoon when I stand."

Defoe opened the refrigerator, opened a beer. "Why Tamerlane?"

"Pyramids of skulls at Dehli built; eighty thousand captives died to sate his thirst."

"This guy that hijacked your truck was a Mongolian?"

"Hey, don't revoke my poetic license; Tamerlane died in 1405. It was the feeling of power and ruthless disregard I was trying to convey. The way he threw me between those parked cars I could have been a dead rat flipped in a dumpster. You said you wanted it in my own words, friend."

"I did indeed. You think the opened door was a setup?"

"I do; what else? Too quick the beast was on me, too soon my rig was gone. And I in the gutter lay, sore beset with ills that ill beset me. Hey, I bet Shakespeare said that somewhere; it's too good to be mine. Get me that Bartlett's over there, will you?"

Defoe's eye followed the outstretched finger and saw a door open beyond the indicated bookshelf.

"Frankie? Who you talkin' to?" The voice was high and quiet, querulous and pleading. "You're not writin' without me, are you?" A girl, twenty years younger than Schaftmaster, wearing black bikini panties and gray woolen sweatsocks, came from the rear of the trailer, rubbing sleep from her eyes. Her small breasts were firm, with hard brown nipples like pencil erasers. Defoe had an eye for detail.

Her total disregard for middle-class propriety made Defoe think once again of Caroline; she had been flickering in the back of his consciousness all morning. Something about her openness and lack of guile reminded him of the cats; do as you please and to hell with the world. He admired that independence in the feline species, but encountering it in his own made him question, in a way that he had not done since his college days, his self-selected position in the universe.

Schaftmaster ran his eyes over the swell of her hips as she passed. " 'The nakedness of woman is the work of God.' Cover thyself, child. This gentleman is from the insurance company; he has other coverage on his mind."

"Oh, hey, pleased to meet you, I'm sure. You make any coffee, Frankie?" She shuffled past Defoe to the stove, ignoring her nudity and Frankie's command with aplomb. The coffee pot was empty, she rattled it on the range, then opened the refrigerator and took out a Tupperware container, selected a piece of fruit, then, clutching the bowl to her breast, said, "Anybody want a plum?"

"Like to plumb that, my friend?" Schaftmaster asked as the girl wandered back to the bedroom. "My weakness, my downfall, my loss of tenure. I have a terminal case of Lolita-itis. I taught remedial reading to college freshmen for six years before they found me out. Caught me with three cozy cooze simultaneously; greedy, greedy!

But I can't deny myself the tight little, pink little—oh; yum-*yum*.
Virgin twat is not to be forgot. Sixteen is fine, but fifteen—divine!
Angie there is twenty and over the hill, but hell, so am I. You a top,
front, or side pisser?''

''What?''

''Jump-shift got to you, eh? Let's start over, fill you in on the
background stuff. You wear jockey shorts or boxers?''

''Uh, usually jockey; how's this connected with hijacked—''

''Okay, most guys do. I think it's the security of having your nuts
constrained.'' He leaned forward and fixed his gaze on Defoe. ''So,
tell me, when you drain your lizard, you shoot him out the official fly
front, do the two-handed presentation, or do you slip the wiener out
the leghole. If you're right-handed, it's probably the left side. I am.
Now some guys jump the waistband and leak over the top, but from
my survey so far, they're in the minority.''

''What's this got to do with anything? What are you leading up
to?''

''Well, redesigning underwear. All that cutting and sewing ex-
pense and extra fabric in your briefs, and if you use the side exit, you
see, what's the use?''

''You're free-lancing in the underwear business, then?''

''No, no, but, well, you see, this hit me one time I was taking a
leak . . .''

Defoe shook his head and laughed. ''I think I will take that beer
now.''

''Wonderful. Me, too. See, some guys go over the top, balls and
all, the whole works hanging out. Like you do when you're wearing
sweat pants? I mean, you got to, with the sweats, unless you want to
drop them around your ankles and squat like a broad. Hey, thanks.''
He took the cold green bottle and tilted it to his lips. ''I like a
leisurely lunch.''

''How did someone with your literary bent wind up driving a
truck?''

''Bent! How appropriate the phrase, eh? I told you I lost my job
for dallying with the lasses; hard to put that into one's résumé with
any positive spin. Besides, hauling freight with a union card pays
eight hundred a week, which you may be shocked to learn is a wee
bit more than an English teacher with a master's degree can earn.''
He leaned back, drained his beer, gestured at the environs with an
all-encompassing wave of the bottle. ''Well might you wonder what I
do with all that splendid loot, considering the state of the palace
herein. The answer lies in my weakness of and for the flesh. Not only
do I lust after the lovely ladies, I tend to forget myself when

lost in rapt abandon; I marry them. Both, the pair, are fecund bitches; I support a litter of heirs, leaving meager leaving for my own humble needs. Fetch us refreshment once again, goodfellow. I think it was a setup."

Defoe put the new bottle on the table, sat, waited for the poet to continue.

"Someone knew where that load was going, fast-set the ambush fast against me, planned to prick me sorely." He sipped his beer, continued, "I left the yard with waybill, knew the pickup was Kennedy and the destination was midtown Manhattan. Reade Industries, they have a warehouse on West Thirty-seventh, off Seventh Avenue. Coming out of the Queens tunnel, you can't get there from here, if you know what I mean; all the streets are one way in the wrong direction, so to speak. You have to slip up on your destination in a most roundabout way. Leaving several spots where I must be in the left-hand lane for a turn. Someone with a modicum of brains plotted this little ambuscade. There had to be at least two of them, no way could one man throw that door in my path and then get out the driver's side in time to run fifty feet up the street and jump me as I left the cab."

"And you say you didn't see him? Not even a glimpse?"

"Launched I was, like a bloody astronaut! I weigh one sixty, seventy; he grabbed my neck and lifted me off the running board with one hand, had to be his left. Put his right under my ass and boosted me, honest to Christ, I must have gone six feet up before I fell between two parked cars. Gave my head a crack, stars were all I saw. Crawled onto the sidewalk. Next thing I remember, a lady's dog was licking vomit off my face."

"No eyewitnesses? I saw no mention of any in the police report."

"If there were, none came forward. It happened in a flash, my friend. Six blocks from my destination. A radio car was there in a couple of minutes, and they got the police helicopter up quick. But the truck had vanished."

"Helicopter?"

"All of our trailers have numbers on the roof, six-foot-high green vinyl decals. Put there for occasions just as this. They spotted four of our trucks within a half hour. But not mine, mine had slipped from sight." He sipped his beer, thought for a moment. "First load I ever lost, and I've been driving eleven years."

Defoe finished his beer, put the empty on the drainboard. "I talked to Arnold Adelweis before I came here. Now I want to see Mr. Tighe." Defoe looked at his copy of the New Jersey State Police report on the crime. "Beauregard Tighe. Lives in Macungie; know the best way to get there from here?"

"Take 29 to Shimerville, go north on 100; 'bout ten miles from here. You won't get much from Beau, though. He's a nut case."

"Ah," Defoe said, and thought, *Takes one to know one.*

If religious fervor could be equated with nuttiness, then indeed Beau Tighe was a fruitcake. The rear of his car bore a bumper sticker that said "Honk if you Love Jesus!" and a replica of the Pennsylvania license plate was in the rear window, spelling out in blue and yellow "you've got a friend in JESUS."

The doorbell chimed "Rock of Ages, Cleft for Me," and the thermometer imbedded in a plastic representation of Our Saviour informed Defoe that it was fifty-six degrees.

Tighe and his wife evidently spent all their spare cash on mail order religious memorabilia; every available surface in the front parlor was covered with plastic, plaster, glass, and wooden knicknacks and geegaws, giving it the atmosphere of a wholesale sample showroom.

A needlepoint tapestry of the Last Supper, done in acrylic yarn on a plastic canvas ground formed a backdrop to a collection of clocks on the mantelpiece. The center of focus was a large bust of Christ who held a digital clock in his hand while around the base ran the motto: My Times are in Thy Hand Psalms XXXI, 15. The clock was nine minutes slow.

"Thelma got that one, for my birthday last year. Nice, ain't it?"

"Yes indeed." Defoe turned from a plastic holographic Jesus that winked at him, flashing "Repent ye: for the Kingdom of Heaven is at hand." Matthew 111, 2. "I wanted to ask you a few questions about the truck you lost, Mr. Tighe."

"Lost, yes. Like the souls lost to our Lord, snatched by Satan's evil ways."

"I understand that you were in the men's room at a truck stop when you were assaulted."

"Yes; I believe he followed me in. I didn't see anyone, you understand, but you know how you can sense a presence when someone is nearby? Then he hit me; how sharp the serpent's tooth! I thought I had been stabbed, it hurt that bad. I suffered some kidney damage from when he hit me; still on the pills. Stings like the devil when I pass water. He shoved me in a stall, took my keys. I believe I blacked out for a moment; I remember thinking 'My Time is at Hand,' Matthew, XXVI, Verse 18."

"Yes indeed. Is there anything else you can add? Did you smell anything odd, hear him speak?"

"Just that I hope the son of a bitch roasts in eternal hell. Remember, 'Vengeance is mine, sayeth the Lord.' ''

"Yes, Mr. Tighe. And 'Forgiveness is better than punishment; for the one is proof of a gentle, the other a savage nature.' '' Defoe smiled and turned towards the door. "Epictetus. Good day.''

José Cañuzi lived in an ethnically eclectic neighborhood in northwest Allentown. Single family residences co-existed with commercial enterprises; a jiffy print and a Lebanese grocery store bracketed the three-story house, clad in green asbestos shingles, that he and his two brothers rented and occupied with their extended families; seventeen Cañuzis, aged six months to eighty-four years, lived in the four-bedroom dwelling.

"I'm telling, jous, Mister Defoe, ees a motherfucker. I got a wife and a si's-month-old baby, I'm making good money driving for IGT. And this happen. Firs' good job I got; I make eighteen fifty an hour wi' benefits, an' this has to happen! My head gets busted, I'm seein' two of everything sometimes. I can't drive like that, right?''

"Right.'' Defoe put the glass of ice water that Marie Cañuzi had pressed on him down on the faded pink countertop. Multicolor boomerangs decorated the Formica and magnified themselves into freeform shapes through the lenticular combination of water and glass. The kitchen of the seventy-five-year-old house had been modernized in the 1950's by a long-gone occupant; pink and gray had been the hot combination of the decade, but the gray linoleum had lost its identity somewhere in the seventies, and in places the plywood subfloor showed its buff and brown random striations. The room was clean; the enamel of the electric range was abraded through to shining steel in spots, but the entire kitchen was actively cringing from the constant onslaught of the Cañuzis. "You didn't get any kind of a look at the man who hit you?''

"Ees like I tol' the cops, tol' Mister Bullfinch; I saw nothing. We stopped at Midway, I go inside for a pees and coffee for me and Marty. Been rolling about fi', si's hours out of Kennedy Terminal; Marty had drove the first leg and was nappin'.'' José sat at the table and tumbled a pack of Marlboros end over end with his hands. "You know, Mister Defoe, I box Golden Gloves when I was a kid, in New York. That's where I met Marie. I could take a punch. But ei-yi-yi! This fucker could *hit*. Caught me back here, in the kidneys, I'm telling you, I went down. Then he pick me up and threw me in a stall. Tha's when I hit my head. I guess I blacked out; ne's thing I remember these two queers was holding me at the sink, washing my face with paper towels. I had threw up, you know? They wasn' such bad guys, they could have cornholed me while I was out, but they di'n. They ain't all as bad as you think. These two queers called the Staties, waited until they got there. Made the cops call me a ambulance. Tol' the cops I had a concussion. Hey. They was right; the hospital took S rays and everything, kep' me overnight. Marie was a mess, cryin' and like that . . . But I didn' see nothing. Except he was big. I could tell you that.''

"You didn't see anything. Just like the other drivers; this big guy hit you quick, from behind. Did he say anything? You hear anything at all?''

"No, nothing; like I tol' you, it was real quick. Pow. Bang. I was down and he was gone.''

"Okay, José, last question, and then I'll leave you alone. You're a good witness, you remember a lot of what happened." Defoe reached across the table and wrapped his hand around the younger man's wrist. "Now. Can you remember any smell? Close your eyes and think.''

José closed his eyes, stopped playing with the cigarette pack. "Yes. The pisser smell, like always, soap and that stuff they put in the urinals. But there was somethin' else; I was down, he bent over to take my keys, and I smelled his choes. It was pi's—yeah, his choes smelled like pi's. I remember, from when I was jus' a kid, we always had two-three pi's at home. Stink like hell, Mister Defoe; I remember.''

"Piss, I don't think I understand.''

"You know, *pi's,* like bacon. Big, pink fuckers; always gettin' loose and they eat anythin', my ol' man feed them garbage he brought home from the hotels, in San Juan. Taste good, but stink like hell when they alive, you know?''

CHAPTER **16**

"They start to stink like hell, you don't dress 'em out quick and tuck 'em in a cooler, you know what I'm saying? I ain't about to haul all that meat around in my truck two, three days, waiting for this man you say deals deer. Now you take me to him, he buys this nice little doe here, and then maybe you and I can do some business. Maybe we'll go out to that place I told you about, take that whole damn pen at one shot." Yearner tipped his dirty yellow DeKalb seed corn cap over his eyes as he scratched the back of his neck. "But until your man proves hisself, Ronnie, we ain't gonna do shit. I don't care what I said the other day at that bar. That was whiskey talk, you know that. Now we sober, we ready to do us a deal. You and me, we take this doe to your man, and it goes like you say, well then, we can do some business. How about it?" Yearner flipped the tarp back over the carcass. A State trooper had stopped a pickup for a taillight violation earlier in the day on I-95 and found the dead deer in the back, killed with a clean head shot, five weeks before the opening of deer season. The driver had posted a hundred-dollar bond with the JP, and Yearner had signed the deer off the State Police log for Official disposal by Game Commission; there were no facilities to hold a fresh carcass for the six months that could elapse before the case came to trial.

Ronnie leaned against his own truck, parked next to Yearner's in the DQ lot. "Yeah, well, I got a problem, Randy. See, I can't go down there with you, I got something else on for tonight. I mean, I only called him up on account of what you and me had going for us; I didn't go get no deer or nothing today. I figured you and me would get them ones out of that pen you told me about. Since we din't, I got me something lined up for tonight. Hell, I didn't even know if you was gonna show, I only stopped here 'cause this is where she's supposed to meet me.'' He looked around the parking lot at the vehicles scattered in the gathering dusk for confirmation of his lie.

''Shit, don't matter to me; I'll take this baby down there by myself, Ronnie. I ain't shy to put the whole hundred in my pocket. But I figured you come along, introduce me to the man, well, next time, you and me together take those damn pen-raised suckers to him, split it up the middle.''

''Hey, don't think I don't appreciate it, man, 'cause I do, It's just that, well, damn. This little piece of pussy I been working on since the summer, and she finally come around, gonna go out and put out, tonight. I can't pass that up, know what I mean?''

''Yeah, so where's this place I'm supposed to go, then?''

Ronnie waited until Yearner pulled out of the Dairy Queen lot before going to the pay phone by the toilets.

Defoe went to the pay phone while the attendant filled his tank and checked the oil in the Jaguar. The current witticism among the auto cogniscenti ran: ''Why don't the English make computers?'' Answer: ''Because they haven't figured out a way to make them leak oil.''

He held his beeper ready and hoped that Caroline wouldn't pick it up. Then again, he hoped she would. He was in a postcoital depression and experiencing an approach-avoidance sensation that made him testy. She was physically quite attractive, an eager and enthusiastic lover. But she struck him as shallow, had a one-dimensional persona. The dinner at Joe's had certainly not impressed her. She obviously was a talented artist, but beyond that there seemed to be little. Maybe it was just her youth, or worse yet, their age difference. *Have I,* he thought, *degenerated from worldly wise to merely jaded?* Last night, he had to admit, she had been attuned to his sense of loss when he told her about his son. And yet, earlier in the day at Sally's, she had played the teenage bitch; superficial and self-centered. Defoe was confused, a situation he was not at all comfortable with.

''Chase! I was hoping you'd call; you disappeared before dawn. No note or anything.''

''It was eight o'clock; there's a note on the stove.''

''So who cooks breakfast? I brushed my teeth; the peppermint toothpaste was all I could handle. I almost threw that up. How much champagne did we have after we got home?''

''Count the empty bottles. Listen, I called to see if there were any telephone messages. How about you go downstairs and check for me?''

It would have been far simpler for Caroline to hang up, Defoe to redial, and on the third ring connect to his answering machine with his remote; get his messages, and hang up.

But he gave Caroline the code for his office door, and waited while she went down to the lower level, punched through the security system and activated the answering machine. They listened to the single message together.

"Mr. Defoe, Harold Askew here, still holding the fort at Sacred Heart. I spoke with Cal Bullfinch this morning, I guess you have talked with him by now, gotten the dope on the fourth hijacking. Appreciate it if you'd fill me in on your progress. I should be out of here in a couple of days, they say I'm coming along pretty well. I heard from that State Police contact I told you about, on the tire print. He got the data back from the FBI today. I've been on the phone for the last couple of hours. That tire is an oddball; let me get the . . . yeah, here it is. Mickey Thompson Performance Tires, Cuyahoga Falls. Ohio. Something called a Baja Belted; real oddball they tell me. And the size is thirty-four by nine-fifty. It's big and it ain't cheap. But here's the real news; Thompson has half a dozen distributors in Pennsylvania, and one of them, in Clifford, about twenty miles north of Scranton, sent a set of four down to a garage right around the corner, about six weeks ago. Shorty's Garage, specializes in what my cop source calls 'bigfoot conversions.' R.D. Lobachsville, back in the willywags somewhere off 73 and 100. Woody, that's Corporal Elwood Shrubb, says they're a rough bunch. He's pretty well convinced that a lot of stolen parts are going through there, but they don't have any proof." There was the uneasy pause that is typical when one is talking to a machine that cannot respond. "Well, I guess that's it; check in with me when you get the chance; I'd stay away from that Shorty's. We have something concrete for me to give the police now, let them do their job. Good-bye." There was the sound of a telephone clattering onto a receiver and a hum. Defoe jotted notes to himself on a three-by-five card, wrote "Baja Belted 34X9.50" on the back of the photograph.

"Chase? Do what he says; stay away from that garage."

"Hey, don't worry. I'm not planning any heroics; just want to stop by there and sniff the air. It's on the way home if it's where he says it is, not more than a half hour or so out of the way. Look for me in about an hour. I'll take you out to dinner, pay you back for last night."

"Pay me back? What's that supposed to mean, hotshot?"

"For the dinner. At Joe's. You insisted on paying the bill, remember?"

"Yeah, but you set it up, chose the place and everything. Well, tonight is my turn. It's all arranged; I have been busy today."

Defoe winced, afraid of what havoc she had wrought with his kitchen. "I thought you couldn't boil water."

"Don't be smart. I called a friend of mine this morning, guy that eats out a lot, and I asked him to recommend a restaurant. I want to personally thank you for your hospitality yesterday."

"I thought you did that last night."

She ignored his remark and continued. "He told me about a place, off the beaten track; it's hard to find, but worth it. An old country store, converted into a restaurant; serves real gourmet food. Only they don't take reservations, we'll have to take our chances. He gave me directions. So how about it?"

"I gave him the directions. He's on his way down there, got a doe in his truck. So how about it, Red, I do it right?"

"Yeah, Ronnie, you done good. We gonna have a little surprise party for that dude. I'm heading over to Shorty's now, to set it up. You go on home, forget all about this, you know what's good for you."

It was dusk as Yearner pulled into the field of junkers beside the garage and killed the engine. He sat, sipping a beer, letting his senses acclimate to the environment. Insect noises rose from the tall grass around the rusting wrecks, parted out hulks with shattered windshields. The whine of tires on asphalt dopplered past as the occasional car sped by. The garage was dark inside, a mercury security light hummed atop a pole and threw white light over the gravel forecourt of the building, throwing the parked trucks, sitting high on their lift kits and fat tires into sharp relief of light and dark, the vehicles casting long shadows in the fading twilight. The red wink of a cigarette flared briefly behind the building and Yearner heard a low cough. He put the beer can on the dash and drew a deep breath, held it for a moment, then let it out in a long sigh. He opened the truck door and picked up the .357 from the seat beside him. He favored the FBI carry; high on the hip, over the right kidney. Good concealment and provided a quick draw, but you sure as hell couldn't drive with it there. He got out and shrugged into the suede jacket with the fringes on the chest, adjusted the coattails over the weapon. He reached under the seat and slipped his handcuffs into his left hip pocket. With two or more adversaries they could be useful.

They would have to come back here, near the highway, to see the deer, make the buy. Or they would have him drive around behind the building for the transfer. Either way, when the arrest went down he would be two steps from his vehicle and the twelve gauge pumpgun behind the seat.

As he walked slowly toward the rear of the garage he automatically

checked behind him, listened for any sign of flanking movement.
Two men stood by a half dozen rusty oil drums that bracketed a
rutted driveway circling behind the cinderblock structure and Yearner
wondered where the others were; the kid had told him that a dozen or
more hunters showed up at these buys. Was he so early that he was
the first? Or had the kid set him up? He shrugged it off; Ronnie
wasn't that bright. He stepped over a black puddle filled with an
uneasy mixture of crankcase oil and rainwater and said, "Hey, boys;
moon's gettin' up; gonna be a night for fun, ain't?" Tacking "ain't"
on the end of a sentence is a peculiarly Pennsylvania Dutch way of
inviting agreement with a statement of fact, and Yearner had learned
to use it as a kind of shorthand to establish himself as a member of
the tribe.

The younger one, six feet two or so, dirty blond hair in a pigtail,
dropped his cigarette on the packed earth and ground it under an
engineer boot with a worn-down heel. He wore a sleeveless denim
jacket over a black T-shirt with red Harley wings across the front and
turned to the older man in the dirty overalls. "This the guy, Jumbo?"
he asked.

Red Gloeckner stepped from the shadow of a three-yard dumpster
with a chunk of swamp oak four by four that he had separated from a
busted skid half an hour earlier. He swung the thirty-six-inch piece of
wood in a sweeping arc that was designed to turn the game warden's
right kidney into a line drive double off the center-field fence.

Defoe rolled to a stop under the mercury light and looked at his
watch. Saturday night, he assumed a place like this would be a center
of activity; kids, the semi-employed, and automotive enthusiasts
knocking back six hundred a week all collected at the local speed
shop, drinking soda or beer, doing business or shooting the shit. A
Saturday night tradition since the postwar days when the V-8 flat
head Ford gave birth to the American phenomenon called the hot rod.
He had expected a crowd and had planned to infiltrate, play the
moment, read the players, and ad lib, find out what he could about a
certain set of tires that had gone onto a jacked-up orange pickup
truck. He got out, closed the Jag's door, walked toward one of the
vehicles awaiting service, wanting a closer look at the towering
trucks that he had hardly given a second glance when he saw them on
the highway.

There was a certain raw macho power to them, sitting six inches
above their frames, their suspension systems exposed like a doxy
flashing her petticoats. Hard black knuckles of rubber protruded from
their foot-wide tires; they all had husky roll bars behind the cab, but
the chromed tubes and the many coats of lacquer on the body panels

made Defoe doubt that these vehicles ever ventured off the road, much less risked overturning. He ran his hand over a pristine lemon-yellow fender as low grunts and scuffling sounds behind the building attracted his attention.

Swamp oak is a hard wood with a twisted grain and not much good for anything but firewood and pallet lumber. After exposure to sunlight and rain and the weather extremes of the seasons it starts to split along the growth rings. When the piece of four by four hit Yearner it contacted his revolver and saved him six weeks in intensive care waiting for a kidney donor to die. The piece of wood broke into two splinters; Gloeckner was left holding an eighteen-inch bayonet that tapered to a vicious point, but his hand was numb from the impact of the stick with the gun and he dropped his weapon. The Smith & Wesson was knocked loose and fell to the ground; as Jumbo and the biker converged on Yearner it was kicked under the rear wheels of Gloeckner's truck.

Before flying free the gun had jumped up and cracked Yearner's lowest rib on the right side, sending a blinding flash of pain through his back. He fell forward and instinctively shot the fingertips of his left hand into Jumbo's throat; the farmer gagged and swallowed the lump of Redman he had tucked in his cheek; tears came to his eyes, but he grappled with Yearner and held onto him with a bearhug once he got behind the undercover agent.

The blond boy began to punch Yearner in the side of the head, drawing blood both from the biker's knuckles and his adversary's skull.

Red had more experience than his assistants and he measured his moves.

Skean said get this bozo off our backs. To Gloeckner that meant time in a rehab center, learning the painful process of walking on legs that had been shattered.

Best way to accomplish that was to run over his femurs with the truck, but this son of a bitch had to be laying down, still, for that to happen. Red waded into the fray, throwing hammer-handed punches at Yearner's head, punches the fucker kept slipping even though Jumbo had his arms wrapped around his upper body and that asshole biker kept slapping shots at him from four feet away, scared to get into the center of the action.

Defoe watched the three-on-one contest for a moment, saw a hubcap full of lugnuts beside a truck on jackstands, and decided to even the odds.

The wheelnuts, sharp-edged hexagonal hunks of steel that weighed a quarter of a pound apiece, were very similar in size and heft to the lead fishing sinker that Defoe had spent countless preteen hours throwing at rats behind the family stables. Because his father had forbidden him to use the single shot .22 without supervision, rat hunting at dusk had evolved into a competition between the young man and his father; Defoe with his four-ounce dipsy went first, then Dad with the snap of a long rifle in the little Remington if a follow-up shot was available.

It became an obsession with Defoe, almost Zen like in intensity, throwing the battered chunk of lead throughout college and beyond, knocking match boxes off a fence at fifty feet with monotonous regularity. Like the violin, perfection required constant practice.

He scooped up the handful of lugnuts, picked one, hefted it, cocked his wrist and threw. The six-sided piece of steel hit Gloeckner behind the ear and he dropped as he threw a punch.

The second shot hit Jumbo in the neck; he released Yearner and turned toward Defoe. The third bounced off his chest and a fourth missile a half second later hit him between the eyes, tearing open a hunk of scalp that would require thirteen stitches to close. The biker took the last lugnut on his raised forearm, tearing a gash in his red-and-blue panther tattoo but doing little to turn him from his concentration on Defoe. He pulled a Phillipine butterfly knife from his back pocket and flipped it open with a flourish. Defoe looked down at his empty left hand. "Damn those five stud Fords, any-way," he said, and looked for an escape route through the auto carcasses in the weeds.

Gloeckner shook off the pain behind his ear and got to his knees; saw the familiar shape of his truck and went for it.

Yearner rolled away from the truck and tried to clear his head, subdue the lightning in his ribs.

Jumbo wiped a meaty hand across his face and cleared the blood from his vision. He bellowed and headed for Defoe.

The biker had Defoe trapped between two wrecks and was ready to stick the runt.

Yearner got up, leaned against the dumpster and pulled his trouser leg above his calf, ripped the .25 Beretta from its ankle holster. He squeezed the double-action trigger, fired a shot into the air. The sound of the small caliber gun was little more than a pop, but in the quiet of the moment it commanded attention. Jumbo and the biker paused, turned toward Yearner as Gloeckner fired his ignition. The big truck shot back, swung wide, and bounced across the rough roadway, disappearing around the far side of the garage. Yearner contemplated a shot at the fleeing vehicle as Jumbo flipped a plastic pan of filthy gasoline and carburetor parts into his face.

He screamed and waved the pistol in front of his face, snapped off a pair of shots, threatening random mayhem as Jumbo and the biker leaped into the other four-by-four and sprayed gravel across the field of battle as they sped away.

Defoe heard the little .25 bullets zing overhead from his position behind a dead Mustang. "Secure from battle stations, pal; they're gone."

"Shit! My fuckin' eyes are on fire. I can't see."

"Hold your fire, I'm coming out."

Yearner sat with his back against the dumpster and the little automatic in his lap. He held both hands over his eyes, softly banged his head against the steel trash container. "Son of a *bitch,* that hurts. I got to get to a hospital, buddy."

"No problem; I guess Saint Joe's in Reading is the closest. Can you walk?"

"I don't know, I think I got a busted rib. Help me up." He yelled as Defoe got under his right arm, supported himself on the lip of the dumpster. Defoe picked up the pistol and deactivated it, handed it to Yearner who dropped it in his coat pocket. "There's another gun someplace, a .357. See if you can find it, will you?"

"Let me bring my car around back. Hang on there." He bounced the Jag over the rutted roadway and aimed his high beams at the scene. The stainless-steel revolver gleamed in the mud where Gloeckner had run over it. "I found it," he said, prying the weapon from the mud. He opened the cylinder and ejected the six cartridges. It would need to be stripped and cleaned but appeared undamaged. He looked at the tireprint in the mud, deep ridges in stark relief under his headlamps. He went to his trunk, dropped the weapon and the ammunition on an old blanket, and picked up the manila folder of hijacking information. He shuffled through the papers under the dim light that illuminated his license plate, found what he wanted, and walked back to the front of the car.

He held the photograph against the reality in the mud in front of him and saw the match. "Son of a gun," he said softly and put the photo in his pocket.

"Come on, friend, ease yourself down here on the backseat. Less chance of that rib doing any more damage if you're lying down. We'll have you at the emergency ward in twenty minutes."

"Yeah. One last favor; stop out front and lock up that ratty-looking Power Wagon. I got weapons and radio equipment in there I can't afford to lose."

Defoe pulled onto the highway and turned toward Reading. "That's a regular war wagon you got there. What line of work you in?"

"Pennsylvania Game Commission. Mostly undercover. I was about to bust up a gang of deer jackers. Only it looks like I'm the one got busted up. Guess I got careless. How'd you happen to show up there? What's your name, by the way?" Yearner lay across the leather seat and watched the red lights dance across his corneas. The smell of gasoline and blood made him nauseous.

"Chase Defoe. I was investigating an insurance claim; several truckloads of expensive clothes, about five million dollars worth, were stolen recently. We traced a tireprint at the scene of one of the robberies to that garage; they sold the tires. I was just nosing around tonight, and found a hell of a lot more than I expected to."

"How's that?"

"One of the guys that jumped you was driving the truck we're looking for."

"No shit! I guess they're into a bit more than just the illegal venison, then. What agency you with? State Police?"

"No, no, I'm just a private citizen. It's a long story, but basically I'm helping out a friend. Here we are. Think you can walk inside?"

An East Indian intern listened to Yearner's list of symptoms and immediately placed him in a wheelchair; a black man in whites took him off to X ray for a picture of his ribs and right kidney. Defoe tagged along; the game warden was a link, however tenuous, to the official world of law enforcement and could be useful.

The intern tried to make him stay in the waiting room with the distraught relatives of accident victims and the recipients of knife and gunshot wounds; it was, after all, Saturday night. Defoe flashed his Naval ID card, carefully covering the word "retired" with his forefinger and told the doctor that he was debriefing an official government agent and that time was of the essence.

"You're a piece of work, you know that, Defoe?" Yearner said, lying on the table as a technician draped a lead shield over his loins.

"Call me Chase. I didn't want you to get lonely in here. Besides, we might be able to help each other out. There's a connection here that I can't see just yet, but I think we're after the same set of people. Only you have an official cachet that I lack. Besides, there's a twenty percent recovery fee from the insurance company, so if we *were* able to find any of the stolen goods . . ."

"Hey, I can't argue with that logic. The heist was worth five million bucks, did you say?"

Internal photography finished, Yearner was taken into a treatment room where a dark-haired RN bathed his eyes with some kind of soothing solution and washed the blood and grease from his head.

They had removed his clothing and he lay on the table in his underpants and an open-backed hospital gown.

"Tell me, darlin', do you look as good as you smell? 'Cause that perfume is overriding the stench of gasoline to a remarkable degree. How about it, Chase? Is she the goddess that I think she is?"

The nurse laughed and blushed and Yearner managed to get her to hold his hand and promise to be there when his vision cleared enough for him to see.

The intern returned with the X rays and clipped them to a viewing light. He studied them for a long time before speaking. "You are a very lucky man, Mr. Claxon, very lucky." He spoke rapidly, with precise diction. "No damage to the kidneys, and the rib is only cracked. I will tape you and you can return to duty. Yes, very lucky indeed."

"Yeah, Doc, but what about my eyes? That's my main worry. I've had busted ribs before."

"Ah, quite so, quite so, the eyesight, yes. Petroleum products can be very harsh. However, the surface of the cornea is remarkably tough, I doubt that you have sustained any permanent damage. We will keep your eyes bandaged for a little bit; they will be very sensitive to light, yes, very sensitive. You will want to wear darkened lenses for a few days. I shall see that you get medication for the discomfort. Sit up now, I will tape your ribs and your friend can take you away."

"Chase, my friend," Yearner said from behind the white bandages over his eyes, "another favor. Call my service; I have to check in with her every so often or she'll put out an alert on my worthless ass. Jot down this number; tell her what happened and that I'll check in with her in the morning."

The pretty nurse came in with a pair of disposable plastic frames with smoked lenses and Defoe went off to track down Yearner's clothing and see that the hospital's paperwork was coordinated with the proper official agency of State government and put a call in to the answering service.

When he returned to the treatment room, Yearner was sitting in a sidechair with the lights dimmed. "How are the eyes?"

"Pretty good. They burn, but these glasses help. How 'bout it, I look like Ray Charles?"

"Not even close. His teeth are whiter."

"Yeah . . . *ow!* Don't make me laugh. So, what's our next step?"

"I have a request in with a stockbroker, we'll find out Monday if the companies that lost the clothing are connected. It's just a hunch, but I think they may be. I have a photo, right here, as a matter of fact. I stuck it in my jacket at that garage. It's the tire print we're looking for. Matches the one back where I found your gun. If we can find out the owner of the tires we are halfway home.''

"Give me the print. I know a Statey out of the Hamburg Barracks, owes me a couple of favors, and I have a real strong personal interest in finding out who this big son of a bitch is. I'll have him check it out for us, get back to you tomorrow. Give me your number.''

"Sure. But don't you want a ride back to pick up your truck? Assuming you can see well enough to drive it.''

"Uh, yeah, I can see fine, gettin' better every minute. Only thing is, that nurse, she already promised to make sure that I got back to my truck; she goes off in half an hour. But I don't think I'll be able to drive after all, so she'll have to take me home. Or even back to her place, maybe; I'm sure she lives a lot closer than I do.''

"You work fast, don't you?''

Yearner laughed, let out a little gasp, and tensed his torso at the pain. "Got to, in this line of work. Never stay in one place long enough. Hey, thanks for the assistance tonight; you saved me from some serious surgical work. Those boys weren't fooling around.''

"If that big one was the same guy that jumped the drivers I talked to today, you're lucky to be walking out of here tonight.''

Defoe was an hour late getting back to the barn; he was overly apologetic and she was overtly worried. They had another hour's wait for a table at Landis Store and it was after nine when Caroline started on her prime rib.

He watched her eat a few minutes, then asked, "What is the next step with your book project?''

She chewed, swallowed, took a sip of wine. "First thing I have to do is find out who these people are that I'm supposed to draw, where they live. I guess the publisher will set up the transportation and all that. I suppose I'll be flying all over. And I got to find a new apartment. They're gonna tear down the place I'm in now. Which is no big loss; now that I got a few bucks coming my way I can afford to look for a decent studio. Only with this book assignment I'm not gonna have much time.'' She sawed off a slice of beef. "See, I need space for my work, good light. Not that easy to find in Reading. I'll probably wind up putting all my stuff in storage, until this deal is finished. Gonna be a bitch, though, not having a studio to work in. See, I'll do the roughs on location, wherever these celebrities are. But then I got to have studio space to do the finished drawings.'' She shrugged in explanation. "That's the way I work.''

Defoe fussed with his sole, forked a morsel into his mouth. "You think my barn would suffice? The daylight is certainly ample.''

She poked at her salad, put the fork down on her plate, looked at Defoe. ''Maybe. I could set my table up there by the windows. Not your classical north light situation, but I won't be working with live models at that stage anyway. But yeah, it could work. You making me an offer?''

He smiled. ''Yes, I suppose I am; I mean, you need a place to work. And the barn's available, I have no plans for a few weeks. Just temporarily, of course, until you can find someplace more suitable.''

''And if I was to move in, well, that would be convenient as hell, right? Roll out of bed and go to work. Just like home.''

''I hadn't thought about that aspect of it, actually.''

''Then you're dumber than I thought. Because I did. This morning. And Chase, I think I'm going to have more fun in the next couple of weeks than I've had in a long, long time.''

''Caroline,'' he said, reaching across the table and taking her hand, ''you took the words right out of my mouth. Let's go home.''

CHAPTER 17

"**W**atch it, for Christ's sake! It feels like you're tearing my fuckin' ear off."

"Keep rutching around like that and I'm liable to. Hold still now." Skean swabbed the thick wound ointment, a sulphurous yellow antibiotic cream, behind Red Gloeckner's ear. It was the fix-all at the game farm, used to treat barbed-wire cuts, lesions, and the hoof slashes inflicted on the does during breeding season.

Red sat on the kitchen table, his head bent forward, nearly between his knees, big hands gripping the edge of the white enamel tabletop. "Hey, Mobay," he said. "Get me a beer, will ya?"

Mobay sat at the table, fat hands folded across his stomach, watching Skean work on the raw wound. "I told you not to let this asshole handle it, right, Joe? But no; it's his doin' this game warden is onto us, you said. Let him get the guy off our ass, you said. Now where are we?"

"Yeah, yeah, I hear you; Jesus Christ." Skean threw the cotton swab in the trash and put the medication back in the cabinet with the other veterinary supplies. He put a four-by-four gauze pad against the side of Gloeckner's head and fastened it securely with strips of two-inch adhesive tape. "Don't fool with that for a couple days, Red. Leave it heal up. So what the hell happened down there?"

Red got off the table, blinked his eyes, touched behind his ear, gingerly probing with his index finger. Skean looked at Mobay. "What the fuck did I just say to him, Mobes? Leave it the fuck alone, right? And first thing he does is go poking at it."

Red opened the refrigerator and popped a beer. "Fuckin' short guy shows up, outta nowheres. Me and Jumbo and the Rat had this dude about put away; next thing is, I'm on my face in the mud, my ear's on fire."

"You dumb fuck." Mobay crushed his beer can with one hand, arced it across the room toward the trash can. "He had backup with him. Prob'ly smelled the setup, that kid Ronnie you're so hot on prob'ly tipped his hand to it."

"Bullshit; wasn't that way at all. We was whaling on that sucker a good while before this other guy jumps in. Didn't have no gun, neither. Else why didn't he use it. He was throwing some kind of shit at us."

"So you cut and run." Skean lit a cigarette, shook his head slightly with disgust.

"Hey. This game warden had a hideout piece, starts shooting. Jumbo 'n' the Rat split; I wasn't about to go up against both them fuckers by myself, Joe. What was I supposed to do?"

Mobay chewed a piece of flesh on the edge of his thumb. " 'S gettin' out of hand, Joe. Game Commission nosing around. Plus this other shit you're into."

"You think I like it? I got more on the line than you do; I'm still on parole, remember? Only thing is, we got customers in the city, screaming for venison."

"So we'll just have to cut back on what we give 'em, just give 'em what we can supply out of the herd. Deer season opens pretty soon, anyhow, we got to shut down then, like always."

"Yeah, okay, yeah, you're right. I'm gonna haul them sides in the walk-in up to New York on Monday. Meanwhile, you got to run that trailer load of shootin' hogs out to Ohio, six grand worth of boars ain't nothing to sneeze at right now, Mobes. And then we'll shut down for a couple, three months. We got plenty to do around here without worrying about running more meat through." Skean stubbed out his cigarette and went to the refrigerator for a beer. *Besides*, he thought, *I got to go up to New York anyway, pick up the balance of the money from that last truck. Four times eight is thirty-two; I can take a long vacation with that kind of money*. To Gloeckner he said, "Red; did that game warden get a good look at you, your truck? 'Cause I don't want to see you out here for a while if he did."

"Naw, it was too damn dark and he was hurting too bad." Red finished his beer and stood up. "I tell you one thing, though," he said, and touched his ear again. "I see either one of them two cock-suckers again, I'll recognize *them*."

"How do I recognize them? The keepers, I mean." Defoe and Caroline stood in his salad garden, surrounded by six rambling and rampant tomato plants, each with a five-eighths basket and a section of the Sunday *Times*.

"Easy. Pick the ones without any blemishes; nicks, bruises, things like that. And bigger than a tennis ball. Remember to wrap each one in a separate piece of paper."

"And they'll get ripe? Green like they are?"

"Right." Defoe laughed. "The tomatoes you buy in the supermarket are picked green, mostly by a machine. Then entombed in cellophane and warehoused for six weeks. They turn 'em red with ethylene gas. Why they taste so awful. Why I grow my own." Vine-ripened tomatoes bruise easily and ship poorly, both negative entries on the cash-flow ledgers of agribiz. And in the business of food, taste and nutrition place far below the factors of yield per acre, shipability, and field-ripening curves. Genetically engineered vegetables have become so prevalent that there is an entire generation that thinks tomatoes are supposed to be round-cornered cubes and crunch when eaten, like an apple. He waved his hand across the ten-foot-square plot. "Only way to get fresh salad food. Grow it. Unfortunately, we live in a temperate climate and tomatoes are tropical. So the first frost kills them. Which, judging from that moon we saw last night, isn't too far away."

Caroline stopped picking green tomatoes and looked at Defoe. "Wait a minute. What has the moon got to do with the temperature? Tides, I heard about, but frost?"

"Don't know exactly, but in the fall, and again in the spring, clear nights and a full moon seem to coincide with a freeze. I personally think it's the lack of cloud cover, surface heat radiating back into space. Surely you know about the old-timers, planting by the phases of the moon?"

"Yeah. What about this other stuff? We going to pick it, too?"

"The greens are hardier; escarole, spinach, endive. The chicory. I'll put a cold frame around the buttercrunch and the deer's tongue and they'll be fine until we get a hard freeze; probably not until Thanksgiving. See, some things are more tolerant of cold than others. Winter hardy, the geneticists call it. Some can stand adversity, others wilt at the hint of winter. Like tomatoes. First touch of frost and they're dead. While something like broccoli, for example, can be frozen solid and survive."

"Why is that? Some things can handle the cold and others can't?"

"Well, I suppose from a purely scientific standpoint, it would depend upon where, climatically, they evolved. I'm not really sure, not being a botanist. The philosophical viewpoint would be that that is their destiny, the essence of their being." He began putting wrapped tomatoes in his basket. "I do know that if we don't get these love apples safely in the basement they'll turn black and die at the first killing frost. Stoop to your chores, Caroline, stoop to your chores."

CHAPTER 18

Walter was a vice president and spent the better part of his day on the telephone with either clients or other members of the multinational brokerage firm, and in order to get anything productive done on his own he had gotten into the habit of arriving at his office at seven o'clock, two hours before the business day began and three before the markets opened. He called Defoe at five after eight.

"Would you rather have coffee or tea this morning?" Defoe leaned around the corner of the wall that separated the kitchen from the main room. Caroline sat cross-legged on the floor with a yellow pad, chewed on a pencil.

"Huh?" She looked up, smiled. "Oh, doesn't matter, whichever is easier." She went back to laying out the first floor of the barn and where she would set up her studio.

"Both the same. But if you want coffee, I have to go down to the freezer for the beans. Stay fresher that way. Then I grind just enough for a pot."

"Don't bother with all that, then. Make tea."

"Surely. What kind? Do you prefer it with milk or lemon?"

"What difference does that make?"

"Well, if you like it with milk you should use the full-bodied India and Ceylon teas. Earl Grey, for example. Lemon, on the other hand, complements China green. Green tea is unfermented; the leaves are steamed but don't undergo the controlled fermentation that the stronger black teas get. Milk in green tea results in a dishwater drink."

Caroline rolled her eyes. "I thought hot water and a tea bag was the extent of the process."

"If you want a proper cup of tea, there are certain procedures that should be followed. Like your drawings. You use all sorts of different pencils, different hardnesses, right?''

Caroline cupped her chin with her hands, rested her elbows on her knees, and smiled at Defoe. ''Right.''

''Exactly. Just as it is with the preparation of food. You may think it a small thing, but there is logic behind these arcane rules. For example, with milk the sugar is added last, but if lemon is used, the sugar is put in first. Because the citric acid in the lemon prevents the sugar from dissolving.''

''You got any Tab?''

''You *are* a philistine.''

''Answer your telephone, Defoe. If it's my mother, you never saw me.''

''Defoe here.''

''Chase, g'morning. Glad I caught you in; I really don't want to have to type all this stuff up for a fax. You ready to take notes?''

''Hello, Walter. Yes, hang on a sec. Caroline, let me borrow your pad. Go ahead.''

''Okay, as I told you Friday, this Reade Industries is trading over the counter. Very low volume, hasn't paid a dividend in years. Right now it's at a buck and a half a share, a five year low. Majority stockholder Quentin Reade, President and CEO. The annual report I'm looking at is several years old; unless a client holds one of these penny stocks, we don't generally update the reports, Chase.''

''I understand. Any connection with the other two outfits?''

''Yes, I'm getting to that. This Gleneagle, was—still is, I guess—a small chain of department stores in the Midwest. Another OTC stock, flat earnings. I don't know how some of these companies get listed.''

''Sure you do, Walter. Guys like you come along and convince the owners to go public, float a couple of million shares. They get to look at their stock listing every day and you put a nice piece of the offering in your pocket.''

''Cynical bastard. Anyway, they were bought out last August. By your Reade Industries. Friendly takeover, one-for-one exchange of shares. Same deal with the other company a couple of months later. Only the Norton and Norton takeover wasn't so friendly. Drexel Burnham handled it. Norton and Norton tried for a white knight LBO with West Point Pepperell, but WPP went after J.P Stevens about the same time, and Reade got control of the board. Of Norton and Norton. You understand, Chase, I don't have too much on any of this, what I have I got out of our mainframe; hooked all the keys I could think of, the three principals, obviously, and a couple of wild cards. SEC filings of intent, things like that. I have half an hour in this project. You really want in depth, I'll put a girl on it for a day or two.''

"No, no, this is enough. Any guess as to why Reade went after these two chains?''

"Well, yes; but it's only a guess. According to the annual report, Reade is a converter. Started out as a spinning mill in the eighteen hundreds. Still operates a plant in New England. My bet would be they're looking for vertical integration. Imports have really been hurting the clothing industry ever since the early eighties when Reagan threw open the floodgates. The rags aren't my specialty, but there's been a lot of winnowing over the last eighteen months. The big boys have been hammering each other pretty hard, billion dollar takeovers. The kind that make the headlines. I suppose the same thing is happening down in OTC.''

"Yeah, the rich get richer. Your gut feeling on Reade?''

There was a pause before the broker answered, and when he did, he hedged. "I really can't say, Chase, from what little I have here. But my guess is the company has to be pretty well stretched. Debt load to capital must be in the high 80's. A bad quarter and the whole thing could come down around their ears. Of course they're not alone, the conglomerate fever of the decade has been predicted on steady growth.''

"Speaking of steady growth, Walter, I have about twenty thousand I'd like to place. A windfall, as it were. Send me your recommendations.''

Defoe hung up the phone. "Caroline, I have to go upstairs for a number and then down for another. Do you suppose you could make the tea?'' He tore his notes off the legal pad and tossed it back in front of her. "Thanks for the paper; what are you working on?''

"Moving in on you. Listen, I'm all weak in the knees about this tea. Tell me what to do.''

"Just boil some water. Kettle's sitting on the stove.''

"That I think I can handle.''

"Let the water run a minute, until it's fully aerated. Cold, of course. Put the kettle on a medium flame and don't overboil it. Loses oxygen, you know. Makes the tea taste flat. Don't *under* boil it, though, that will make it taste weak, no matter how long you steep it. Oh, and rinse the teapot with hot water to warm the pot. I already filled the tea ball with English Breakfast. Just pop it in the pot and pour the boiling water over it. It's a small-leaf tea, three minutes should do it. Never fear, I'll be back by then.''

"Shit,'' she muttered. "I should have taken notes.''

Defoe pulled several pieces of paper from his wallet, looking for the number that he had written down at the hospital, then remembered that he had used a five-dollar bill and found it in his trouser pocket, the pair he had worn to dinner with Caroline. Good thing he wasn't a big tipper.

"Hello, good morning, this is Chase Defoe. I spoke with you the other evening, told you about Mister Claxon's accident? JoAnne, right?"

"Yes, sir, this is JoAnne."

"Yes; I wanted to get in touch with him, we had tentative plans. Has he checked in with you?"

"Yes, sir. I heard from Mister Claxon last night. He is recovering nicely but won't be working today, his eyes are still bothering him. Can I take a message?"

"Why don't you just give me his number and I'll talk to him directly about it?"

"I'm sorry, sir, I don't have a number that he can be reached at right now."

Bullshit. "Okay, JoAnne; I understand your position. As soon as he makes contact with you, tell him that Chase Defoe wants to talk to him. Let me give you my number here, I'll be at it for about an hour."

"Yes, sir. I'm logging your message at eight twenty-seven. G'bye."

That's the blondest-sounding girl I've ever talked to, Defoe thought, breaking the connection and heading down the spiral stairway to the basement. "Be there in a flash," he called as he passed the main floor.

He keyed into his office and snapped open the clasps of his attaché case, pulled out the fat leather five-by-eight notebook that was his memory bank. DEFOE. About a dozen entries, followed by DE KOONING, W; [Elaine] NYC. An address and a Manhattan telephone number preceded the date 1967. Has it really been that long? The entry he was looking for was newer:

DELPHI NYC. 37 W. 37th Street NAVINTEL77-(PCOAT). As he dialed the number, he hoped he had kept abreast. It had been at least five, maybe six years. He looked at his watch. Nearly nine; the Oracle often slept till noon.

The telephone rang a long time but Defoe knew to hang on. Finally it was picked up. "Yes?" The voice was detached, asexual, bored.

"Good morning. Chase Defoe calling for Delphi."

There was a clatter that boxed his ears; he could picture the receiver being dropped on a marble-topped hall table, heard hard footsteps on the tile floor receding. An infinity passed before the handpiece was picked up, a husky voice said, "Chase, darling, is it really you? That lovely piece of barkcloth you sent me from Africa, I absolutely *treasure* it. It was all *over* that year's scarves, although I'm sure you didn't notice. You naughty boy, it's been a decade."

"Has it really? I'm living in eastern Pennsylvania now, retired from the Navy. If it would be convenient, I'd like to get together with you, get us up to date with each other. Would today be possible?"

"Today?" Delphi laughed a low, throaty chuckle. "He hasn't talked to me in ten years and wants a same day appointment. I keep kings and princes waiting, Chase darling."

"Yes, but you're trying to sell them something, aren't you? I, on the other hand, might bring you a little tidbit."

"Well . . . Hans has my appointment calendar in front of me; I *could* squeeze you in about noon, if that would do."

"Perfection. Couldn't be better."

"Hmm, well, just for a few minutes, dear boy. I'm extremely busy, you know."

"Chase, I think this tea is ready; I mean, it's been three minutes." Caroline yelled down the stairs.

"I'm on my way." He picked up his briefcase and locked the door behind him.

"I couldn't remember all the stuff you told me, about the milk and lemon and all." She handed him a white china mug. "So I just put in a dollop of honey and about two fingers of sour mash. What do you think?"

He sipped and smiled and shook his head. "It's a real eye opener."

The phone rang and he picked up the cordless from the counter.

"Defoe here."

"Defoe. Yearner Claxon. I hear you're looking for me."

"Right. What did you get on that tire print?"

"Shoot; my contact was off this weekend, I should hear from him today, tonight, though. Anything new with you?"

"Yes. Hot data from New York; I'm heading up there now, take a look at the companies that lost the trucks. Strong possibilities that there was inside involvement. Either an insurance scam or a straight hijack. All three companies are owned by the same outfit."

"What I can't figure is how this bird with the truck figures into it. You sure about the tire print?"

"Looked like a match to me."

"Yeah. You like some company today? That New York? There's some kind of connection, the deer and the trucks. That much meat's gotta be getting into the restaurant pipeline. Besides, I can't sit around here all day, waiting for my contact to find out about those tires. I got to have something to do.''

"Your nurse didn't pan out?"

"Hey, that's where I am. Only she isn't; has seven-to-three today. Left here at six, I fell back asleep. JoAnne woke me a minute ago.''

"You're still without transportation, then.''

"Oh, hell, we picked my truck up yesterday. Came back here for some therapy. For my . . . ah—contusions and abruisions. The eyes are okay, though. I sure would like to ride along with you today.''

"I don't see why not. I know a couple of places in New York that serve game, venison; maybe we have time, we can check them out. Meet you someplace?''

They decided on the Turnpike entrance at 309 and nine o'clock; time for Defoe to breakfast, shower, change, and kiss Caroline a lascivious good-bye. Time for Yearner to find, prescribe, and take a pair of Darvon capsules; wash, dress, and leave an appreciative note on the pillow, hoping it was the first place she would look.

The Jag wouldn't start; the morning air was moist and British motors are peckish in the damp. Caroline cranked the starter while Defoe muddled under the bonnet; a squirt of ether in the carbs solved but did not cure the problem.

Yearner's truck fired more readily than its driver. He spotted the golden arches a mile from her apartment, parked and took a pint of juice and a coffee to a table, waited for the Darvon to kick in. The Ray•Bans kept the body parts from separating completely.

She lived in a transitional zone between gentrification and terminal welfare and he had strayed across the line. Black winos, already in layered overcoats that anticipated the ensuing frosts, came in and ordered large coffees, took four, five plastic shots of ersatz cream, pocketed a dozen envelopes of sugar, the main meal of the day, and shuffled to a booth, where they sat in stultified silence, absorbing the dextrose and caffeine, a side order of nicotine to cut the fog.

The women, on their way home from cleaning jobs in offices or heading out to the same in white folk's homes, loaded up on breakfast pies and other high carb delicacies; believed the TV's exhortation to have a Coke instead of coffee.

Yearner sighed, looked at his watch. Bought a pair of sausage-and-egg delights, another magnum of coffee to go. Stopped at the 7-Eleven for gas and ice to refill the cooler, an early bar for a brace of six-packs. Defoe was waiting at the Turnpike entrance.

Twenty commuters' cars were parked on the graveled verge and Yearner made it twenty-one.

"Yearner?" Defoe approached on the traffic side. "Somehow I

thought that had to be your truck. It looks different in the clear light of morning.''

"Ah, Defoe." Yearner came upright in his cab, squinted through his shades. He swallowed phlegm, touched his temples. "Rough forty-eight hours, pal. Took more of a beating than I thought. 'Course all that damn rum an' Coke didn't help, Saturday night, or yesterday or whenever. I can't handle booze.'' He reached across the seat and extracted a can of Coors from its plastic yoke. "How 'bout a breakfast brew?''

"No thanks, not for me.''

"Yeah, pretty lightweight, but hell, it's not noon yet. I got a six-pack of Colt 45, if you want.''

"I just had a tea and bourbon, thank you. And I suppose I'll be driving.''

"Yeah. You really don't want to go to New York and back in this. Y'all don't mind; taking your rig up there?''

"Not at all; I don't blame you, I wouldn't want to take this thing too far from home, either.''

Yearner got out, adjusted his sunglasses. "Hey, don't be bad-mouthing the old lady, Chase. May look like shit, but I keep it up. 440 under here.'' He smacked the hood with the flat of his hand, winced. "Over air shocks and damn near new radial rubber. But with the four-wheel drive she's a ball-buster at speed; and we'd be yelling ourselves hoarse all the way up, the way these tires sing. Besides, I got a Mossberg pump and a State issue Heckler and Kock .308 behind the seats. Not to mention the Glock 9mm under the dash, and this .25 Beretta ankle gun.'' He pulled up his trouser cuff and unstrapped the Velcro holster, tossed it under the seat. "I can't take any of this stuff into New York, you know the damn laws they have?''

Defoe raised his eyebrows. "That reminds me, I have that Smith and Wesson revolver of yours in the trunk; cleaned it up a little, yesterday. Just poked the mud out of the major parts; rear sight appears to be off a bit. I suggest you check it out before you depend on it too much.'' He opened his trunk and handed over the weapon wrapped in an old T-shirt, watched Yearner shrug into his suede jacket and adjust the Stetson. "Regular Crocodile Dundee, aren't you?''

Yearner looked down at his chest, fluffed the fringes with his fingers. "I guess it is a bit much for the city. Let me see what I got in back.''

He opened the camper cap and rummaged inside, switched his boots for a pair of Hush Puppies, and slung a tweed sportscoat over his shoulder. "My teaching assistant disguise. Knit tie and horn rims complete the look. Suit's at the cleaners," he added, settling himself and a six-pack into Defoe's car.

"How about one of these sausage things?" He offered a sandwich to Defoe, who glanced over, shook his head.

"No thanks, I had something before I left. You always drink beer for breakfast?"

Yearner laughed. "Naw, I had coffee and juice already. This is just to get me back on line. Damn. I feel half naked without a gun on, I'm so used to wearing one. Or two."

Defoe switched lanes, accelerated around a tractor trailer. "Dutch courage. Like any mechanical device, they're never there, or functional, when you need them. You know Murphy's Law?"

Yearner folded his can, put it on the floor between his legs. "Sure. Anything that can go wrong, and all that?"

Defoe looked back at traffic. "Right. And then there's Thoreau's Corroboration. 'Simplify, simplify.' You sound as though you were from the South. Virginia?"

"Maryland; 'Merlin,' as we say down home. Town of Hudson, near Cambridge, on the Eastern Shore?" He glanced out the window at the anonymous North Jersey landscape, second-growth ash surrounding a man-made lake the color of a dirty dime. "Watermen, the whole clan. My daddy drowned, the way most of 'em do, sooner or later. Tonging oysters. 'Austers.' That's when I lit out. Seventeen, just got out of high school and saw myself following Daddy's footsteps too close. Man, at his funeral I took a good look around. At my uncles; most of 'em missing fingers and toes, mashed-up hands. Look seventy at forty-five. You'd think a man knew he was going to spend sixty, seventy hours a week on the Bay would learn to swim, right? You wouldn't believe how many sink like a stone, they fall in. Don't wear a life jacket, gets in the way of work. I joined the Marines." He opened another beer and watched the traffic eddy on the Interstate.

"I was over in Lebanon when they blew us up. Pulled my buddies out in pieces. I mean that, literally. 'I got me a black left arm here, wedding band; anybody got other parts to go with?' Shit." He took a swallow of beer. "I bet you were an officer, you were in the service."

"Right. Navy. I was a captain, as a matter of fact. Put in nearly twenty years."

"I knew it. You got that officer way about you. You look old enough to have been in 'Nam."

Defoe shook his head. "Naval Intelligence. But I never got within a thousand miles of Southeast Asia. Cambridge, that's south of Annapolis, isn't it?''

"Yessir. About forty miles. Other side of the Bay, of course. Waterfowl country, duck hunter's dream land. Or was, before pollution turned the Bay into the world's biggest toilet bowl. I tell you, I got kind of homesick after eight years, and I went back down there. And then I just plain got sick, see how it had changed. Chase, I think I'd rather eat a can of lye than risk a raw oyster nowadays. That's what I started out to do, I got out of the service. Tried for an environmental job in Maryland, but there wasn't any openings. I was MP in the service and Pennsylvania had this Game Commission position. So I took it. Temporary, I thought, until I can get back down home, kick some polluter's asses.'' He finished his beer, laughed quietly. "Funny, I get up here, I find out a good part of the problem is runoff from Pennsylvania farmland. Fertilizer, ag chemicals, find their way into the Susquehanna, hit the Bay at Havre de Grace. So anytime I'm out around Harrisburg, the Lancaster area, I poke around the farms, look for a hillside that hasn't been contoured, point it out to the farmer. They're mostly pretty good guys, nature lovers, when you get down to it; respect wildlife. Got to, they expect to make a decent living off the land. They just don't realize, a little pesticide runoff from a three-, four-acre piece of land that's really too steep for corn, ought to be in hay, that runoff gets into a little old three-foot-wide rill. Well, I pull out a topographical of the area, after shooting the shit for a while, show them just exactly where their farm is, the field we're talking about. Let them pick out the stream, follow it down to the feeders that empty into the Susquehanna. You know, Chase, a lot of those old boys recreate down the Bay, got a boat at Conowingo, maybe a trailer home, a summer place, along the Bay. They remember how good the fishing was, thirty, forty years ago. Crabs, oysters. Duck hunting in November. I don't push them; don't need the hard sell, these fellows are outside every damn day all year long, they hear the geese going over in March. I let them figure it out, maybe ask a question or two, guide them along.'' He crumpled his can and set it on the floor next to the others. "I guess I'm doing as much good up here as I would be running around inspecting sewer plants in Baltimore County.''

Defoe drove without responding for several minutes. "World War Two,'' he finally said. "That's when the big change came, right after. Took a week, ten days by ship to reach Europe. Now it's a few hours, and not just people, either. All this stolen clothing we're looking at? Came in by air. The Interstate highways, hard to believe it, but they were started during Eisenhower's presidency. You're too young, I was just a kid, but I can remember old Route One, ran from Presque Isle, up in Maine, down to Key West. Two lane, blacktop and concrete. Ran right the hell through the middle of every town and city for two thousand miles. Thirty-five, forty miles an hour, you were moving right along. Now we have instant everything, from satellite TV to microwave meals, but I don't think the quality of life has improved; hell, if anything, it's worse. We're running faster, but I don't see that we're going anywhere. That's what attracted me to the area I live in now. In a lot of ways it's still back in the forties. My neighbor has a 1949 tractor that he uses every day for barnyard chores. Drives a '53 Ford pickup. He's pushing ninety himself. Every chance I get, I hang around him, kind of basking, I guess you could call it. Because when he goes, him and the few others, it really will be the end of an era. I don't know if I'm making any sense. It's not nostalgia; I don't long for the good old days, I know they weren't all that good in a lot of ways. I don't want to trade penicillin for the hand-cranked telephone on a party line.''

"Yeah, I know what you mean. I guess I feel the same way, I'm out in the woods, sitting like a rock on a stump, and I see a flock of wild turkeys move across an abandoned field. There used to be elk in Pennsylvania. And eagles. And now there's sandwich wrap that we pull out of the stomach of a dead otter thirty miles from the nearest highway. Modern man seems to be running in circles, hellbent on being everywhere at once. And leaving a trail of crap behind to prove he was. What did you find out about your hijacked trucks?''

"Same parent company; pretty obvious that's where the culprit lies, in one form or another. I want to stop at a source first, see what background I can pick up. Here we are, now, if I can find a parking place.''

They walked along, the lunch hour crowds moving at a Manhattan clip around them. "Hey,'' Yearner said, looking at a girl in a leather skirt and tight sweater jiggling toward them, "how'd you like to homestead that piece of real estate?''

Defoe watched the young woman as she passed. "Nah. There's not a flat piece of ground to build on. Here we are.''

Delphi Silks occupied a brownstone on the fringes of the garment district, showroom on the first floor, living quarters above. In addition to designing scarves and neckties for Oscar, Calvin, and Ralph as well as the house label, Delphi wrote, under the pen name Oracle, a weekly gossip column for *Women's Wear Daily*, exposing the famous and socially notorious of New York to the biting wit that had been a trademark for thirty years. Defoe had first met Delphi when he was investigating what he called the Peacoat Scandal and had found the Oracle invaluable in leading him through the labyrinthine world of Seventh Avenue.

They were led up the narrow stairs by a blond young man who kept looking over his shoulder at Yearner with appreciative glances and a sly smile. Delphi lounged on a chaise in the sunny studio, surrounded by potted plants and dressed in a patterned silk kimono, open at the throat, leaving little doubt that it was the only article of clothing on the svelte form. A flawlessly made-up face of ageless beauty smiled at Defoe, then looked at Yearner.

"Well *hello.*" Delphi turned back to Defoe, asked in a throaty voice, "Is this the tidbit you promised me this morning, darling?"

Defoe smiled. "Perhaps. Although I thought my company would be enough. How have you been; you look the same as ever, haven't aged a day."

"The miracle of surgery, dear boy; nip and tuck. Who *is* this rugged young man?"

"Yearner Claxon, ma'am. Pleased to meet you. I'm just a country boy, awed by this here big city." He held out his hand and Delphi took it, caressed its palm before leaning back against the chaise, letting the kimono fall open to reveal a pale thigh. "Rustic, too; how absolutely delightful. Tell me, Chase, does he tug his forelock?"

"Go easy, Delphi, appearances can be deceiving. Yearner's a field agent for the Pennsylvania Game Commission. Tracking deerslayers at the moment. Perhaps he's gotten a bit far into character."

"Uhm. You'll both join me in a glass of Chartreuse; Hans!"

"Delphi, I'm interested in knowing what you can tell us about Reade Industries. A series of trucks were hijacked and all were carrying clothing destined for Reade or its subsidiaries. Naturally enough, it looks as though someone at the company is responsible."

Hans reappeared with a small tray, a decanter, and three cut-crystal sherry glasses. Delphi poured and distributed the liqueur, dismissed the factotum. "Reade. Chiefly owned by Quentin Reade, about your age, darling, as a matter of fact. A privately held company until rather recently, the last six or eight years, I would guess. Goes back to the Civil War; Quentin inherited from his father, oh, I would say in the mid-seventies. The son took the company public soon after. Began an acquisition campaign with the proceeds of the offering. All this was in last year's annual report; quite a splashy one, the company's hundred and twenty-fifth anniversary. I know all this because Reade himself is rather an item. Recently shed wife number two, or possibly three, and on the prowl again. A sportsman, big game, I think. Or is it balloons? No, that's the financial person, that publisher, what's his name. Isn't it a shame, dear boy, when the mind starts to go before the body?'' Delphi chuckled and sipped the spicy liqueur.

''Anyway, the company is highly leveraged at present, due in no small part to the disastrous performance of the market last year. Their debt load has to be positively enormous, and servicing it must eat up every cent they can scrape together. Of course the textile market is recovering, so things will have eased up a bit, but still. I'm surprised they haven't had to sell off a few divisions; Lord knows an awful lot of people bigger than Reade have been forced to do that. Look at Manhattan Industries. Who, incidentally, were looking at *us* with a rather greedy eye last year. I think it was my absolute decadence that put them off.'' The Oracle laughed and stroked a silky throat, caressing the surgically tightened skin with slender fingers.

Defoe stood and put his glass on a low table. ''Thank you, Delphi, as always, you've been a fountain of information. Now I think we'll go and beard the lion in his den. Oh, and I promised you something. For your column. I was chatting with a friend in Washington a few days ago. It seems that the President's latest Supreme Court nominee has a rather colorful incident in his past. The FBI found that someone else took his bar examination for him. The Senate committee will get the report on Thursday; for both our sakes I think you had better wait until then to publish, eh? Spreads out the source potentialities a bit.''

They walked the few blocks to Seventh Avenue. ''Hey, that Delphi is one sexy number, Chase. Maybe getting on a bit, but still prime cut.''

Defoe laughed. ''Right, Yearner, Delphi has got to be at least sixty. And was born in the Bronx. As Melvin Fiermann.''

''What? A *guy*, a trans whatayacallit? No shit.'' He smiled and shook his head. ''Welcome to New York, Yearner.''

The receptionist smiled, too, and it was obvious that she had spent forty-five minutes with a WaterPik preparing for the moment. Every crevice between every tooth was pristine; the pink gums above the dazzling enamel had a Disney purity that belied their organic origin. Mr. Reade was not yet in but his executive assistant would see them; she indicated an open door at the end of a broad hallway behind her Post Modern desk.

''We gonna just waltz in here and tell 'em who we are, ask questions?''

''Why not?'' Defoe replied as they walked along the hall. ''We're not cops; I don't care who stole the clothes. They have to prove their innocence to us, if they expect the company to cover the losses. As far as the insurance company goes, it's guilty until proven innocent.''

The assistant appeared in the doorway of Reade's office, backlit, three-quarter profile, a single sheet of paper in her hand. She looked at them for a moment, then turned and went back through the doorway.

In a concentrated fifteen-year study of the subject, Yearner had determined that a remarkable rear end, all curves and dimpled convolutions, was generally preceded by a rather uneventful front, as though the celestial sculptor had used most of his materials and enthusiasm on the derriere.

Conversely, a magnificent breastworks, jutting proudly forward, self-supporting as a truly well-engineered mammary department should be, was inevitably followed behind by a gluteus that was hardly maximus.

To find an exemplary example of both fore and aft in the same individual was a rare enough occurrence to cause a true aficionado like Yearner to experience heart palpitations and a tightening in the throat.

"My God, Defoe," he said, stopping. "Benchmark pussy. They should cast a master mold of that one."

Defoe elbowed Yearner, introduced himself and his partner.

"Hello," she said, extending her hand and smiling. "I'm Viola Dagamba. Mr. Reade's personal assistant."

A native of Kenya, Reade had discovered her working as the coffee girl in a Nairobi travel bureau. The slender, elegant teenager took New York by storm and three years of high fashion modeling and five *Vogue* covers transpired before she developed the rounded curves that attracted Yearner's discerning eye. She still could, and occasionally did, model swimwear, but Reade had discovered her other, less obvious talents, and she now seated the two men in front of the leather-topped desk fully versed in the details of the hijacked loads of clothing.

"Mr. Reade is not yet back from his weekend." She had a soft voice with a trace of England that seemed an echo of colonial Africa. "He has a lodge and preserve in the Adirondacks where they shoot in the fall." She waved her hand across the expanse of the room, thirty floors above the street. "As you can see," she said, "he is quite the hunter."

Yearner and Defoe both took in the array of trophy heads: eland, gazelle, and oryx, along with several of the more esoteric ungulates of the world.

"He has taken the Big Five; they are at his place upstate. I do hope you have come with a settlement for us. Mr. Reade is most anxiously awaiting some word from your company."

"Not quite finalized, Miss Dagamba. You're African, are you not? Kikuyu, perhaps?"

She smiled and inclined her head slightly. "You have a discerning eye, Mr. Defoe."

"Possibly. But that's Mount Kenya in the background of that photograph of the elephant, and, I assume, Mr. Reade. The Kikuyu are the dominant ethnic group. How do you feel about westerners harvesting your wildlife to adorn their office walls, Miss Dagamba?"

She grinned, showing white teeth and a pink tongue. "Please call me Viola. There is an American Negro saying, Mr. Defoe. 'Different strokes for different folks.' "

Both he and Yearner laughed. "Well put. However, I am disappointed that Mr. Reade is not available; we really won't be able to do anything until I can meet with him."

Viola leaned forward in the swivel chair behind the desk, sharing café au lait cleavage with the two men. "Well then, let's try and reach him in his car." She touched the intercom. "Marnie, get Mr. Reade for us. Try the Jaguar first." She sat back in the chair, smiled through the steeple she made with her slender fingers.

"The problem we have is that all of the trucks hijacked from IGT over the past week or so were carrying goods either for Reade Industries or companies owned by Reade. Rather a coincidence, eh?"

She hesitated only a fraction of a second before replying. "That, I think, would stretch the bounds of credulity, Mr. Defoe. Someone, either inside our small company, or an outsider with a grudge, is obviously behind this. Mr. Reade and I discussed both possibilities before he left on Friday. He took copies of the pertinent manifests with him and planned to give the matter deep thought over the weekend." A light flashed and Viola picked up the receiver. "Mr. Reade. Mr. Defoe, from the trucker's insurance company, is here and will need to meet with you regarding the losses. They have discovered what we just found out ourselves and are obviously concerned that all of the losses are connected." She paused for several seconds, her face a mask of anonymous beauty. "Yes, sir." She handed the receiver to Defoe.

"Hello, Mr. Reade. Chase Defoe. I obviously have some serious doubts about these claims and would like to meet with you as soon as possible."

"Not any sooner than I do, Defoe." There was a wow and crackle overlaying the transmission, adding an exotic urgency to the call. "Listen; I'm about two and a half, three hours from the city, and that's cranking this baby when I hit the thruway. How about we meet for dinner, at my place, we can hash this thing out. I've got a few ideas on this.''

''Well, it certainly beats driving back up here tomorrow.''

''Great! I'm in Trump Parc. Central Park South. Let's say six o'clock. Hope you like game; I've got a trunk full of pheasants I shot this morning. In the meantime, go talk to Barry Lyndon. He's my head designer, but more important, he's got thirty years in the rag trade. I'm a money man, I admit I don't know shit about the clothing end of it. Tell him I said to give you every cooperation. And put Viola on again.''

Defoe smiled and handed the telephone to Viola without comment. He always got a kick out of big shots.

Barry Lyndon's office was the antithesis of Reade's. Four-by-eight tables were piled with swatches, samples, muslin concepts pinned and basted together. The cork walls were covered with pastel sketches, sometimes two and three deep. A duplicate fit model, wearing bikini briefs and goosebumps, stood on a low platform, staring vacantly out the window as two young women draped crepe de chine over her torso while a middle-aged man watched and smoked a cigarette. ''That's good, I like that,'' he said, coming closer. He reached out and pulled a fold of fabric tighter at the breast, defining the nipple. ''There, yes, do that up, darlings. With the piqué collar, absolute dynamite. Hi, guys.''

''Mr. Lyndon?''

''In the flesh, boys, in the flesh.'' He patted his jowls with the backs of both hands. ''You can't be buyers, because Marnie only knows two things, and one is that buyers are absolutely forbidden to get within a thousand miles of this room. So I suppose that leaves the police. Although your suit, sir, had to have cost you a thousand dollars, and I suspect was tailored in London. While you, young man, appear to have slept in your jacket. It's a nice piece of tweed, though. You really should have your off-the-rack altered; a man your age with a thirty-inch waist should *flaunt* the son of a bitch!'' He held out his hand to Defoe. ''Barry Lyndon.''

''Chase Defoe. My associate, Yearner Claxon. We had hoped to see Mr. Reade about the insurance losses. I just spoke with him on his car telephone; he passed us along to you.''

''Ah, Quentin, the dear boy. We just lost, irretrievably *lost*, about fifteen hundred pieces of this season's best of Europe, and he retreats to the wilderness to assassinate rabbits. Take that jacket off, young man, it's bothering me. Janice! Steam Mr. Claxon's jacket, dear, we can't have him looking like a street person.'' He touched Yearner's forearm. ''I spent twenty years in menswear. That's where you have to know your stuff; can't fake it the way we can here. Women's clothing, anyone with a fist full of markers and a sketch pad can call themselves a designer. Am I right, Mr. Defoe. London? Made to measure?''

"About ten years ago."

"I thought so. You stay in shape. My middle-age spread is gaining ground."

"Well, a few suits at what this cost can be quite an incentive to stay the same size."

"Yes. Unfortunately, New York has about twenty thousand restaurants, each better than the previous. How can I help you gentlemen?''

Yearner finally entered the investigation. "Mr. Defoe has some questions about the clothing that got swiped. Meanwhile, I'll just look around, okay? While Janice is pressing my coat." He sauntered down the hall toward Reade's office and Lyndon watched him go.

"We have four thefts, Mr. Lyndon, all involving companies owned by Reade Industries." Defoe picked up a pencil sketch, glanced at it. "It seems rather obvious that the culpability lies here. I'm not sure whose jurisdiction it falls under, that's for New York City and the various state agencies to resolve. Possibly the federal government, because of the interstate commerce involved. I'm not a lawyer. But I can assure you and Mr. Reade that the claims will not be settled as long as these loose ends remain."

"This comes as a shock to me, pal. I thought we were talking about one load of designer dresses. Which are an absolute loss. Timeliness is everything in this business, and with high fashion, reorders are out of the question. They are already cutting next season's line. *Four*, you said?''

"Norton and Norton, Gleneagle in Ohio, and another I don't have specifics on at the moment. But all subsidiaries of Reade. Who would have access to shipping information? Dates of arrival, value of the loads, that sort of thing."

Lyndon rested a buttock on the edge of a table, shook a cigarette from his pack. "Jesus. This looks bad. Things have been tight, Mr. Defoe; we've grown rather rapidly in the last two, three years. But we had a good fall and the cash flow should improve. Only with these thefts; well, all of those goods should be on the selling floor right now. There is absolutely no way to replace them. Even getting substitute merchandise will be a bugger of a job. I suppose our buyers will get out there and come up with *something*. Without insurance money, though, it will be next to impossible. The money end is not my forte, you understand, but I seriously doubt that our line of credit is sufficient at the moment."

"Yes, I understand all of that. However, you did not answer my question. Who has access to the data?"

Lyndon exhaled a cloud of smoke, folded his arms, looked at the ceiling. "Well, Quentin, obviously. Me, Miss Dagamba. Any of our five buyers, assistant buyers. Who are spread across the face of the globe at the moment; Hong Kong, Paris, Milan. A couple are closer to home. I don't keep track of them, Quentin would know their whereabouts. But, really, Mr. Defoe, anybody, with a little effort, could get into the files and learn what you are asking. For that matter, people from the mill are down here on a weekly basis. Did you know we own a textile plant in Massachusetts? And any of the store people; they have their own buyers, who are in the city regularly, of course. I am honestly not the person to talk to about this; I design the three House lines, four collections a year for each one. I don't have time to get involved with other aspects of our business. But I do have healthy stock options and am too old to start over. I came over from Perry Ellis when the dear boy passed away. Resolve this, Mr. Defoe. I have a gut feeling that without this insurance money we are up to our tushies in alligators."

"Well," Defoe said with a smile as he tossed the tissue onto the table, "then there is little to worry about. I understand that Mr. Reade is quite the hunter. I'll let you get back to work while I see what Mr. Claxon is up to."

Mr. Claxon was up to an after-work cocktail with Viola and was attempting an escalation to dinner. As they left the building, Yearner said, "You concentrate on this Reade character, Chase, and I'll put a full court press on Miss Viola, do a little undercover work."

"Yes, indeed," Defoe replied. "But under whose covers?" He scanned the curb for a cab, saw one up the street, and hooked it with a New Yorker's eye. "Let's use what's left of the afternoon to check out some of these restaurants, find the venison connection."

Quentin Reade parked in his slot and extracted his briefcase and the canvas boat bag containing a double brace of cock pheasants from the trunk of the XJ sedan. He rode the elevator to his two-bedroom apartment in the Tower. Its three thousand square feet included twin terraces that overlooked Central Park and had cost him pocket change of less than two million dollars.

He tossed the birds on the kitchen counter and called for Sancho, the elderly Basque who served him as chef, valet, and housekeeper. "Four for dinner, amigo; do something exotic with the pheasants. And run out for a few bottles of a good wine to go with whatever you decide. Power dinner tonight." He put a fistful of ice in a stubby crystal tumbler and poured Ezra Brooks over them. "I'll be in the shower, put the machine on when you go out."

He hit a number on the auto dialer while he undressed, tossed his Levi's and Tony Lamas in the direction of the closet. "Mary, honey; Mr. Reade. Listen, I know it's short notice, but I need the twins for dinner, couple of hours after. Can you help me out?"

He carried the telephone and his drink into the bathroom, turned the shower on hot. "Thanks, sweetheart, it's really important, or I wouldn't do it to you, I know how it can fuck up your life. I'll look for them about seven. Promise they'll be out the door by ten." He put down the phone, swallowed bourbon, and stepped under the stinging water. *Unless I need them for the night*, he thought.

Ten minutes later he stood in front of his closet, contemplated the smoking jacket with an ascot, then the tuxedo, before selecting a dark three-piece suit. Always a possibility that this insurance guy wouldn't understand the other outfits; probably a mope from Scarsdale whose idea of a big time is Singapore Slings at the Pirate's Cove, the Surf and Turf special.

Quentin Reade had the insouciance of an Edwardian aristocrat. It came to him by birth and early training, first at Groton, and later, at Williams College. His father's textile mill had provided a solid, if unspectacular living for the Reade family since the 1860's. After college, Quentin had worked for his father for a year, saw it as a dead end, and went to Wharton for his MBA. Ten years on Wall Street taught him the secrets of money manipulation and New York sex. When he took over Reade Textiles upon his father's death he was ready to map out an expansion for the company that would see its revenues increase from a million and a half to nearly a hundred and forty million dollars a year.

"I'm a hunter by nature, Mr. Defoe. A predator, I'll admit it. Some of us are sheep, others wolves. I doubt that it's genetic, my father was most certainly a sheep. But I get my rocks off, out there in the business jungle, hand-to-hand combat. And then there's this." He waved his hand at the six-hundred-square-foot living room and the ample evidence of his prowess on safari. "I've done Africa six times, taken the Big Five. You hunt, Defoe?"

Defoe swirled his Scotch and looked at the amber liquid, then shifted his gaze to the pair of Cape buffalo horns above the wet bar. "Oh, a little, Mr. Reade. Nothing on this scale, of course, some smoothbore now and again. To tell the truth, I don't really see the challenge in it anymore; I mean, what's the purpose? Going up against, say, an elephant; a hundred yards distant, with a point six hundred Nitro Express. And a dead shot white hunter on your off-hand side, for insurance.''

Reade smiled slyly. "Point well taken; and the same conclusion I came to a couple of years ago. Let me show you my solution.'' He put his drink on a glass-topped coffee table whose base was formed by the interlocking horns of the Lesser Kudu and opened an ebony gun cabinet with ivory fretwork set into the double doors. "Handguns. I've become exclusively a handgun hunter, Defoe. Puts the challenge right back into it.'' He handed Defoe one of the dozen revolvers and automatic pistols displayed within the cabinet. "Have to stalk to fifty yards for a decent kill, closer for something like the Buff.'' He gestured with his chin toward the horns above the bar. "Forty-eight inches between the tips, Defoe. Hell of a brute, however it was taken. Actually, I used a Westley Richards .470 express rifle, from my guide's kit. But the range was less than twenty-five yards when he finally dropped, and that pumps the adrenaline, amigo.'' He pointed at the weapon. "A .44 Magum, Smith and Wesson Double Action. Probably the biggest handgun you ever saw, right? Shoots a 240 grain bullet at around twelve hundred feet per second. Well, next to these other custom single-action revolvers, it belongs in a lady's purse.'' He offered Defoe a pair of weapons, butt first. "The Freedom Arms .45 Colt and a Casull .454. Both throw a three-hundred-plus grain bullet at fourteen hundred feet per second. They deliver twice the energy of that forty-four mag. A thousand dollars worth of handgun there, pal. Each. But money is of secondary importance when a couple of tons of rhino are coming at you flat out.''

Defoe handed the guns back. "A bit heavy, aren't they?''

"Three pounds, plus. More, with five in the cylinder.'' He returned the stainless-steel revolvers to their cabinet.

"Well, it's certainly a very impressive collection of artillery, Mr. Reade.''

"Hey, I haven't shown you the latest in the power escalation derby. It's still in my briefcase, Sancho hasn't had time to clean it yet. I was breaking it in this weekend, ran about a hundred rounds through her.'' He pointed to a red welt in the crotch of his thumb and forefinger. "Hang on, let me go get it.''

Defoe sat on the couch, ran his hand over the zebra-hide upholstery, an abstract in black and white, and looked out at the lights of the Upper East Side coming on across the dark expanse of the foreground that was Central Park. Reade was really pushing the macho image. Interesting. He sipped his drink. Wouldn't think that a man with his background and position would feel the need. He got up and walked to the windows, looked down at the park; the trees, just beginning to shed their leaves, were dimly illuminated by the lights that lined the paths. Another kind of jungle, he thought.

Yearner looked at the view from Viola's window. "You live right on the edge of the woods, don't you? A regular forest over there."

She laughed and handed him a glass of white wine. "Central Park. Hardly a forest."

"Not for you, no, I guess not. They have lots of jungle where you come from?"

"None at all, Yearner, at least not the kind you're thinking of. Plains and grassland. Hot; my country lies astride the equator. And yet there are glaciers in the higher elevations of Mount Kenya. A country of interesting contrasts. As is yours. How, for example, does a handsome country boy get into the boring profession of insurance adjuster? I somehow pictured them as old men with dandruff and bifocals."

"Yeah, well, you'd have to take that up with Defoe, I'm just his assistant. New on the job. That's why I invited you out for a drink, after work. Because frankly, I don't know what the hell I'm supposed to be doing, investigating this hijacking thing. So I figure, we have a couple of cocktails someplace, you'll tell me something I need to know. What that is, to tell the truth, I have no idea. But the company will pay my chits, and hey, drinks, maybe dinner with the best-looking woman I've been with in since I can't remember, what the hell? Only we end up back here instead; you say you want to change out of work clothes before we go out. That caftan. It's pretty, I mean the print, the pattern. But it don't look like something that you'd want to go out in public in; sort of a housecoat, that's what my momma would call it."

She laughed and came close. "Dashiki; a native garment. Hand-woven cotton, block printed, a traditional design. Feel the texture; like a bedsheet, yes? But you are right, in this country I would not wear it in public." She threw her shoulders back and her bare nipples pressed against the rough fabric. "Too revealing." She took his wineglass and put it on an end table with her own, then gripped his biceps, pulling him to her. "Tell me, Yearner Claxon, from Chesa-peake Bay, Maryland. Have you ever kissed a black woman?"

"Look at this black bitch, champ. The ultimate in handguns." Reade offered Defoe the weapon. "I'm planning on going after the most dangerous game with that, the big cats. Either tigers or the lion, India or Africa; not sure which just yet. Depends on what season I can get away.'' He sat and put his feet up on the coffee table. Defoe noticed that Reade wore hand-tooled ostrich skin cowboy boots with his business suit.

"Linebaugh Special. I had Jack make it up for me, on the Ruger Bisley frame. Six-inch, fifty-caliber barrel and a new five-round cylinder for the custom cartridges. That's the major problem; we had to use the .348 Winchester brass, cut it down to 1.4 inches, and expand the mouth. I have a gun nut over in Jersey hand load my bullets. Made up a special die, to Linebaugh's specs. They're the rounds we tested this weekend. 460 grain bullets at 1,200 fps. In wet newspaper we got thirty-five inches of penetration. I can't wait to hit live flesh with it.''

Defoe held the single action revolver out at arm's length, sighted down the barrel at the black blankness of the terrace doors. "A regular hand cannon, Mr. Reade. I pity the lion. Do you suppose we could discuss these hijacked trucks?''

Reade stood, took the revolver from Defoe, held it at port arms. Smiled with a wry twist of the lips. "After dinner. Pleasure first, business later,'' and left the room to the sound of the Westminster chimes that Defoe recalled was Reade's doorbell.

"Yes," Defoe said under his breath. "Although I'd have put it the other way round.''

Yearner looked at Viola's naked body in the dim light that the moon and the city sent through the window of her apartment, marveled at the contrast of the dark flesh on the white sheets. "Now, my friend,'' she said, turning toward him, "I suppose you would like something to eat.''

"Defoe,'' Reade said, coming back into the living room with a young woman on either arm, "Our dinner guests. I took the liberty of arranging companionship; I hope you aren't put out.'' He looked at Defoe with a daring smirk and introduced the two girls. "Lisa,'' he said, disengaging his left arm, "and Liza. Quite a pair, *N'est-ce pas?*''

Sancho came into the room with a tray that held a pair of fruit-based cocktails; evidently the young ladies' tastes were known.

"Identical twins, Mr. Defoe. The evening's challenge is to distinguish them. But dinner first. Sancho!''

Sancho knew rustic, peasant cuisine, the best thing to do, after all, with game, and could prepare bird, boar, stag, or hare in the styles of rural France and Spain. The pheasants were fresh and the budget free. He had selected a Pomerol and new potatoes with carrots and small onions. A bakery on the Upper East Side supplied a fresh and generally unappreciated bread while Reade anticipated the vinial desires and poured.

"I am going to the kitchen and see if I can find us some food, Yearner, dearest. An omelet perhaps, and a tin of caviar and crackers. Meanwhile you rest and regroup for a fresh onslaught. And finish that bottle of wine; I'll bring another." He rolled onto his side and admired the sway of her hips as she sashayed from the room.

Defoe finished dissecting his pheasant and laid knife and fork on the side of his plate, sipped the wine; pleasant, but could have been left to breathe a bit longer. He smiled at the girl across from him. "I suppose you are often asked, but how *does* one tell the two of you apart . . . er—Lisa?"

She smiled, caught his eye, dropped her gaze to her dinner, let Reade pick up the thread of the thought.

"Difficult to differentiate, aren't they, Defoe? Lisa, Liza. Show the gentleman. I think, after all, we are ready for dessert."

The two young women, on cue, put down their forks and, a hand behind their backs, wriggled their shoulders as they unzipped matching dresses. The tops dropped, their braless breasts exposed. Defoe stared across the table at a fulsome pair, faint line of fading tan demarking the zone between sun and swimsuit. He turned toward the twin on his right; her breasts were equal to her sisters, but for the nipples. They stood erect, pink against the pale skin and pierced by tiny golden hoops.

"Liza," Reade said with a chuckle, "is the one into kinky sex. Does the idea of a little pain turn you on, Mr. Defoe?"

"Perhaps giving pain is a pleasure for some, Mr. Reade, but receiving it rarely is, contrary to the popular beliefs." He folded his napkin in half and laid it on the table. "While I appreciate your efforts to wine, dine, and otherwise entertain me, I think it would be more productive if we sat down and discussed your insurance claims."

"You don't fool around on the little woman, right, sport? Or do I misread you? I can get a couple of *boys* up here, like that." He snapped his fingers with a pop that made the girls start and Defoe react inwardly to the vehemence of his delivery.

"As a matter of fact I am single and serenely heterosexual. But a bit old-fashioned, I am afraid; it has nothing to do with the obvious charms of these two lovely young women," he said, and smiled at the twins. "And I apologize for their ineluctable disappointments."

"At least accept my offer of brandy and a good cigar, Defoe," Reade said. He had escorted the two young women to the door, tucked a pair of hundred-dollar bills in separate cleavages, and cupped their buttocks with an affectionate squeeze before closing the door. They found their own way to the elevator.

The two men went through the ritual of clipping, piercing, and lighting the cigars and swirling, inhaling, and finally tasting the brandy before Defoe spoke. "Quite frankly, Mr. Reade, the company finds it an unacceptable coincidence that four separate thefts all come to roost at your door. Until we are persuaded that Reade Industries is not responsible, no payouts will be made."

"Caviar," Viola said, caressing, "seems to have remarkable restorative powers; I see that you are once again rising to the occasion, Yearner."

He looked down at himself and laughed, lay back on the pillow. "I think you may have more to do with it than these fish eggs. Only thing is, my ribs're hurting a bit from our last go round."

"Well then," she said, throwing her leg over his loins and guiding him into her, "just lie back and let me do all the work this time."

"Just relax a minute, Defoe, and let me work on this thing." Reade put his cigar in an ashtray and refilled his snifter. "Accept for a moment that I have nothing to do with this hijacking thing. Suspend your disbelief." He drank, picked up his cigar, and blew a cloud of smoke across the room. "You see, I'm leveraged to the hilt right now, things are tighter than a bull's ass in fly season, to quote the fellow that runs my lodge up in the Adirondacks. I made several acquisitions over the last few years that really stretched us. But you got to stretch to grow, right? Anyway, the last market glitch really put us up against it, and the only way I've been able to hold on to those companies is by heavy borrowing against them. Most of my creditors I can hold off; contractors, fabric brokers, domestic suppliers. The spinning mills. They can wait sixty, ninety days, they're used to it in this business. The bigger ones are factored anyway, and I can work with their banks." He finished his brandy and stood up. "What I'm about to tell you is in the strictest confidence, Defoe. It can't go beyond this room." He paused for a dramatic moment. "I've been using my margin account to keep us afloat until our fall receivables come in. And I've been getting margin calls that I can't meet, not without selling down my own position in Reade. My account executive has been covering the situation so far, but he called me last week in a panic. The SEC is going through their books, because of some goddamned junk bond scandal, and he says it's only a matter of time before both our butts are on the grill. I need cash to cover my position, and I need it quickly." He stood over Defoe and opened his hands, offered his palms to the man before him. "That's the truth of the situation and the reason I want a quick settlement from your company." He waited a beat before continuing. "And anything I can do for you, to help expedite the settlement . . . well—just tell me what you need." He poured a measure of brandy into Defoe's glass.

"Oh, God, that's good!" Viola moved rhythmically against Yearner, increasing the pace until she collapsed forward, burying her face in his neck as the orgasm washed over her. He felt her tighten and grip him as he came for the third time in as many hours.

That, Defoe thought, sounds suspiciously like the offer of a bribe, but he said nothing, instead sipped his brandy and examined the ash of his cigar. Finally he looked at Reade. "All very well; I can appreciate your position. But doesn't that make it all the more tempting to hijack your own merchandise as a way out of your cash crunch?"

Reade laughed without humor. "Jesus, you're a hard man to do business with, Defoe. Let me get my briefcase and take you through it by the numbers. Help yourself to the brandy."

He spread the manifests on the coffee table, tapped at a calculator as Defoe looked over Reade's shoulder. "Five million, more or less, the total value of the loads. That's cash money, already spent. We paid up front. With letters of credit two, three weeks ago, when the goods were shipped from Europe. Now, nobody . . . well, hell, you know this, nobody will insure for more than eighty percent. So if you were to write me out a check right now, I'd be out a million bucks."

Defoe started to say something and Reade interrupted. "I know what you're going to say. I would be able to pick up some quick dollars from the stolen merchandise. You're thinking that surely someone in my position would know how to get rid of hot clothing. Sure, I suppose I could ask around; I do know the retailers that handle off price merchandise, the job-lot boys. That's where we get rid of last season's dogs. They buy with no questions asked, but at ten cents on the dollar. We might raise a million, but let's be optimistic and say we get two out of the clothing. Leaves us with a million profit after all is said and done. On a five-million-dollar investment. Not a real good return, Defoe. Not when you figure that the five million worth of clothing, delivered into the pipeline, would have returned us ten, twelve mill in thirty to sixty days." He tossed the calculator on the table with the papers. "Any way you look at it, my friend, I'm going to take it in the ass."

Viola snuggled beside Yearner, nibbled his earlobe. "Satiated, Mr. Claxon? Incapable of movement?"

"Dead and paralyzed. Call me in a week." He lay on his back, inert, with his eyes closed.

"Uh-hmm," she chuckled, her tongue probing his ear as her fingers traced a delicate track toward his groin. "Would you be terribly shocked," she whispered, "if I told you I liked it in my ass?"

"It doesn't feel good, being in this position, Defoe. You're all but accusing me of engineering these thefts, while the police have not even been to see us. I assume that *they* have a better handle on the case than you do. But you're putting us in the position of being guilty until proven innocent. I thought insurance claims were paid and *then* a recovery was attempted." Reade picked up his cigar, found it dead. "Let me assure you, Mr. Defoe. If any of the clothing turns up, we will gladly return the insurance money for the merchandise. Especially the designer pieces. For all intents and purposes those dresses were sold when the buyers placed the orders; they had specific customers in mind. We aren't in the habit of ordering dresses, gowns that can sell for five to ten thousand dollars, and hanging them on the selling floor in the hope some little gal wanders in and likes what she sees. At this level, the buyers know their customers, their tastes and needs." He relit his cigar and refilled his snifter. "Everybody is going to take a bath on this one."

"Hey." She poked Yearner with a toe. He was sprawled across the bottom of the bed, where he had collapsed after his final orgasm. "You okay?"

"Yeah," he chuckled, his voice muffled by the crumpled bedcovers. "I just had a funny image. I was a kid, my buddy kept rabbits. First time I saw them breed it blew me away. The buck gets up on the doe, goes at it, fast and furious, about like we just did. Only when he comes, he falls off her, lays there like he was dead. I thought he was, first time I saw it. Now I know how that old dude felt." He rolled off the bed and stood. "I need a shower."

She reached for his trousers as he closed the bathroom door, waited until she heard the water before going to the telephone.

*   *   *

"Excuse me a minute, Defoe." Reade took the cordless phone that Sancho had brought him and followed his servant back to the kitchen.

"This Yearner Claxon, supposed to be Defoe's man? ID says he's with the Pennsylvania Game Commission. Is that like casinos or something? I don't get it."

"Shit. No, it's game like in hunting. But all Defoe's been talking about all night is insurance. I don't get it, either. Call Willard and tell him about this; he's supposed to meet the guy later, for the payout. He needs to know about this. I'll call down there, in case he hasn't left yet."

Reade came back into the living room, looking at his watch and shaking his head. "Damn buyer in England. Didn't realize it's nearly midnight here. She has lined up two thousand dozen Shetland pullovers. Only they want cash. You'll have to excuse me, Defoe. I have to make a couple of calls, wake up some bankers that are going to be pretty pissed. You see why I need that insurance money. Next step is the six-for-five boys whose office is a street corner. Do what you can on this, for Christ's sake."

"Willard's not here. Who's this?"

"Viola. Where is he."

"Working."

"Where, damn you? I got to talk to him. He's not still at the warehouse, is he?"

"Not yet. Said he had to take a load someplace, be back there, though, to drop off the truck. Then we's going to meet, at Wink's, around one. Party time, Momma."

"Yeah. He's going back to the warehouse, though?"

" 'S what he said. Just to drop off the truck. You want to catch him there, you better hustle your bustle."

"Winks. I can't keep up with your new places; activity clubs. Where's that?" She pulled a spiral steno book from her purse and picked up a pencil.

A glass pressed against a hollow core door is a poor substitute for a stethoscope, especially when a shower is running in the background. But it enabled Yearner to pick up about every third word that Viola spoke, enough to know that she had mentioned his name several times and was looking for someone named Willard. He heard her come toward the door and put the glass back on the sink as she came in.

"Honey, much as I hate to, I got to throw you out." Her British accent faded to black as she put on a shower cap and stepped under the water. "Mr. Reade just called; some kind of emergency just came up, and I got to go back down to the office. I sure would rather stay here and fuck you.''

''Mr. Reade, huh? I didn't hear the phone.''

''Yeah. Well, you were in the shower, honey. I mean I can hardly hear you talking, and you're right here. I'd say stay here, wait for me, only I could be down there all night, on the phone to Europe. It's tomorrow over there already.''

He tilted the steno pad and looked at the impressions under the raking rays of the bedside lamp, rubbed the pencil over the page, and then tore it off. She called for cabs and they left the building together. ''Tell him the Port Authority. Buses run out of there all night. Unless you want to catch a train to Philly.'' She touched his arm as he opened the cab's door for her, kissed his cheek. ''You're one hell of a lover, lover,'' she said, and slid across the seat. Yearner held the slip of paper under the interior light as her cab pulled away from the curb.

''This mean anything to you, pal? Winks? MacDougal Bleecker?''

The driver turned and looked at Yearner through the scabrous wire mesh that protected him from his passengers. ''Airport? You want go Kennedy? Port Authority. Big hotels, I know all big hotels. Where you want?''

At the Port Authority Yearner found a telephone book with the relevant pages intact. Plenty of MacDougals and Bleeckers but none connected in a single name. Winks drew a blank in both yellow and white pages. He approached a pair of cops in their car.

''I don't know what Winks is, pal, but MacDougal and Bleecker are streets. In the Village.'' The cop looked Yearner over. ''Down Washington Square. Where the fairies hang out.''

The other cop leaned across from behind the wheel. ''Watch your ass, you go down there, buddy,'' he said, and laughed.

''Yeah, I'll do that, much obliged. How do I find a cab driver that knows how to get there? Last cabbie hardly spoke English.''

Both cops laughed. ''You don't want much, do you, pal? This time of night all you got is fuckin' Chinks and Iranians. Take the subway there, the A train. Get off at Fourth Street, Bleecker's a couple a blocks south.'' He pointed at the steps leading down to the subway. ''Just follow the signs down there; remember, A Train. Long as you got your Uzi, couple a grenade launchers, you won't have no problems.''

Both cops laughed as Yearner went toward the subway entrance, stepping over a sleeping derelict and around a leather-skirted transvestite who asked him for a date in a bored baritone. New York, New York. Rude by day and lewd by night.

*   *   *

"Joe ain't here. Who's this?"

"I'm . . . ah—a business associate of his, from New York. We're involved in a trucking deal. It's pretty important that I talk to him; any way I can get hold of him tonight?"

"Trucks? Hey, you the guy with the rigs we grabbed? Me and Hunch?"

"Who is this?"

"Gloeckner, Red Gloeckner. Me and Hunchie are the ones nabbed the loads for you, took 'em up the place there, Seventh Avenue."

"Red, yes, Skean mentioned your name. Listen, we have a problem developing, why I have to talk to Joseph."

"Well, fuck, he's up *in* New York, hauled a load of meat up there this after. Ain't back yet; but he told me he's got to stop and see that Willard guy, Borzillo. Pick up the rest of the loot. For that last truck. Hey, how come you don't know this?"

"Because I left it up to Willard to make the payout. Did he say where they were going to meet?"

"No; New York, is all. What's the problem?" He stood at the wall phone, looked across the kitchen at the girl at the table, put out his left fist, thumb and little finger extended, made a drinking motion. She brought him a can of Miller's from the refrigerator, popped the top for him.

"I've been entertaining a fellow named Defoe, from the trucker's insurance company, all evening; trying to expedite a payout on those loads. But I just found out his associate, a man named Yearner Claxon, is not from any insurance company. He's an agent for the Pennsylvania Game Commission. I think Skean needs to know about this."

"A Gamey! Fuck. I had a little tussle with one of them dudes last night. I wonder it's the same guy. What'd he look like?"

"I haven't seen him."

"How about this other one?"

"Defoe, Chase Defoe. He's in his mid-forties, I'd guess. Short, about five six or so. Well dressed; looks pretty fit."

"Son of a bitch. Sounds like the fucker half tore my ear off last night, we were set to do a number on that warden. I'd guess you got the two of 'em up there, pal."

"I don't like it. Either way, the trucks or the venison, they could be getting close to the whole thing. We have to act, before this situation falls apart. Listen, Red. Joe tells me you're the one who jumped those drivers, says you handled it real well. Here's what I want you to do. Get to this Defoe's place, break in if you have to.

But find out about him, who the hell he is. If he's with the police we need to know. He left me his card, has his address on it. RD Topton; 474 Berne Road. Think you can find it?''

"Yeah; wait up a minute, pal. Suppose somebody's home, calls the cops, throws down on me?''

"Don't worry about it, he's single and too straight for a girlfriend, you know what I'm saying. Besides, he just left here. You have two or three hours, at least.'' Reade paused for a moment, thinking. "You handle this right, Red, there'll be a real nice bonus in it for you, you got that?''

"I got that. The fuck I do with what I find there?''

"Call me at this number. You as good with a gun as you are with your fists?''

Red paused for a moment before answering, working out what the man was getting to. "Yeah,'' he finally said, and hung up.

"I need to go run an errand, honeypot,'' he said to the girl. "But we got us time to finish up what we was about, when he called.'' He put down the beer can and smiled at her, drawing his lips back over his teeth. "I believe,'' he said, "you were about to suck me off.''

CHAPTER **19**

Yearner came up out of the depths of the New York subway system, got his bearings, and headed east to MacDougal then south to Bleecker, marveling at the fauna of the urban jungle at one A.M. He noted the Cafè Borgia and Le Figaro across the way, then spotted a Chinese restaurant on the northwest corner and realized he had eaten little since breakfast. As he approached the entrance he spotted the pulsating sign several doors up the street. An extremely graphic depiction in red neon was bracketed by the words "Winking Sphincter" and he knew he had found what he had come for.

The cab stopped and Willard Borzillo got out, leaned back through the open door, and said something to Viola. Yearner saw and recognized her, the exotic beauty of her face momentarily illuminated under the interior light of the taxi. Their eyes locked for an instant as he turned away. It was dark and he was hardly expected here and wore the horn-rimmed frames; surely she had shrugged it off as a coincidental resemblance.

He had the bulk of a sumo wrestler, wore greasy denim and black leather punctuated with silver stars and studs. He shaved his head and affected a large gold hoop in one ear. Yearner watched him go into the club, then bought an eggroll and a quart of beer, dined against a wire trash basket in front of the Chinese restaurant and waited.

Willard and a man left the bar, Yearner watched them walk fifty feet up the block, stop and talk beside a van.

He passed them with a shuffling stagger, turned, and noted the Pennsylvania tags, memorized the numbers.

Skean got behind the wheel, headed west as Borzillo walked east on Bleecker toward Yearner, who picked up his pace.

An alley loomed, dark on the left, and Yearner decided to stop and pee, let the Neanderthal pass, and follow him. He was fumbling with his fly when the punch hit him under his cracked right rib and he gasped, going down.

"Viola's boyfriend," Willard laughed. "Ain't too bright, are you?" He aimed a kick at the prone and writhing Claxon who skittered away and got to his feet, deeper in the alley. "She seen you, in front of Winks. You dumb fuck. How'd you get down here ahead of her?" He pulled a lockback out of his jacket and opened the blade with a loud click. "And how'd you get onto the trucks? Not that it matters now. 'Cause you going *down*." He lunged at Yearner who skipped back a step, shallow breathing in little puffs to favor his side, buying time as he checked his rear, flicking his eyes over his adversary and the weapon. Six-inch blade, held low in a grip that said he knew how to use it. The man was big and Buddha fat, but muscle-rippled under the lard. The fire had been reignited in his ribs and he wished to hell he had brought his anklepiece along, fuck the Sullivan laws.

He feinted with his left and Willard slashed his forearm, cutting through the tweed to the flesh.

Quick, too, Yearner thought as the red haze of pain mixed with the adrenaline of the moment, canceling the sex and alcohol serenity that had dominated the evening. He went again with his left, might as well cut it up good and settle this one way or the other. With his ribs he couldn't go the full fifteen rounds. The blade cut him left again, deep, as his right thumb went into Willard's eye socket and he felt the jelly sphere against his nail.

The man screamed and hacked to his right as Yearner withdrew, brought his left leg up, toes extended, snapping his knee for full acceleration into his adversary's crotch.

A quarter second after contact, Yearner vowed to never again fight while wearing Hush Puppies; his big toe broke with a crack that was audible above the scream that announced Willard's wounded balls. As the big man doubled forward, Yearner whirled away and threw his right heel up in an Oriental move he had rehearsed but never used before in anger. His heel caught Willard full in the throat and crushed his larynx; he died, thrashing in the alley, with the sounds of a flushing toilet clawing their way out of his lungs and the stink of voided bowel in his leather pants.

Death by asphyxia takes the full three minutes, longer for a nonsmoker. Yearner watched him go, shallow breathing in little whimpers against the alley wall, cradling his ribs and arm, the crippled foot extended along the line that joined brick and asphalt.

Yearner slashed his sleeve to see and read the wounded flesh; folded the knife, dropped it in his pocket, and holding his forearm tight against his side, limped from the alley, cursing the pain in his toe.

It was not until he sank into the back of the taxi that he began to shake. Two blocks along he opened the door at a traffic light and vomited in the street. Eight years in the Corps; Lebanon, Grenada. And he had never killed another human, until tonight.

"Hey, I appreciate it, y'know? Most guys flash on the fuckin' floor." The cabbie turned in his seat as he pulled away from the light. "You all right, pal? Looks like you got more than a little too much sauce to deal with."

"Hey, you speak English; Christ." Yearner sank back in the seat, relaxed an iota against the familiarity of a fellow American in a foreign land. He coughed a laugh at the ridiculous premise; he was in New York, not Beirut. "Yeah," he said, struggling to sit up. "But I could use some first aid. Think you can find an all-night drugstore?"

The cabbie was from Brooklyn and moonlighting three nights from his regular job as a body-and-fender man at Midtown Mercedes. On account of his daughter was a Sophomore at CUNY and wanted to transfer to Cornell and be a vet. He handed the plastic bag to Yearner and gave him the change from the twenty. "You sure you're okay? I mean, you look like *shit*, pal. Lemme run you over Bellevue; this time a night it won't take ten minutes."

"I haven't got time; I'll be okay." And no way do I want to answer any questions about knife wounds to a New York cop. Yearner cracked a beer from the six-pack, offered the driver a can.

"No way; thanks anyhow. I got two hours to go, I have a frostie now, I'll fall asleep."

"Yeah, well." Yearner eased back and drained half the can. Coming down from a combat high, the brain does silly things. Reach out and hold a fellow human, grab a buddy and hold on. "That girl of yours, she's serious about being a vet, I could fix her up with a summer job, down Philadelphia, the New Bolton Center. Just washing cages, pitching hay, that kind of stuff. But she'd get a taste, see if it's real, or that teenage wet dream." He leaned forward and stuck his card through the mesh. "University of Pennsylvania runs it, their veterinary school. Nip and tuck with Cornell, know what I mean? Only right now, I got to rent a car, get back to Pennsy."

They tried Budget and Hertz, both of which closed at midnight, but found that Avis, trying harder, was open twenty-four hours on East Forty-third, in the shadow of the United Nations, and Yearner took the fifty out of his belt's zipper pocket, reminded the cabbie to give his card to his daughter.

He doctored in the men's room as the girl did the paperwork on a

Chevy with a big engine. A full roll of two-inch tape reinforced his ribs and another five yards from the second allowed him to walk on his left foot. The forearm took a little more work. Yearner used hot water to soak the shirtsleeve from the maroon wound. At one-thirty no one was around to hear him yell as he peeled the cloth from the cut. He pressed gauze pads against the slashes and wrapped his arm with the remainder of the tape. Stitches would have to wait.

Ms. Avis gave him a look as he gimped to the pay phone. He considered calling JoAnne; but he wasn't due to call in before morning and saw no reason to wake her. Instead he dialed the number for the Pennsylvania Department of Motor Vehicles. Radio calls were answered around the clock, but the telephone was a curiosity after five P.M. Finally, the duty officer picked up the phone and he identified himself. The van was registered to Joseph Skean and the game farm's address was given to Agent Claxon.

The door was open and the lights were on. A half-dozen wrinkled sketches of the cats were foot-scuffled and scattered across the floor; a box of charcoal sticks was crushed into the warp of the carpet. At the stairway he saw Magnificat.

Sprawled like a blind-sided road kill, the black fur was matted with coagulating blood; his brains and intestines were a dark smear across the Oriental rug.

Defoe smoothed and studied one of the charcoal portraits of the cat. Her talent was stunning; Caroline's work had the instantly recognizable style of draftsmen like Hirschfeld and Herblock combined with a realistic rendering of her subject that was the equal of any of the Wyeths. With a few soft strokes of a stick of charcoal she had created a portrait of the animal that Defoe at first mistook for a soft-focus photograph. He'd had no idea that she possessed that kind of raw talent; but then he should have guessed. Botticelli had never praised his mechanical skills.

A low meow made Defoe look up. No Name crouched on the steps above him, shivering.

He picked her up, sat on the iron stairs and held her against his face, softly stroking her fur as he looked at the room below. Several minutes passed before the cat relaxed and began to purr; he put her down, got a large bath towel and wrapped the remains of the black cat in it. He walked slowly around the big room, through the kitchen, then took a five-cell flashlight back outside.

In the powdery dirt and frost beside the Jaguar he spotted the now-familiar tire print, faint but unmistakable.

There was no sign that the intruder had been to the lower level.

JoAnne answered on the third ring, and he had to drive the catch from his voice before speaking.

"This is Chase Defoe; I called you this morning, asking for Yearner. I'm sorry to wake you, but this is important."

"Don't worry, it happens all the time, Mr. Defoe. But I haven't heard from him for some time now. He's not due to call me until eight."

"Yes, I know, I left him in New York, several hours ago. In good hands. But he was expecting information from a state trooper, an address on a suspect. Have you gotten it yet?"

"Yes, sir, he called today; but I don't know if I can give that out to you, not without Mr. Claxon's authorization."

"JoAnne, it's imperative that I have that address. He and I are both working on this together, did he tell you that?"

"Well, yes, I guess he did; I mean, he said he was going up to New York with you, and—"

"Exactly. And he's still working that end, while I'm following a new lead back here."

"I suppose it's okay then. But it's two addresses, where the guy lives and where he works. Gloeckner, Stanley Gloeckner. He lives in a trailer park, outside of Trexlertown. That's what's on his driver's license. But his truck registration lists the Hunter Game Farm as the address."

"Give them both to me, then. And make sure Yearner gets them as soon as he calls in.".

A battered athletic locker in one corner held two tennis rackets, a can of stale balls, several bamboo fly rods, a tackle box, and a Winchester 16 ga. pump gun. Defoe took a handful of green plastic shotshells from a box on the top shelf and dropped them in his pocket.

"Hello?"

"This is Gloeckner."

"Who are you calling, sir?"

"Who's this? I'm calling the guy up in New York, with the trucks. He there?"

There was a pause; Red could hear conversation in the background. Reade came on the line. "Mr. Gloeckner, I'm afraid I don't know you—"

"Red, this is Red. I talked to you a couple hours ago. About busting into that guy's house? Hey, while we're about it, I don't know your name. I mean, I'm supposed to be a part of this, I figure—"

"Right, Red; my omission. I'm Mr. Reade. I assume you have news from Defoe's residence."

"Yeah. Not what you wanted to hear, guy. You told me he lives alone. Not entirely true. I got out there, asshole's a half mile back a lane, I figure I got, like you said, a hour or so to nose around. Only there's a broad there. Drawing pictures. Fucker lives in a barn, only he's turned it into a house, sort of. Anyhow, I see the lights, I drift up to the door, cut the ignition so's not to, you know, so I don't make no noise. I peep in the window, see her there, with the chalk. But I guess she hears the truck. Anyway, the dumb cunt opens the door. Makes it easy for me, y'know? I don't have to kick it in. So I figure I'll play it cool, I ask for this Defoe, tell her he's a pal of mine. Told me to drop by for a brewski when I'm in the neighborhood. She's lookin' a little spooky, him not being there and all, but still cool. And then this fuckin' *cat* comes by. Size of a goddamn raccoon, rubbing against my leg. So I stomp the fucker. Shit, I can't stand cats, make my skin get all funny. Like snakes, y'know? Then, all of a sudden, no reason, she's a fuckin' firecracker; all over me, so I whacked her around a little. Then I grab the broad and split." He paused for breath and a slug of Miller and Reade jumped into the opening.

"Okay, Red, you did well," he said, controlling his anger. "What happened next?"

"Next? Nothing. I come back here, the farm. Tied the bitch up with some baler twine and parked her up the barn, stashed her in the grain room. And called you. Where the fuck's Joe?"

"Wait a minute, Red. You kidnapped this woman?"

"Well, what the hell. I mean, you told me there wasn't going to be nobody there, only she is. What the hell am I supposed to do?"

"Did you find out anything about this Defoe?"

"No; what the hell. With her and the cat and all, I split. I tell you one thing, though. She looks like a real piece. I'm gonna check it out better, things get sorted out."

"No, you sit tight there, by the phone. I haven't heard from Willard yet, but he has to have met with Skean by now; Joe's going to be back there any minute." Reade looked around the big room, gazed out across Central Park at the late-night lights that delineated the apartments along Fifth Avenue and bit into the knuckle of his thumb as though it were a Pennsylvania Dutch hard pretzel. *Shit!* "Sit tight," he said again. "When Joe gets back, tell him I'm on my way down there. We're going to pay this Defoe a visit."

Reade put down the telephone and yelled to Sancho. "Get my leathers out." He went to the ebony cabinet and after a very brief pause, selected the new .50 and a box of handloads. "Serve the son of a bitch right," he said, putting the gun and the cartridges into a canvas day pack along with a ballistic cloth web belt and holster.

The arm was throbbing now and he wished he had thought to have the cabbie buy a bottle of aspirin along with the rest of the first aid supplies. He opened another can of beer instead. Traffic was sparse through the tunnel and lighter still by the time he reached the turnpike entrance. He took a ticket from an automatic machine and accelerated back to speed. Now, at least, he could devote a little of his concentration to the events of the evening, sort things out.

It didn't make sense, the pieces didn't add up. Viola had been a bitch in heat at her place, and then she fingered him to that gorilla. He hadn't told her anything of consequence; she must have gone through his wallet while he was in the shower. And seen his ID. Nothing else in there to cause that kind of reaction. But how the hell could she be connected to deer poaching in Pennsylvania? Defoe had better know about this. His headlights bounced off the reflectors on the big sign. New Jersey Turnpike Authority. Rest Area Ahead. One Mile. Fuel. Food. Phone. Yearner eased off on the gas and dropped down to sixty-five in anticipation of the access lane.

He bought a package of painkillers from a vending machine in the men's room and called Defoe, looked around the rest stop while the telephone rang. A few late-night travelers sat scattered at the tables, hunched over their coffee. Truckers in insulated vests worked the cigarette machine, kidded with a tired girl at the cash register. Defoe didn't answer; Yearner left his message on the machine.

Yearner sipped the hot coffee and drummed his fingers on the rack of telephone books as he watched a young Hispanic with a sleeping child on his shoulder waiting by the doorway marked Women. He called JoAnne.

"Honey, I hate to wake you, but I got a bit of trouble right now. I tried to call that Defoe fella I went to New York with, but I can't get hold of him. I want to let you know what to tell him, in case he calls for me."

"I already talked to him, Yearner, about an hour ago. He called here, wanted the information on those tire tracks. He told me you and he were working on the same case. I hope I didn't do wrong."

"What? You gave him the info?"

"Yes, I did. He sounded so—*authoritative*, I guess is the word. I'm sorry, Yearner, I know I shouldn't have."

"No, no, JoAnne, that's okay, you did right. Only thing I don't understand is why he called you in the middle of the night. We'll have to coordinate this with the State Police, probably need a search warrant. This thing is going to take a day or two, what's his hurry? Did he say where he was calling from?''

"No, he didn't; just apologized for waking me."

"Okay. Better let me have the suspect's name, address."

"Yes. And Mr. Defoe did make a point of telling me to be sure you got the information when you checked in. I have two separate addresses, by the way. A trailer park on the license, but the vehicle registration lists a game farm up in Lehigh county."

"Game farm?" Yearner reached in his shirt pocket. "Not the Hunter Game Farm?"

"Yes, that's it. The truck's registered to a Stanley Gloeckner, same as his driver's license. But with the game farm's address."

"Aw, damn. Excuse my mouth. That's the same place a van I just saw in New York is from. Listen. Defoe calls back, I don't expect he will, but if he does, you tell him to stay the hell *away* from that place, wait to hear from me. And try calling him every half hour or so; he may not be back from New York yet. But I got a bad feeling that he is. I'm heading for that place, the game farm, right now. You don't hear from me by—'' He looked at his watch, thought about where he was, and estimated travel time to the farm. "You don't hear from me by six o'clock, call out the troops. Send the Staties to this game farm."

He bought a Pennsylvania map from a vending machine and saw that the quickest way to the game farm missed his truck and its armaments by twenty miles. Sometimes you just had to go into battle naked. He'd done it earlier in the evening and come out, if not a winner, at least the survivor. Somehow, though, he didn't think the men at Hunter's Game Farm would be armed with just a lockback hunting knife. He accelerated up the entrance to the turnpike.

The trailer park had narrow roads with speed bumps every hundred yards and a sprinkling of potholes between. A dog began to bark as Defoe drifted past at ten miles an hour, looking for the number he had jotted on the scrap of paper. Most of the trailers were dark; blue light flickered from a window here and there, signifying insomnia and the *Late Late Show*.

He found Gloeckner's trailer, dark and silent, no sign of vehicle or occupant. A detailed map of eastern Pennsylvania was in the glove box of the Jaguar and Defoe unfolded it, training his flashlight on the roads, plotting his trajectory to the game farm.

The faded sign had been painted thirty years earlier on a four-by-eight sheet of plywood, and simply said HUNTER GAME FARM.

EXOTIC WILDFOWL, but it was enough to slow Defoe on the winding secondary road. Moonlight illuminated the gravel lane that, not unlike his own, disappeared through the woods. He parked a hundred yards farther along and noted that he had not seen another sign of habitation for several miles. He loaded four shells in the Winchester, pumped a cartridge into the chamber, and set the safety. The moon was bright enough to leave the flashlight in the car. He thought about entering through the woods, but it was predominantly second growth and promised slow passage. He would use the lane, with caution.

The rutted gravel tracks bracketed a central hump of kinder soil that supported a spotty growth of grass, green fading to brown with the onset of fall. The moonlight bounced off the ice crystals forming on the leaves and they crunched underfoot.

He had steadily climbed since turning north at Allentown and was now another five hundred feet above the level of his own farm; *I'm glad*, he thought, *that we picked the tender crops before tonight.*

He stopped and turned up his collar against the cold, watched his breath against the night, and listened. *God, let her be all right.*

The lane made a gentle curve to the right and the treeline gave way to open ground on his left. A single strand of barbed wire, chest high, delineated the boundary between field and road. He walked along for fifty yards before finding a fencepost, an eight-foot-length of creosoted utility pole, braced on both sides by massive angled beams. The barbed wire was fastened to the pole on either side by a wrist-thick coil spring and a porcelain insulator. A second wire, offset into the field by a section of two-by-four, was strung at ankle height.

High tensile fencing, developed in New Zealand and now found around the world, used the principle of tightly stretched wire to contain or deter the most determined animal. Charging buffalo in Wyoming bounced off the wires strung by the National Park Service. A decade earlier they had routinely trampled a hundred miles of chain-link fencing into a tangled mess. Elephants in Tanzania ravished the orchards bordering the Serengeti Park until the singing wires were stretched. Add an electrical charge and even the horse, dumbest of domestic animals, quickly learns the boundaries of their domain.

A snort and a nasal whistle in the dark told Defoe that deer were to his left; he paused and watched the phantom shapes move in the night, then turned his attention to the farmhouse a hundred yards down the lane.

A herd of deer surely meant no dogs were loose, but he stopped and watched and listened nonetheless. White fluorescent light radiated from a ground-floor window of the farmhouse, probably the kitchen. A pale-yellow glow from a small window in the upper level of the barn drew his attention to that structure. It stood at the far end of the farmyard, against a slope that rose into the woods to the north. A solid board fence enclosed the forecourt facing him; even from this distance and in the dark he could see its substantial construction. "Horse high, bull strong, and hog tight" was the expression his ancient neighbor used in describing such a fence. Whatever was in there was meant to stay behind its confines.

A pickup truck sat high on its chassis midway between the barn and the farmhouse; Defoe somehow knew this was the vehicle whose tire prints had become his grail. But where was Caroline?

Mobay took the Carlisle exit and exchanged the turnpike for Route 81. He'd bypass Harrisburg and Lancaster to the south, go north through Frackville and Mahanoy City, head east past the coal country towns of Tamaqua, Jim Thorpe, Lehighton, and drop down on the farm from above. Nine hours with an empty trailer and six thousand cash in the glove box, he wanted to get back home, sleep in his own bed, share the trip with Joe. He drained the last cold drops of the turnpike coffee and looked at his watch. Nearly three. Another hour and he'd be there.

Sudden movement draws the eye and Defoe hugged the shadows of the fenceline, silently cursing the full moon, drifting slowly toward the lighted zone of the farmhouse, running over the possibilities. The big guy with the truck was here, the one he had encountered what now seemed so long ago at the garage. Two others had been with him when Yearner had been jumped.

He assumed that Caroline was here, else why was he? The other two. Four in a pickup's cab? Maybe one other. *Shit, Defoe, you're stalling. Make your move.*

Red crumpled the can of Coors and bounced it off the wall. *Fuck this shit!* Sit around and wait for everybody else. Go the hell up the barn and snatch a piece, before the others get in line. But first another brew.

The three-thousand-year-old dictum of warfare was "take the high ground," and Defoe heeded the advice. He ducked under the barbed wire, skirted the barnyard, and reemerged on the upper side of the pasture, having flanked the barn and the farmhouse.

*   *   *

Red opened the bottom door and stepped into the barn. The hogs stirred briefly in their shallow, feral sleep as he felt his way toward the steep stairs that led to the upper level. Lights would wake the fuckers, turn them into a squealing mass demanding feed. Let 'em wait for Joe. Or that asshole Mobay. "Don't mess wiff my pigths," the fat fucker said. Fine then; feed 'em when you get home. I'm going upstairs for a piece a pussy. The treads creaked under his weight.

Defoe came up the ramp and stopped at the big doors. It was dark on the north side of the building; the treeline filtered the moonlight to a pale shadow. He could make out a small door set into the left of the larger pair, its boundaries delineated by the hand-wrought hinges on the right and the opposing iron latch. The occasional crack in the aged planks glowed with the yellow of the incandescent bulb inside. He rested the shotgun against the wood and eased the iron across the opening with both hands, striving for stealth.

Red swallowed the last of the beer and was about to crush the can in his fist when he heard the sound of the keeper sliding across the rusty latch.

Skean stopped at the Sunoco off the interstate, pissed while they gassed the van, then worked the machines beside the register for coffee and a Baby Ruth. He threw a twenty on the countertop, waited while the boy made change.

"Gimme some quarters, kid," he said, leaving a dollar bill on the greasy plastic. He let the phone ring a long time before hanging up.

"Dickhead," he said under his breath as he left the warmth of the oasis.

Defoe eased through the board-and-batten door and was reaching back for the shotgun when Red hit him between the shoulder blades with a right jab.

He arched his back, fell forward, and sucked air with a truncated scream as he hit and caromed off a corner of a cutting table. Under the feeble light of the single bulb he took a quarter-second inventory of the loft as he went down; rough plank flooring, three inches thick with a scant covering of stale hay and straw, a pair of battered stainless tables, and gambrels hanging from the beams by rusty chains. Freshly fleshed hides, salted and racked on wire frames around the room; the black rectangle that was a feed chute to the livestock floor below.

Red was on him as he rolled; quick for such a big man, he used a hammerlock to immobilize and a forearm across the throat to sharpen the attention as he hauled the smaller man to his feet.

Defoe instinctively tried to bring his knee up into his assailant's groin and found himself crushed against the poplar siding by Gloeckner's bulk. A head slap from an open right hand set off sharp stabs of light; he lost track of reality as the baler twine bit into his wrists.

He struggled back to consciousness as he felt Red's hands paw his pants, then settle on the inside pocket of his suit, opened his eyes as Gloeckner fumbled his wallet open, extracted his driver's license.

"Well, well, well. So you're this Mr. Defoe." He smiled down at his captive, all pink gums and shiny teeth under the swaying light bulb. "You the fucker what like to tear my ear off last Friday night, ain't you?" He folded the cash from Defoe's wallet and tossed the billfold on the floor, tucked the money in his jeans. "Sure get around, don't you, little man?"

He turned and touched the bandage across the side of his head. "You and that Game Protector. Huh. I was about to do a number on him, you showed up. Well, fuck it." He had tied Defoe's hands behind his back with several lengths of sisal clipped from the bales of alfalfa that were stacked against one wall. He prodded Defoe with the toe of his high top. "I guess I'll just have to do me a number on *you*, instead." He grabbed Defoe by one foot and dragged him across the floor to the air compressor, hit the control switch. The light dimmed momentarily as the half-horse motor kicked in, chugging steadily as the tank built pressure.

Gloeckner picked up the red rubber hose and popped the valve, bleeding a jet of air through the needle.

"Time I get through with you, you gonna look like that Michelin Man." He lifted Defoe by the right leg until just his shoulders touched the floor, wrapped his left arm around the calf, and jabbed the needle under the skin at the Achille's tendon.

The pressure of the air began to tear the dermis from the muscle below; it burned like liquid fire as the bubble began its inexorable progression toward his knee. He screamed.

Red laughed. "Bet it feels about like my ear did, the other night, don't it?" He shifted his grip, giving the pressure bubble access to a new section of Defoe's leg.

His pulse pounded in his ears and sweat chilled his skin; he felt his bladder let go. Defoe threw his free leg back over his head in the direction of the compressor in a desperate attempt to stop the air that was tearing his leg apart. He thrust his foot between the V belt and pulley that connected the motor to the pump. The rubber squealed against his shoe, dragged his ankle against the edge of the pulley, giving him another, newer, pain to deal with.

His foot finally was sucked into the tangent of belt and pulley, jammed there; the motor hummed and heated, sent its thermal message back to the basement of the farmhouse where a tiny dollop of lead melted in the fuse and shut down the line to the barn. The light went out.

"What the fuck?" Red dropped Defoe's leg and looked around in the blackness of the barn. "Blew the fuckin' fuse." He kicked out at Defoe in the dark, connected with a thigh. "Don't go nowheres, pal." Red laughed and slowly shuffled his way toward the door, cursing once under his breath as he stumbled against an unseen object.

Defoe heard him work the latch, saw the blackness of the wall change to the dark gray of the doorway, watched the darker shape of Gloeckner pass through, listened to his footsteps recede. He rolled on his back, willing the fire in his leg to lessen, tried to clear his mind, set a course of action. "Chase!" he thought he heard, "Chase!", but the pounding in his temples shut out the reality of the world outside his head; he was so focused inward he did not react until the banging brought him back to reality.

"hase! *Answer* me, for God's sake!"

"Caroline?"

"Chase!"

"Caroline! Where are you?"

"In here. Get me out."

He rolled to a sitting position, then got to his feet, gasping with the intensity of the pain as his muscles worked against the separated skin. His night vision began to improve and he could make out shapes in the feeble moonlight. To the right of the doors he saw the bulk of the walk-in cooler, on the left the board-and-batten door of the grain room. He hopped toward it, trying to keep his damaged leg from contacting the floor, for each touch sent pain like shards of glass up his leg.

A rough wooden latch, pivoting on a sixteen penny nail, held the door fast. He pushed it with his chin until it was vertical and the door opened. She stumbled out, arms in front of her, bumped against Defoe, who cried out.

"Chase; oh, God! What did he do to you? I heard you out there. Hold me, Chase. Please."

"I can't, my hands are tied. Our captor was amusing himself with an air hose. Listen. We have to act quickly. You get out of here, right now. Can you walk?"

"Yes, sure; what about you? I'm not leaving by myself!"

"You have to, Caroline. I can't walk; my right leg's shot."

They leaned against each other in the gloom; she raised her hands in front of her, touched his face. He felt the rough twine that bound her wrists together against his cheek. "I'm not leaving you here for that *monster*," she said. "We'll go together; I'll help."

"No good, we'd never make it. I told you, my leg is useless." He heard the tenacity in her voice and took a deep breath, regrouped his thoughts. "We've got to get these ropes off if we're to have any chance at all. Try to find my wallet; he took the cash I had and threw it on the floor, over by the tables."

"Chase! Never mind your wallet, we've got to—"

"Listen. Do as I say. There's a single-edged razor blade, behind the credit cards. Find the wallet and we may have a chance. We'll prepare an ambush for that bastard."

She began to search the floor, mostly by feel, shuffling her feet in the straw. After several minutes she stopped. "Oh, it's useless, Chase; I'll never find it in time." There was panic in her voice. "Can't you walk, just a little? Lean on me."

Defoe had pushed the pain to the back of his mind and was able to concentrate on their situation. "Caroline. I haven't been thinking clearly; here's our way out of this; listen. The house is a hundred, a couple of hundred feet away, and it's dark out. Takes a minute or two to walk it, especially now, at night. He said I blew the fuse; that means he went to fix it. When the light goes on we have at least two minutes before he gets back. So we get ready." Defoe hopped over to her, stood in the center of the loft, canted to one side on his good leg. "When that light goes back on, take a deep breath and look for the wallet. It's going to be right in front of us; it's black, will show nicely against all this straw." He spoke slowly, trying to calm the panic he had felt in her voice. "Pick it up, open it. The credit cards are in a slot on the left side. Pull them out. The razor blade has a cardboard sleeve to protect the edge. If you can't get it off quickly with your hands tied, use your teeth. I think I'm about under the light bulb; when it goes on I'll turn and you cut the ropes. You got that?" He paused and took a breath, fought against the frustration of his bonds.

"Yes, right. I'm ready."

"Good. Now, the next thing. We aren't going to have time for me to cut you free also. You can run, your hands are tied in front of you. As soon as my hands are free, get out of here, head up into the woods. Keep going, no matter what. He won't come after you, in the dark, not with me here. You understand?"

"Chase, I—"

"Don't argue!"

Caroline employed the ultimate argument against Defoe's logic. She began to cry. She had been punched, slapped, kidnapped, bound, and locked in a musty-smelling room with sacks of feed and the skitter of rodents in the dark for half the night. Listened to Defoe being tortured by that animal with the obscene grin. Somehow providence had reunited them, but Defoe was intent on splitting them apart; committing suicide to ensure her flight to safety. She hung her head and wept, her will spent; tears coursed down her cheeks as

The light came on.

"Okay. Calmly. Look for the wallet. We have plenty of time, Caroline." Defoe moved to her side, looked at the floor. He began to quarter the area with his eyes, searching in segments as he said, "Feel with your feet; pick a lane, move forward, sweeping the straw, slowly; don't miss it. Plenty of time." He scanned, saw nothing, went back in his mind to the moment when Gloeckner had torn the wallet from his coat, saw the image in his inward eye, the big man stuffing the bills in his jeans, tossing the billfold aside.

"There! Look over by the compressor, around the walk-in box. I'm pretty sure that's where he threw it." More than a minute had passed since the power had returned, and he knew that their freedom of movement was rapidly dwindling. And the knowledge hit him in the chest with a thud; he broke out in a cold sweat, smelled the stink of fear in his armpits and felt the flush upon his face. Shit. How had he forgotten; the pain inflicted by the air hose must have completely ruined his reason. The goddamned shotgun, resting just outside the barn doors. You damn, dumb, stupid son of a bitch, Defoe! Could Caroline handle it, her hands tied? Too late now. Can't risk distracting her concentration. Have to hope she finds the wallet finds the wallet finds the wallet

She felt with her feet as the agonizing seconds passed. And picked it up as Gloeckner came through the door. The shotgun at port arms.

"Found this little Sweet Sixteen outside the door. Brung me a present, did you, old fucker?" He looked at Caroline, drew his lips back in a parody of a smile. "Hey, honey pot. I guess you know each other, hey? And you know what? I got so interested in Defoe here, I forgot all about you, tucked away there." He turned to Defoe. "I fixed up the electric for you. Real good. Ain't no more fuses, so I put a penny in the box. We gonna have all the air we want now. No more interruptions, old man." He took two steps forward, raised the gun butt, and drove it into Defoe's chest, knocking him back across the loft.

He thought his sternum had ruptured with the force of the blow; he couldn't catch his breath and he lay on his back, saw the purlins and their overburden of slate pulsate as he struggled to retain consciousness.

Red grabbed Caroline and she dropped the wallet as he threw her against the stainless-steel cutting table, laid the shotgun across its top. "Hey, you old fuck," he said. "Pay attention now. Before we get on with your skinning, I want you to watch this." He looked over at Defoe, who had gotten to his knees and was gasping for air.

Red held Caroline's hands with his left, snatched at her waist with the right, pulled her pants down and off, did the same with her underpants, and forced her to lie back on the table, her legs hanging over the edge. Still holding her hands, he fumbled with his own trousers, dropped them around his ankles. "I'm going to show you how to fuck a woman, old man." He stepped forward, levering her thighs apart with his own.

Defoe fell onto his side and groaned, rolled onto his back, felt the smooth leather of his wallet against his wrist.

Gloeckner leaned his weight on Caroline, reached down with his free hand, forced his cock into her, turned his head and smiled at Defoe as he began to move his hips in the rhythmical thrust of sex.

Defoe moved onto his side in the shadows and worked the blade at the bonds. Gloeckner had snugged the rough sisal tight, and the tissue had swollen since the knots had been tied. Defoe sliced as much flesh as baler twine and the blade became sticky with blood. He was past pain and continued to cut in ever-increasing arcs. He was well aware that the imminent little death of Gloeckner foreshadowed by but a moment his own far more final demise.

Red's attention switched from Defoe's agony to the woman beneath him as he approached his climax and he was oblivious to Defoe's sudden shift from subjugation to attack.

The singletree was four feet of hickory with wrought-iron end caps, the sole vestige of long-gone harness; the leather traces, collar, and martingale had faded with the last plow horse half a century before.

Defoe swung from his knees and hit the back of Red's; the big man buckled, fell away from Caroline, and grabbed the Winchester as he went down in a tangle of trousers around his heels.

Defoe swung again and missed as Red got to his feet, aimed the shotgun at Defoe one-handed and squeezed the trigger.

The safety did its job and nothing happened. Defoe thrust the singletree up at Red's face; the bigger man parried with the barrel of the gun and grabbed the piece of wood with his other hand.

He pulled and Defoe let go. Red staggered backward, clutching the gun and the length of hickory, his ankles hobbled by his pants. He lost his balance, stepped backward over the black hole that was the feed chute to the pens below.

Defoe heard him hit in the wet mud.

The hungry hogs moved in on the exposed genitals first, going for the soft and easy parts. Red released the safety and fired once before the boars took over.

CHAPTER 20

Caroline pulled her clothes back on and listened to the frenzied screams overriding the lower, guttural sounds coming from the dark hole, looked over at Defoe. "What's *down* there?"

He shook his head, eased himself into a sitting position against a table leg. "Don't know. Some kind of animal that needs a high fence. Whatever it is, Mr. Gloeckner won't be tormenting us anymore. Are you all right?"

"I'm okay, physically. Some bruises; that son of a bitch hit me a couple of times, back at the barn." She crawled over beside him, reached out for his hand. "I don't want to think about the other part, the mental. I'll probably fall apart if I do."

"Come on then, Caroline, help me with this leg. We have to get out of here before any of the others show up."

"Others?"

"He had two helpers at the garage the other night. And Gloeckner hardly struck me as the brains behind anything more complex than a mugging."

Caroline cut a burlap feed sack into strips and wound them tightly around Defoe's lower leg, immobilizing the separated skin against the muscle beneath, told him about Red's arrival at the barn and the death of Magnificat while she rolled his sock up over the makeshift bandage.

"Someone sent him there, gave him my address. But why?" He looked at the drying hides. "These have to be the people that Yearner is after, the poachers. Only Gloeckner, or at least his truck, was at the hijacking of one of the loads of clothing." He shook his head. "Doesn't make sense, not yet. But the two are connected." He put his arm around her, pulled her to him, touched her cheek. "I'm sorry you got involved in this, Caroline. God! If I'd thought in a million years—"

"Hey, I know that, you dummy. You think I blame you for any of this? Hell, you're my *hero*; you rescued me from that big scumball." She turned and cupped his face with both hands, kissed him gently. "Sir Chase, my savior."

He stood and tested his weight on his leg, shook his trousers with his fingertips and laughed. "Some hero. I pissed myself, when he shoved that air gun into my leg. Come on, Caroline, let's get away from this place, I haven't saved anything yet."

Red's truck was locked and Defoe's leg was pooling fluid. He sat on the running board, touched his calf. "I'll never make it all the way out to the road, Caroline, this lane is longer than mine. You'll have to bring the Jag in here. It's a few hundred yards up on the left, key's under the seat. Hurry."

The damp of the night had congealed in the Jaguar's electricals once again and Caroline was trying to figure the secret to opening the beast's bonnet when the lights of the van presaged its arrival.

"Thank God you came along, sir," she said, crossing the road as the driver rolled down his window. "The car won't start and it's kind of an emergency; I wonder if you can help?"

"Don't know nothin' about foreign cars. I can run you out to that all-night Exxon on 209. Ain't much they can do much for ya, though, 'cept send the tow truck. Them foreign machines're tricky, lady."

"No, I can't; I mean, my friend's injured, I can't leave him."

"Yeah?"

She nodded. "Back down that lane, down there a little. It's a long story, but he hurt his leg, and I have to get him out of there."

"Well, come on then, get in, let's go fetch your friend."

Caroline ran around the other side of the van and climbed in, offering her thanks, and Mobay started up and turned down the lane to the game farm.

Defoe saw the lights, knew they were not his own and rolled under the truck before realizing that it sat so high on its chassis that he was a sprawling, if not sitting, duck.

Mobay pulled past the pickup and parked beside the farmhouse. Defoe watched Caroline get out, and then the driver, and he crawled from his tentative cover.

"I couldn't start your car, Chase," she said, "and luckily this man stopped. He's offered to take us to a garage."

"Lucky indeed," Defoe said, extending his hand. "That's hardly a well-traveled highway out there, not at four A.M. Chase Defoe."

"Mobay. Lady said your leg's hurt. What're you doin' back here?" He produced a pouch of chewing tobacco and filled his cheek.

"Our car broke down. Caroline said you offered to drive us to a garage, and I much appreciate it, sir. Think we could head out?"

"Yeah. Where's the guy owns thisth truck?"

"I don't know," Defoe said, and looked at Caroline. "We came back to use their phone, but nobody's home."

"You hurt your leg before or after you walked the lane?" Mobay worked the quid, spat. "Come on. Let's go inside once, set down and figure this out." He took Caroline by the arm and assumed that Defoe would follow.

He watched the big man move toward the farmhouse. Too many years before, Defoe had competed in the modern pentathlon; run, ride, and swim. Fence and shoot. He had been in the peak of conditioning, placed fourteenth at Tokyo. He wouldn't have gone up against Mobay then. He followed.

"Now then," Mobay said, having pulled out two kitchen chairs and pointed Defoe and Caroline into them, "What the fuck'th going on? Where'th Red?"

Defoe drew a breath and attacked. "We've been monitoring your operation for months now and moved in tonight. Obviously we miscalculated; Gloeckner was the only one here and he died resisting arrest. I have a backup team down the road, waiting for the rest of your bunch to arrive. You're the first; very fortunate, for you. Cooperate with us and I personally guarantee that your assistance will reflect favorably on your case at sentencing."

"Red's dead? Who the fuck are you? What's this all about?" He swatted his face, rubbed his bristly stubble with a hand the size of a grizzly's paw and muttered, "Goddamnit, Joe, where the *hell* are you?"

Skean parked beside Mobay's van and stock trailer and flexed his shoulders, rotated his head, taking in the starry sky as his skull slowly spun, easing the kinks out of his neck.

"Mobes! You're back; I didn't figure on seeing you until tomorrow. Who're them?"

"Guy says they been watchin' us for months, the operation. Says Red's dead. Don't make no sense to me."

Skean said, "Who are you?"

"Said his name's Defoe, Joe."

"Defoe! Willard told me about you, couple hours ago."

"Who'sth Willard?"

"Uh, guy up New York, Mobes. You don't know him."

"Yeah. You still foolin' with that truck shit, ain't you?"

"No, no. I took the load from the cooler up, like we agreed. This

Defoe guy is connected with the Game Commission, someway. Or at least a dude with him is. It's kind of complicated. You remember the one Red tangled with, Friday. When he got his ear tore up. They were nosing around New York, last I heard. How'd they wind up here?"

"They was here when I pulled in. I don't know nothin' about this, Joe. But I don't like it."

"Yeah, yeah, I hear you. Listen, Defoe. You better start telling me what the hell's going on, you want to stay happy."

"At the moment the only charges against the two of you are receiving illegally harvested wildlife. That involves civil, but not criminal penalties. You'll get off with a fine. Continue to hold us here, though, and you're interfering with a federal officer in the execution of his duties and you're looking at ten years, mandatory. In a federal penitentiary."

"You don't look like no federal nothing to me, Defoe. Who's she?"

This one seemed twice as bright as the other two, together, and Defoe decided to try a different version of the truth. "Look, just let us go, drive us back out to my car and you're off the hook. The only evidence against you right now is a bunch of deerskins in your barn. Be tough to make much of a case on just that. Especially since we're here without a warrant. By the time someone from the Game Commission gets in here with one, those hides might not even be there. Blame the whole thing on Gloeckner. The only reason I'm here, is he broke into my house, kidnapped her." He nodded toward Caroline. "His truck's registered to the game farm, you can say the whole thing was his doing."

"Yeah, that's right," Skean said. "What's this about Red?"

"Guy said he was dead, Joe. Rethisthing arrethst."

Skean shook his head, went to the refrigerator, and opened a can of beer. "What about it, Defoe?"

Defoe sighed, leaned back in the chair, eased his leg out straight. It felt numb. "In the top of your barn, up there. We fought and he fell into the yard below. Whatever you have down there got him."

"Jesus! The pigths, Joe. He fell down the feed chute. God*damn*."

Skean put down the beer can on the drainboard and lit a cigarette. "Yeah," he said under his breath, exhaling smoke.

"So," Defoe said, "that make's it neat, right? Red kidnapped my associate here, brought her to the farm. Tried to kill me. Serious charges, if he were alive. But the two of you, you can walk away from this right now. The key is 'right now.' Come on, Caroline. Let's go out to Mobay's van. He's going to drive us back out to the

Jag, help me start it.'' Defoe got up, leaned on the table, tested his leg against the floor.

"Soundths like he's making senseth, Joe. I don't want to hear about no *kidnapping*."

Skean leaned against the sink and smoked, watched Defoe and the woman. "Yeah." Except you don't know about the trucks, Mobes, and how Willard says this Defoe was all over Reade's case today. Of course with Red gone, Hunchie is the only one who can connect that with me. We get shed of this Defoe and there nothin' holding us here. With the money Mobes brought back from Ohio we got close to forty thousand, cash. Enough to get us a good start a long ways off. He dropped his cigarette in the beer, listened to it sizzle. "You got a deal, Defoe. Run 'em out to the road, Mobes." While I pack.

"Now who the fuckth's that?" Mobay looked out the window as the motorcycle passed the vans and the rider rocked the machine back on its kickstand.

"Well, Mr. *Defoe*," Reade said, pulling off his helmet under the fluorescent fixture. "An unexpected surprise. I anticipated going hunting for you." He turned to Mobay. "You must be Red."

"No, this is my partner. Mobay."

"Where is he? I spoke to him earlier this evening. I assume this is the woman that he picked up at Defoe's."

"Defoe says that Red's dead; fell in with the boars. We was just getting ready to run them the hell out of here. They got nothing on us, Quentin."

Reade turned and looked at Defoe. "Leave? Oh, no, that's quite out of the question. Isn't it, Mr. Defoe?" He took off his leather jacket, then removed the holster, revolver, and box of cartridges from the day pack. "Defoe has surmised far too much about our activities for him to leave, Joseph. Far, far too much." He looked at his watch. "But it will be light enough to see out there before too long. Dawn; a most traditional and appropriate hour. And then we can solve all of our problems, the ones here, and in New York. Right, Defoe?" He turned and smiled at Skean. "The way we dispatched that minor annoyance last week; remember, Joseph?"

Defoe tried to stall, hoped that some opportunity would arise. "I still don't understand it, Reade. What's the sense in hijacking your own trucks? How does ten cents on the dollar solve your margin problem?"

Reade looked at Defoe and grinned. "Haven't you figured it out? These boys delivered the clothing to my New York warehouse. The following day all of the garments were shipped to their original destinations. Willard, my dock foreman, saw to that. With new paperwork cut, there's no way to identify the goods. Besides, who'd think to look for the stuff in my own stores? You're as stupid as the rest of them, Defoe."

Yearner drove slowly along the secondary road, but missed the lane in the dark.

"Don't be a damn fool, Reade. Conspiring to hijack your own trucks is one thing, but killing me and an innocent woman is a bit more serious. And certainly not the solution; Agent Claxon and I have been in contact, he knows that I am here."

"Does he now?" Reade smiled at Defoe and paused for a moment, then resumed his measured task of putting cartridges in the revolver. "I'm afraid your friend is a thing of the past. You see, Viola spotted him, pointed him out to Willard. Isn't that right, Joe?"

"Yeah, he nodded me onto the guy from the Game Commission. I don't know what happened, though. I headed back here after Willard gave me the . . . uh—what he had for me there."

"Rest assured that Willard took care of the problem. He's very capable; no, Mr. Defoe. We needn't worry about your Mr. Claxon."

"And how the hell do you think I found this place? The State Police traced Gloeckner's truck, they'll be here soon. Show some sense, man!"

Reade jumped across the gap and began to slap Defoe furiously with his gloved hands, screaming, "Shut up, you puling coward! Shut up and face the inevitable; and try to do it like a *man*."

Yearner's lights picked up the familiar shape of the Jag and he stopped. The car was not locked, the key was in the ignition. Defoe had seemed to have an abundance of that "situational awareness" they loved to talk about at Camp Lejeune. Not the sort of man to leave his keys dangling at the start of an operation. The hood was cold; hoarfrost advanced across the windshield. He shook his head slightly, wiggled the fingers of his left hand and felt the tendons rasp against his cuts, then got back in his rental car and drove slowly for another half mile before turning around and heading back. Be nice if the .357 was still in Defoe's trunk.

"Hey. I don't know what's going on between you two, but I'm not going to thit here while you thstart killing people. All we done is buy some deer out of season, thell the meat. Like he saysth, it's nothin' but a damn misdemeanor. Joe, tell him. Count us out of thisth shit."

Reade stood over Defoe, daring him to fight back. Then he turned to the table, holstered the big revolver, and looked at Skean. "Yes, Joe. Tell me. Tell me about the forty thousand dollars I paid you to hijack those four trucks; remind me about your assurances that you had good men to do the job. This one of your 'good men?' "

"Hey," Skean said, "ease off, both of you. Just cool it."

"What'th he talking about, Joe? You told me you just grabbed one truck, you wasn't gonna do it no more."

"Ah, holding out on your partner, Joseph? What did you tell him about the driver that we shot here last week? Or doesn't he know about that, either?" He threw a sardonic smile at Defoe. "Good help is hard to find." He laughed and slapped Skean on the arm. His eyes brightened. "Come on, take the two of them outside. Moon's still high enough to see our way; no need to wait for dawn for the execution. Same spot as the other?"

The toe had solidified during the drive from New York; the hike up the lane loosened it enough to start a throbbing that telegraphed up his leg as a dull ache. He stuck to the grass. At least the Hush Puppies made for silent movement.

Yearner left the cover of the trees and studied the buildings and vehicles from a crouch before moving forward, toward the big truck that stood separate from the others. The same one at the garage. He felt a tingle in his groin. A chance to meet up with that bastard again.

Through the rear window he could make out the shape of a rifle rack in the moonlight. He flowed over the tailgate, eased his arm over each side, tested the doors. Locked. He took out the folding knife and attacked the thick gasket of the back window. After several minutes he had worked a six-inch piece free and wrapped it around his right fist, braced his legs against the bed, and pulled.

It slowly came away like a rubbery blacksnake in his hand; the glass slid free. He reached in for the rifle, worked it from its rest, began to ease it from the opening. There was movement by the house. They came out of the corona of light at the open door and he tried to watch obliquely, preserve his night vision. Five.

Skean held Defoe by the upper arm and pushed him ahead, leaving the light that came from the kitchen, marched him toward the high board fence, a moonlit slash of tan against the dark backdrop of the earth and woods. Reade followed with Caroline, kept her moving forward with little jabs in the spine from his black-gloved fist. An uneasy Mobay brought up the rear.

They stopped halfway between the house and barn. After a brief conversation Skean shoved Defoe forward. He stumbled and fell as Reade took Caroline, moved back toward Yearner and the truck.

Away from the building and its spill of illumination they were shadows in the moonlight. He saw the gleam of the big fifty as Reade unholstered his weapon.

"Get up and run, Defoe," Reade called. "Let's have a little sport for the blooding of the Linebaugh."

Defoe got to his knees, pushed himself upright until he was at an uneasy stand. His armpits were wet and stank; the sweat of fear, not exertion. He turned and faced Reade. Saw more the revolver than the man, fifty feet off in the night. *He has taken Cape Buffalo,* he thought, *the big cats with a handgun. And I am supposed to gimp off into the gloaming, to provide this turd some sport. There is some shit I will not eat; I will not kiss your fucking flag. Hell of a pompous note to go out on.* Pratt's statue of Hale in front of Connecticut Hall flashed across his memory. Class of 1773. A double loop of rope casually wound round his ankles, hands behind his back; you had to look twice to see the bonds. Good, solid features cast in bronze, hooded eyes looking across the campus and into the future. *I only regret that I have but one life to lose* . . . hardly fitting, either. He drew a breath, slowly. *It may not be much of an epitaph, but what the hell, at least it's mine. Caroline, I wish we'd had more than these few brief days—and what's that shadow moving over Reade's shoulder, even as he cocks that damn single-action canon?*

Yearner watched the tapestry unfold, recognized Defoe in silhouette, pulled the rifle to him. The scope caught on the rack and he wrenched it free. The time for subtlety was passed.

He glanced down at the receiver; bolt action. Worked a round into the chamber and threw the scope to his eye, rested his left forearm on the pickup's roof as Reade dropped on target. Picked out the back of his head in the dim light and centered the crosshairs, squeezed off the round as he had done a thousand times on the combat range. A silver Expert badge had graced the left breast of his dress blues.

The 30-06 recoiled, barrel rising against the beefy black roll bar and its array of off-road lights.

The bullet passed high and to the right; Reade heard it sing, turned, fired Defoe's earmarked round through Gloeckner's windshield, blasting a cloud of shards through the cab and out the rear, tearing Yearner's trousers in their passage. A second shot a second later exploded a bulb six inches from Yearner's face, tattooed his cheek with tiny bits of glass. He rolled over the tailgate and scuttled into the deeper shadows of the treeline as a final round tore through the cowling, seat, and front bed, mushroomed to full expansion before punching through the tailgate.

Defoe employed the three-second interregnum to stagger to his right and leap over the steep bluff that dropped to a tangle of *Rosa multiflora* permeated with second growth sumac and archaeologically interesting bits of farm machinery. Brer Rabbit, you knew what you were doing.

Skean grabbed the girl; he and Mobay headed for the house as Reade threw a final volley in the direction of Yearner's retreat before following.

Defoe hit in the cushiony tangle and felt the thorns tear at his clothing and exposed flesh, put his arms across his face and blundered deeper into the thicket.

Yearner moved on knees and elbows, cradling the rifle; at the moment it felt sweeter than an M-16 and a full bandolier.

"Kill that light!" Reade stood inside the door, pistol at port arms across his chest, looking around the jamb at the farmyard.

Skean shoved Caroline into a chair, wrapped a length of rope around her torso several times, secured it with a half hitch, then pulled the chain that hung from the fluorescent halo in the center of the room.

"Man thaid, first thing, Joe, he had a backup team, up the road. Was waiting to catch all of us. And we was about to deal with him, thith asshole thartsth with the shooting."

"Shut up, you fat fuck!" Reade turned from the door, sat, and began to eject empty cartridges from his revolver. "You sound like a goddamned old woman. What do you have in the way of weapons in here, Joe?"

Defoe circled the darkened farmhouse and climbed back up the slope into the woods. His calf was a raw aggravation that stayed below the threshold of agony. He worked his way to the lane, was wondering at the identity of his ally as he heard a hiss from twenty feet away.

"Defoe. Over here. And quiet down, you sound like a damn herd of cattle, crashing around out there."

Defoe scuttled across the road and ducked behind a pile of rocks. "The reports of your death, as they say, are greatly exaggerated, Yearner."

They compared injuries and brought each other up to date. "Let's get the hell out of here, come back with the cavalry, Defoe."

"Can't. Caroline, the woman I told you about? They've got her, inside."

"Shit! Okay, I'll stay here, keep 'em pinned down while you take my car and go for help."

"Think it through, Yearner. It would be a couple of hours before I got back here with the police. It'll be light by then. And there's three of them, with who knows what kind of firepower in there."

"That was my next question. What the hell was that guy shooting at me?"

"That was our Mr. Reade. With his new toy. A fifty caliber single action. Five rounds. Slow as the devil to reload, but if he hits you it's all over."

"Yeah. And he seems to know how to shoot the thing."

"Remember that Cape Buffalo rack in his office? He's got another set, over the bar in his apartment. Forty-eight inches between the tips; told me he took it with a handgun. And there was a reference in there a few minutes ago that leads me to believe he killed the missing truck driver, right here. What do you have there?"

"An '.06, with four rounds left, got it out of that truck. And I knocked the scope off, getting it out. I need to fire one more shot, to realign it. But that'll leave me with three."

"Think there's any more in the truck?"

"Could be. You want to risk going out there to look?"

"We got a choice? They can't see us from the kitchen; if I keep the pickup between me and the building I can get to it, check it out. Beats sitting here, waiting for daylight. When they can go out the other side of the house, flank us the way I came, or behind the barn."

"Yeah. Well, if you're game, I'll shoot across the lane and cover you as best I can. But I'm not likely to hit anything until I zero this damn thing."

Yearner faded into the shadows and Defoe crawled toward the pickup dragging his leg. He was sure its sound against the stones was louder than tin cans tied to a mongrel's tail.

He eased himself up and reached through the rear window opening, unlocked the driver's door.

"I got a .38 pistol and an 8mm Mauser, with a scope. Mobay's got his .22 pump gun is all."

"Well, that's a whole lot more than we're hearing from out there." Reade turned from his observation post at the doorway. "I don't know who it is, but they sure aren't showing me much strength. Go get those guns; the three of us will work a pincer movement and take the fucker out. And scrape what's left of Defoe up while we're out there. Come on, move it."

Mobay followed Skean out of the kitchen and up the stairs. They used the hallway light to find their way into the bedroom where the guns were. "Don't be doing this, Joe. That man's crazy down there, talking about going outside, killing people." He dropped his voice to a whisper, shook Skean's arm with an engulfing grip. "Now think about it, Joe. Let's you and me go down there with the guns, 'n' take his away. There's some kind of cops out there, that Defoe said he's a federal man. We ain't going to shoot our way out of this.''

Skean went to the window, looked out at Gloeckner's truck, isolated in the barnyard. ''It's not that simple, Mobes,'' he said, turning back and going to the closet for the guns. ''Reade killed a driver here, last week. I had to get rid of the body. That makes me an accessory. I go down for that I'm inside for a long time.''

Defoe eased the door open and the little button in the jamb eased out and the interior light came on.

Reade stepped outside and fired a shot into the truck's cab; the bullet tore through the passenger side and missed Defoe's head by three inches before ripping a fist-size hole in the driver's door. Defoe reached for the fuse box and furiously ripped at the wires and fuses until the light went off.

Reade fired once more as Yearner sent a round into the stone wall a foot from his head, peppering his face with fieldstone fragments. He ducked back inside and turned his attention to the woods.

''Skean! Get the hell down here with those guns.''

Defoe had seen the shotgun behind the seat in the first flash of the interior light. By feel he discovered that it was an autoloader; he worked the action on an empty magazine. Expecting another round to tear across the seat at any second, he searched for ammunition on the seat, floor, found nothing. He hoisted himself inside the cab, groped for the glove box. His hand scrabbled through the contents, closing on a plastic cartridge holder. They felt the right size for the 30.06. A cardboard box rattled loosely, yielded a half dozen twelve-gauge shells. Finally, something to fight back with! He had no idea if they were birdshot or rifled slugs, but he loaded them in the shotgun, the anger of his pulse pounding in his ears as he worked the cocking lever, then shoved the barrel through the shattered windshield and fired at the kitchen window before sliding back out the driver's door and limping off. A futile gesture; but *God* it felt so good.

The pellets tore the muntins from the sash and sent a shower of shattered windowpanes across the room.

Caroline tipped her chair over, shrugged free from her haphazard bonds, crawled under the kitchen table, bits of glass biting into her palms. Mobay and Skean came back down the stairs.

''What the hell was that?''

Reade turned from the door. ''Someone opened the door of the pickup truck, took out that window with a shotgun. There's two of them out there.''

''Red's Mossburg. And I bet that rifle is his aught six. Means they ain't cops.'' Skean turned to Mobay. "Got to be that Defoe. We got a chance to get out of this yet.''

"Right,'' Reade said. ''We'll flank them, the way I said. Big boy, you stay here, keep their attention with that twenty-two. Skean, circle around the barn. I'll go the other way.''

"Fuck that, Quentin. No way am I going up against that autoloader full of buckshot in the dark.''

Reade looked at his watch. "It's after five, dawn's not far off. We'll wait until we have enough light to shoot by. You can stay out of range with that Mauser, pick 'em off. The guy with the rifle had two chances at me and missed both times. He can't shoot for shit; I've taken tougher fire from the Cong, and stood my ground.'' He zipped his leather jacket, holstered the revolver. "I'll work my way up into the woods from the left, wait until there's enough light for you, then try to draw their fire, give you a target. But we have to move out now, while it's still dark.''

Skean went to the window, looked out at the dim outline of Red's truck a hundred feet away and the fields and woods beyond. "I don't know,'' he said softly, "I don't like it.''

Yearner hissed under his breath. "Over here. What did you find?''

Defoe crawled behind the tree, rolled over on his side. "Shotgun, handful of shells. Don't know what load they are, too damn dark to see.'' He pulled the rifle cartridges from his coat pocket. "Picked up these for you.''

Yearner began pulling the rounds from the plastic carrier, started to feed them into the rifle's magazine. "Shit! They won't chamber.'' He compared an .06 round with the new ammunition by feel. "Yeah, they're shorter; probably .308, 8 millimeter. At least we have another weapon. Help me resight this rifle, partner.''

"Are you sure you want to do that? You only have three bullets left, can't go wasting them on sighting in.''

Yearner smiled. "Show you a trick. Moon's hitting the plastered wall there real nice. With the scope I can see where my last shot went, high and to the right of the door, and I know about where I aimed, where he was in the doorway.'' He reached in his pants pocket, handed Defoe a dime. "See these two screws on the scope? Windage and elevation. I'll hold the sight on the doorway, where he stood, and you crank the scope up and to the right, until I holler it's where the shot hit. Presto. The scope and the bore are realigned. More or less. But a lot better than what I have now.'' Yearner lay prone, nestled the rifle against the rocks, and took a deep breath, tried to remember where Reade had stood in the darkened door.

"Okay. Easy, don't bump the barrel. Yeah, that's it. One more click. Okay. Now the elevation. No, the other way. Got it." He eased the rifle from his shoulder and sat up. "Rough and ready, but it'll have to do. Now what's the plan? Don't suppose you brought along a couple of cold ones, did you?"

"Hey, you need some incentive to storm the palace, there's beer in the refrigerator in there. I already have enough reason to go back in." He sat back against the tree, cradled the shotgun. "It's funny; I've only known her for a couple . . . three days. And the first twenty-four hours, I thought she was a shallow bitch." He looked up at the sky, picked out the familiar constellations, fading against the dawn. "I looked death in the eye, twice in the last two hours, Yearner. The first time I pissed myself." He snorted a little laugh. "The second time, I ran a quick inventory and found my sole regret was losing her." He looked over at Yearner. "You ever fall in love?"

"Hell, yes, Defoe. I try to make a practice of it, at least once a week." He laughed and sighted the rifle on the farmhouse, looked for movement with the scope.

"Yeah, I forgot, the ultimate assman of Semper Fi. How did things go for you up in New York?"

"God's honest truth, I was out of my league." He dropped the rifle from his shoulder and let the stock stand loosely between his legs, bounced it back and forth with his fingers. "Oh, hell, Viola and me, we got it on just fine. Woman flat out *fucked* me, Defoe. I truly believe I'm spoiled for whatever is left of my life. You remember I called her 'benchmark pussy'? Well, let me tell you, pal. That was benchmark *sex*. Only I find out later, she's using me. Set me up." He shook his head. "I don't really know what the hell's going on, even now, but I saw shit up there, experienced shit; well, I'll tell you, Chase, that New York's no place for amateurs."

"Yes." Defoe chuckled. "It's an exciting city, all right." He looked east to the salmon-hued horizon, streaked with cirrocumulus clouds, a mackerel sky. Red sky at morning, sailor's take warning.

"You know what it always makes me think of? Rome, the way it must have been, about twenty minutes before the Visogoths arrived." He pulled himself to his feet, stretched the stiffness from his limbs. "Come on, let's resolve this situation."

Caroline crouched against the wall, listened to the three men talk. They were going to go outside, stalk and kill Chase. They had forgotten her, given her an opening, a chance for action. What was it that gnawed at the back of her mind; something from the terror in the top of the barn. Fuses, he had said. He put a penny in the fuse box.

She knew enough about wiring to realize how stupid that was. If she could short the line she could start a fire, burn the bastards out. And her with them; what the hell, anything was better than this. She felt along the wall, found a socket, slipped the ballpoint pen from her pocket and folded the metal clip away from the plastic body, eased it into the outlet, and moved it until sparks flew.

"What the hell was that?" Reade turned away from the doorway that had become his stand. "The bitch, she's loose! Get her, Joe."

Skean ducked under the table, grabbed Caroline and pulled her out, threw her against the wall.

"The two of you fucks're crazy; I'm going for the woods." Mobay walked to the doorway that led to the back of the building. "I'll make my way," he said, and lumbered from the room.

"You'll make your stand with the rest of us, trooper," Reade said, and cocked his revolver. "Turn around and take your position. Joe and I are going out." He lowered his sights on the massive back.

Mobay glanced over his shoulder, turned back toward the rear of the farmhouse.

The fifty-caliber explosion deafened the four occupants of the kitchen as the sound bounced off the stone walls and numbed their eardrums.

Mobay fell forward into the hallway, his chest blown away.

Caroline screamed involuntarily at the sound and sight.

Skean saw his partner of a dozen years fall and swung the Mauser's butt in an upward arc, catching Reade behind the ear.

Caroline scooped the stainless-steel revolver, realized that its operation was beyond her, and flung it through the gaping window opening.

Skean turned Mobay with gentle hands and looked from the hole in his chest to the sightless eyes.

Defoe looked toward the farmhouse, heard her scream, and ran, oblivious to the pain, shotgun thrust ahead.

Yearner dropped behind the rock, breathed, raised the rifle, and sighted on the fire zone. The Corps instinct on the line.

Skean dropped his Mauser and pulled the .38 from his belt, grabbed Caroline as she turned toward the outer door. He snuggled his left arm across her throat, whispered, "You and me, babe," and eased her through the door.

"Okay, Defoe," he called, the pistol at her neck, "me and the lady's coming out." He stopped at the exit, framed in the doorway as the sun came over the horizon.

"Throw the shotgun. Throw it hard, or she gets one in the ear." He watched Defoe, twenty feet away. "Me and her, we're taking a little ride. Out of here. Follow us and she's dead; I mean it." He took two steps toward his van. "Go on, throw the gun."

Defoe set the safety and slowly swung the autoloader in a lazy arc, let go, and listened to the weapon crash unseen in the weeds.

Yearner exhaled, held the scope on Skean, saw a scant six inches separating his chest from the heaving breasts of Defoe's woman, hoped he had done the sighting-in by the book. He touched the trigger.

Blood blossomed from the wound as bits of tissue spattered Skean and Caroline and both went down under the impact of the round.

Reade shook his head and got to his knees, crawled forward over the scattered glass on the floor, pulled himself up at the counter. Gunfire behind him, get out the other side! He went over Mobay's body and through the door, crouched beside his bike.

He opened the zipper on his leather boot, reached for the Colt snubnose revolver with the $+P+$ hot loads and thumbed the motorcycle to life.

Defoe reached Caroline and Skean as Reade circled past the shot-out wreck of Gloeckner's pickup. He saw Yearner coming toward the farmhouse, out of the woods, the rifle held high.

Too close for the scope to focus, he pivoted at the hip toward the motorcycle and its rider, fired, missed, worked the bolt and loosed his final round.

Reade rose from his crouch over the handlebars, opened the throttle, and swung his torso left, targeting Yearner.

A rifle bullet hit the front fork, the impact shoving the speeding motorcycle to the right. Reade squeezed off three shots, concentrating on his target in the dim light, locked on, remembering Cong in the highland dusk, feeling the thrill of it. *Combat.*

The fence, its double knives lurking at thirty-inch intervals, ran at a tangent to the lane. So did the motorcycle.

Reade looked back across his shoulder, throttle wrung against its stop as he tracked his target in the bloom of dawn. The wire slid beneath his helmet and the first barb bit into his throat.

At forty miles an hour the teeth lashed by at fifty feet a second.

The mind is but a concept; intangible, existing in the ether world of thought. The brain, however, is a biological complex of sensors and receptors, ten billion marvelously evolved nerve cells powered by oxygen-laden blood and controlled by electrochemical impulses. Deprived of its power, it is still capable of receiving data, interpreting it, sending directional signals—continuing to function for a remarkable length of time.

Reade felt the wire's touch, experienced an odd sensation that was not exactly pain. He heard the receding sound of the motorcycle, caught a glimpse of his leather jacket above the blood-red taillight. Then he saw the sky for an instant, and trees upside down, before the impact with the gravel lane jarred his vision.

When he opened his eyes again the world seemed darker, as though the newborn day had flickered by and night was falling. Forty feet away he could see the shape of the motorcycle, lying on the lane, someone pinned beneath it. In his leathers. In his leathers. His.

He tried to open his mouth to scream and in the waning seconds of his life went completely mad.

His arm was still tight around her throat; she had fallen with him, locked in an obscene embrace. Defoe pried her free, pulled her from Skean's grasp, held her head against his chest, and smoothed the damp dark hair. "Easy," he said softly. "Easy. It's over now."

He looked back up the lane at the motorcycle, the helmet in the road, Yearner. He sat against the plastered wall, feeling the warmth of the rising sun chase the frost.